ALSO BY JARRET KEENE

Kid Crimson Western Series

Gunpowder Mountain

The Guns of Goblin Valley

Stagecoach to Oblivion

PRAISE FOR GATEWAYS TO ANNIHILATION: STORIES

"Keene's collection is quietly magnificent. I can think of few things better than spending your time reading his words."

— MERCEDES M. YARDLEY, TWO-TIME BRAM STOKER AWARD-WINNER

"Spectacularly imagined, eerily romantic, and fannishly reverent, Jarret Keene brings a majestic voice to his collection of *Gateways to Annihilation*. All the stories here are fantasies rife with edgy nostalgia, and you will see your own love for popular culture and risky spec-fic storytelling reflected throughout. Other writers would sound cheesy or kitschy if they wrote about these subjects; Keene is a master at making them zing with delight and dread. This isn't just grindhouse grizzle and glee. You will feel something real on every page you turn, because each and every swing Keene takes at your emotional core connects like a Louisville slugger on a lobbed softball and the impact sends you sky high. *Gateways to Annihilation* is a home run."

— MICHAEL ARNZEN, BRAM STOKER AWARD-WINNING AUTHOR OF *PROVERBS FOR MONSTERS*

GATEWAYS TO ANNIHILATION

GATEWAYS TO ANNIHILATION

STORIES

JARRET KEENE

Gateways to Annihilation: Stories
Paperback Edition
Copyright © 2025 by Jarret Keene

Dark Wolf Books
An Imprint of Wolfpack Publishing
1707 E. Diana Street
Tampa, FL 33610

www.darkwolfbooks.com

Edited by My Brother's Editor

Paperback ISBN 979-8-89567-894-7
Ebook ISBN 979-8-89567-893-0
LCCN 2025938551

CONTENTS

Contents

for Steve Ditko (1927-2018)

GATEWAYS TO
ANNIHILATION

CONJURE ME

An operating table. A scalpel. The Good Doctor was carving her up. Each incision released a torrent of blood. His grinning face was splattered, his white lab coat drenched. She screamed and screamed. Suddenly, it was over. Straps removed, blood gone, he handed her a bouquet of red roses.

"I'm sorry," he said, tears running down his face. "But these instruments are useless."

His eyes rolled back, his body began to convulse, and she watched in horror as a black cottonmouth emerged from the roses and crawled against her thigh.

This was Josephine's nightmare.

In the morning, she walked through the courtyard behind her quarters, removed her robe, and stepped into the laundry basin. The charcoal was still glowing; the water was warm. She lathered a rag and scrubbed her neck and arms. Afterward, she put on her new white dress and slippers, pulled back her hair, and tied it with a red ribbon, twisting strands of her hair into curls that hung before each cheek. She fastened the gold earrings the Good Doctor had given her. She was proud as she examined herself in the fractured mirror above the sink. Then she went into the house to prepare the Good Doctor's breakfast.

She made a spoon bread and veal hash. She brought out silk napkins and the finest silver and placed a bowl of fig preserves in the center of the table. She took a moment to think of their future together and the prospect of a wedding breakfast bloomed in her imagination. But her fantasy was soon spoiled by a noise upstairs. It was the Good Doctor's wife, Celeste, moaning again. Josephine listened for his voice. Usually, the Good Doctor soothed Celeste with gentle words, then called for Josephine to bring the calomel and a little wine. Right now, though, he remained quiet, most likely using a cold wet cloth to wipe perspiration from the dying woman's brow.

A few blocks away, the cathedral bells tolled the hour. As if provoked by the clanging, the cannon in the Place d'Armes fired. The powder blasts were intended to purify the disease-ridden air and stave off the bayou's fetid vapors. Inside the Good Doctor's home, the windows shook and the china cups vibrated on their saucers. Accustomed to the sudden explosions, Josephine didn't flinch and continued cooking. She'd just started the coffee when he came downstairs. She couldn't remember him ever having looked so fatigued. Yet despite his rumpled clothes and sallow complexion, he was handsome beyond measure.

"You need rest," she told him.

He placed his hands on a chair and leaned forward. "She must go to the hospital."

Josephine repressed the urge to kiss him. She didn't

know anyone who had left the Charity Hospital alive. "Is she that ill?"

He nodded and sat down wearily at the table. "I gave her something to make her sleep."

The water in the kettle was boiling. She poured it over the coffee grounds, then cut a slice of bread and scooped hash on top of it. When he was done, she approached, stroking his wispy blonde hair. Determined, she let her hands linger against his cheek.

He petted her arm and choked out, "I'll never forgive myself for allowing her to stay."

When the epidemic had begun to spread, he stayed behind out of a sense of duty. On her part, Celeste wouldn't leave her husband's side. Now it was summer and everyone in the quarantined city was dying. Victims lay on the floors of the Charity Hospital where the Good Doctor had volunteered before his wife contracted the fever. Ever since the Sorceress had announced colored people were immune, Josephine stopped worrying about getting sick.

"I forgive you," she said, pressing her mouth to his throat.

At first, he remained impassive; he did not succumb. But certain his defenses were ruined from exhaustion, she removed her dress and untied her hair.

He took her on the parlor table.

As he dozed on the sofa, she went upstairs to retrieve the *gris-gris* from under the wife's mattress. It was a small chamois bag that contained strands of hair plaited together; scrapings of dried blood, hers obtained from a menstrual napkin, the Good Doctor's from a towel he'd used to dab a shaving cut; a tiny heart of red wax. The room smelled terrible. Surrounded by mosquito netting, the dying woman lay asleep in her great mahogany bed, drawing ragged breaths. Standing naked over her, Josephine reached inside herself to smear the Good Doctor's seed on the *gris-gris*, then returned the charm to the mattress. Briefly, she considered pressing a pillow to the bleached face. But direct intervention was unnecessary. The spell had been improved; the woman would be dead by nightfall. She would never make it to the hospital.

Josephine bathed in the porcelain tub, using the expensive sweet-smelling soaps. It was her second bath today and she felt a sumptuous delight in drying herself with her paramour's inscribed towel. She redressed, walked out into the yard to gather sprays of jasmine that grew on the trellis, and carried them inside, placing them in a vase atop the mantelpiece. Throughout the morning, she sat quietly in the parlor and worked on her sewing, rocking back and forth in her chair. She filed her nails with the dying woman's emery board. All the while, the cannon boomed and dogs howled and death carts clattered. During a lull, she heard a muffled whimper from the sofa. It was the Good Doctor, having just awakened, his face buried in a cushion, weeping. She put her arm around him and felt his body shudder.

"Hush," she said. "It's almost over."

———

In the afternoon, they received a visitor, Dr. Tallant, the Health Warden in charge of the Fourth District and, confronted with the spectacle of mass death, an unrepentant drunk. He prescribed whiskey for medicinal as well as inspirational purposes and at dusk, he could be found hovering near the chain-ganged slaves in the cemetery, letting them swig mightily from one of his many bottles, keeping them at their grim task of digging trenches for the growing piles of corpses.

"Liberal and frequent," he said. "Liberal and frequent potations of whiskey will rescue us from the Black Angel." He was pouring himself another drink in the Good Doctor's study.

The Good Doctor refrained, as liquor made him tired and careless. Instead, he sat numbly in his leather chair, checking his pulse against the clock on his desk, waiting for the cocaine to do its work.

"More rumors," Tallant continued, spilling whiskey on his vest. "There's a shortage of gravediggers and the people are fearful. They suspect we're burning bodies."

"Are we?"

"Of course not. The stench would be hellish. Even worse than the tar."

"Still. Perhaps the Roman custom isn't such a bad idea."

Tallant snorted. "Nero's human lamps. No, what we need are more slaves. Big, strong, stupid, fever-resistant, liquor-prone slaves. Give me just twenty and we could bury the entire city."

"Be careful what you wish for."

The Good Doctor was about to go upstairs. He was gradually achieving clinical detachment. He no longer saw the dying woman as his wife, but as yet another condemned patient mutilated by absurd treatments. He felt detached from his own actions, from the world that was collapsing around him. He was burdened with the awful knowledge that nothing he did mattered. His abilities to heal had been all along a mirage. Would everything be taken from him? He wanted to get down on his knees and plead for Celeste's recovery. Or else demand a speedier oblivion. Either way, he was running out of tears.

Tallant pulled out tobacco and rolled a cigarette.

The Good Doctor shook his head. "I'm taking Celeste to the hospital."

"I wouldn't recommend it."

"The Sisters of Charity might help."

Tallant sighed, struck a match.

"Nothing works," insisted the Good Doctor. "I've tried everything. Bleeding. Blistering. Quinine."

"Calomel?"

"It ulcerated her gums and tongue. Her teeth fell out."

"The fever spares no one, not even the Sisters. Better she passes away here, where it's clean and quiet."

The Good Doctor swallowed and said, "Yesterday, three fever victims walked out of the hospital. In sound health."

"Easily explained. They were not fever victims, but individuals with minor complaints who assumed they were stricken. No miracle, sir."

"I'm killing her." He removed his glasses and pinched the bridge of his nose.

"What?"

"That damnable opium. I'm killing her with it."

Again, the cannon discharged. It seemed, at least to the Good Doctor, that Death himself was bombarding the city.

Tallant silently raised his glass as if saluting the noise.

"Let it come down," muttered the Good Doctor to

no one in particular. He shuffled the papers on his desk in search of an editorial from the *Crescent*. "Another rumor," he said. "The witch-woman plans to resurrect the dead." He handed over the clipping.

"I've heard," said Tallant, waving it away.

Josephine knocked and entered the study. "She's awake, sir."

"All right," said the Good Doctor. His voice thickened. He was hesitant to say anything more, fearing Tallant might discern their secret.

When she left, the Good Doctor wanted to ask Tallant if he thought Josephine was beautiful, but the question was foolish. Of course he did; he saw it in the way he stared at her, sizing her up and down. Her wide hips and round breasts, her dark hair and green eyes. At nineteen, she was already a vision. Indeed, the single flaw in her beauty was that she was aware of it.

"Tomorrow night," Tallant continued, "there will be a ceremony in the bayou."

"Will it be stopped?"

"No. The authorities are too busy. Let the Blacks have their little party. Soon, we'll all be food for worms."

"Josephine said the strangest thing the other day. She said the fever doesn't attack colored people."

"She's in for a shock," said Tallant, laughing.

"I'm a doctor. This is a doctor's house. Where does she get an idea like that?"

———————

THE OPIUM WAS WEARING OFF. Celeste drifted in and out of consciousness. During the day, the window was kept closed, but now, at night, the burning had lessened and the cannon had stopped, so Josephine threw the shutters open. She lit a lantern and pulled a chair to the bed. With the bowl in her lap, she wrung the excess water from the rags. Her hands shook badly as she bathed the dying woman's forehead. She set the rags down for a moment to collect herself. She wanted very much to strangle the Good Doctor's wife.

She brought to mind the afternoon she and the Good Doctor rode through the city in his carriage, stopping at every clothes shop. He never considered his own attire, always settling for old shirts and shabby coats. He was meticulous only when it came to choosing Josephine's dresses, which were elegant. He also bought her shoes and a pair of green silk gloves. She wore the gloves in the coach on the way back.

"I hope you like them," he said.

"Oh yes." He had inherited her as a teenager from his aunt a year earlier. The daughter of a favored house servant, light-skinned, and adorable from the day she was born, Josephine had been doted on her whole life, sleeping in the big house and cherished by the Good Doctor's younger cousins. His aunt and uncle had loved her until their deaths from cholera and malaria. Loving him reminded her of those golden days.

That week his wife had displayed the early symptoms of the fever. Josephine hoped the Good Doctor would soon be hers.

But the next evening, when the Good Doctor's wife refused to die, Josephine went to see the Sorceress, Queen of the Voodoo. Some people said the Sorceress consorted with Satan, who sometimes appeared to her in the form of a snake called Zombi and protected her from the Whites. Other people claimed she was a thief and blackmailer. The mistress of a legion of men. That she had committed murder. So it had seemed likely that she possessed the means to realize Josephine's desires— the magic a slave girl needed to conquer a White doctor. But now the slave girl's heart was filled with anger and disappointment. The charm the Sorceress had promised would bind the Good Doctor to her had failed.

She stepped out onto Canal Street. The air was a scourge of buzzing biting mosquitoes. The tar barrels positioned on every corner palled the city with smoke. For weeks, people had been pouring out of New Orleans, breaking the rules of quarantine. Everywhere, porters were securing trunks atop carriages as waiting passengers—the plague clearly visible in their mottled features—coughed into stained handkerchiefs. The poor hurried along the sidewalks, luggage and children in tow, out of breath, on the verge of collapse. Josephine had no idea how these doomed souls expected to evade the armed sentries patrolling the bayous. The streets also swarmed with packs of stray dogs. Josephine watched a street cleaner carefully proffer a poisoned sausage to a mutt, its mouth flecked with foam. She passed a thin, bespectacled, White man, wearing a heavy black coat, clean shaven, plugs in his nostrils, who tipped his hat and smiled at her. In his mouth was a piece of orange peel.

Josephine drew her shawl around her and pushed on.

She went to the edge of the city, where the cobble-stones abruptly ended. Gripping the pole of a gaslight, she stopped to rest and survey her surroundings as bits of afternoon light faded from the sky. Beyond stretched a dank swamp spotted with grass. Along the riverbank, a servant was ruthlessly beating a carpet with a stick. Josephine made the mistake of drawing a big breath and inhaled an insect. The coughing fit was severe. She applied some more camphor to her skin. After dabbing her slick forehead with a handkerchief, she plunged into the darkness of St. John's Bayou.

The moon was full, lighting up the moss that hung from the oak branches, reflecting off the swamp water, but the stars remained invisible, as though the moon had siphoned their energies. Lightning flashed; thunder rumbled in the distance. Fireflies flickered among the palmetto leaves. A frog croaked so obscenely that Josephine felt a chill run through her body.

She reached the clearing in time. The Sorceress was still reclining on her throne, a wicker chair with a high back atop a wooden platform. She wore a short garment made of scarlet handkerchiefs sewn together. Around her waist was a heavy blue cord and about her shoulders a red shawl with black fringe. Her hair was bound in a *tignon*, its gray-streaked knots standing above her head. Her scrawny feet were bare and on each leg was an anklet ornamented with tiny bells. Her bead necklace hung to her waist and gold bracelets covered her arms from wrists to elbows. Shiny rings adorned her fingers.

The Sorceress sat motionless, eyes wide open and staring at the fire in the center of the clearing. Her followers were nowhere in sight, but Josephine could sense them moving around, stalking the perimeter of shadows.

The old woman leveled her intense gaze at

Josephine. "Girl, come here. No need to hide in the bushes like a rat. Remove your clothes and speak your troubles."

Josephine stepped warily into the firelight. She stripped off her silt-streaked dress and muddy shoes. Standing before the Sorceress, she wore only her white camisole, as was the rule. Years ago, the old woman had barely survived a knife attack by the agent of a rival priestess. Soon after, she decreed that whoever sought her help must approach in their undergarments, so that no weapon could be concealed. Josephine ascended the stairs and knelt before the Sorceress.

"Closer."

Josephine scooted forward until she was inches from the old woman's face. Her cheeks were marked with grotesque scars, her breath foul. "Does your man belong to you?"

"No."

"Then someone has discovered us. Has he another woman? Is he impotent with you?"

"No."

"Perfume. Sprinkle some of your perfume on the *gris-gris*."

"Sorceress, yesterday I made the *gris-gris* stronger."

The old woman looked at her in surprise. "What have you done, child? Tell me."

"The charm is marked with his seed. It lies under his dying wife's mattress."

For this, Josephine was brutally slapped.

"Stupid girl! That *gris-gris* was a love spell. Now you've made it a dagger. And why did you not say the man was married? Oh, the *loa* are angry and will require a sacrifice."

Still on her knees, Josephine rubbed the sting from her cheek. She set her lips tightly together and said, "His wife must die. He cannot love me otherwise."

The old woman held up a gnarled finger. "If she's not dead, then he has found the charm and removed it. He knows!"

"He knows nothing."

The Sorceress stood and stretched out her arms, bracelets jangling. "Walk the land for a thousand miles. O, devil-o, you are a swamp thing. Black ghost. Whore of Dambalah. You will walk and walk, the dead among the living. You will walk and have no peace. Not until your death is avenged." Then she cocked her fist.

Josephine jumped down from the platform, gathered her clothes, and ran, tripping over the roots of cypress trees. She looked back once, relieved that no one was following her.

———

TALLANT WAS PLAYING a minuet in the parlor. The Good Doctor's eyes hurt from lack of sleep. He fought against the numbness in his heart. He wanted to feel physical pain, but there was only the incessant racking and choking of misery and regret. Finally, he resolved to leave grief behind and know it no longer. It was replaced by an entirely different sensation—cold curiosity. Curiosity as to whether he would come out of this epidemic alive to see sunlight fall across a young woman's face as she walked among the squirrels in Congo Square. He struggled to raise himself and swung his legs to the side of the bed. He glanced at the mirror. A picture of absolute wretchedness. He left the guest room, entered the kitchen, and drank several cups of strong coffee. He was in his shirt sleeves, his trouser legs thrust into the tops of his boots. He saw Tallant standing awkwardly by the piano. The Good Doctor took his coat from the rack and slipped it on.

"I'm ready," he said.

Tallant cleared his throat. "Josephine is gone. Her obedience is questionable, I think."

The Good Doctor looked away, then back at Tallant. He shrugged. "It's just as well."

Together they went upstairs, where Celeste's body lay peacefully in bed.

"Let's wrap her in the sheets," Tallant suggested.

They pulled the sheets from the bed. The Good Doctor heard something hit the floor.

"What is that?" said Tallant.

The Good Doctor stooped to pick it up and answered, "*Gris-gris.*"

"Well, what's it doing here?"

"That little slut."

———

SHE RAN until she was exhausted, famished. Then she walked. On the banks of the river, an old man gave her chunks of salted fish. She continued eastward until she reached the port, at which point she left the riverside and meandered back up through Esplanade. There were noises everywhere. The tolling of bells. The slow clumping of hooves. The rattling of wheels on cobble-stones. The moans of the dying. She saw two men cram-ming a woman's corpse into an undersized coffin. The men jammed the lid shut, mangling her lifeless face and crushing her skull so that the flies swirled in agitation.

It was midnight when she reached the house. On the porch, a filthy gray dog raised its head to growl at her. From the front yard, she seized a fallen tree limb, keeping it between her and the dog. She paused at the door, afraid to enter because of her disheveled appearance. She pressed her ear close to the door. Silence.

"Hello?" she called out. No answer.

She walked through the house and into the kitchen for a glass of water. In the courtyard, she removed her soiled clothes and took a bath. Inside her quarters, she put on her sleeping gown and got into bed. A few minutes later, her door creaked open.

"Is that you?" she murmured sleepily.

The breathing she heard was unfamiliar. Her heart started beating frantically. A ringing filled her ears. She lay completely still with her face in the pillow. She could not turn to look at the stranger she knew loomed above her. Was the Sorceress's curse coming true so quickly?

Tallant threw the blankets to the floor. He took hold of her gown by the neck and yanked it. She heard it tear, and she was naked, scrambling to the other side of the bed. He grabbed her by the arm and pulled her to him. He stank of whiskey. Gripping her fiercely, he wrapped rope around one of her wrists to fasten it to the bedpost.

She started to struggle, but knew it was futile. Her fate was sealed.

He was behind her now, pulling her hips toward him so that she was on her knees. He took her long black hair in his fist. He pressed the pillow to her face, muffling her screams. When he was through, he flipped her over.

She felt the knife cutting into her.

IN THE FOURTH DISTRICT CEMETERY, the fires were always burning. As the cart drew closer, Tallant dropped the reins for a moment so he could pull on his gloves. He took the flask from his coat. Then he lit a cigarette and picked up the reins. He'd been going to the cemetery every day for the last six weeks and it always made him happy. Tonight, things were different. He saw that the slaves were being directed by Dr. Matheson, an elderly physician with a penchant for overseeing the slaves with a rifle, bayonet affixed. Dr. Matheson was waving his rifle now, signaling to Tallant that the proceedings were without flaw.

Tallant brought the cart to a halt and slowly got out, enjoying his task. He gently lowered the rear gate. He pulled out a sheet-wrapped body, dragged it to the edge of a pit, stood it on its feet and shoved. The body tumbled down the incline until it landed on a pile of lime-dusted corpses. Humming to himself, he sauntered back to the cart. He treasured the sight of so many dead people. He didn't mind the terrible smell, a rank odor hanging above the cemetery. *Mephitisme*, the French called it, the smell of death. They believed it caused milk to curdle and wine to turn to vinegar. Now he dragged the second body to the edge and pushed it. After emptying a sack of lime over the pile, he went back to the cart again and closed the gate. Then he walked to the edge of the cemetery, drawn by nothing more than the chaotic flames of a tar barrel. He lit a cigarette, suffused with the satisfaction of his crimes.

A slave by the name of Robert approached, leg shackles clanking.

"Mr. Tallant, sir!"

"Yes, Robert, what is it?" he demanded but handed over the flask.

"One of those dead bodies you brung. Ain't dead!"

"Of course it's dead. You don't suppose I'd bury a living person, do you?"

"I swear I saw it crawl off somewheres."

"How could it crawl if it was wrapped in a sheet? Goddamn it, give me back my whiskey!"

"It got loose," Robert continued, handing over the bottle. "A dead girl, I think."

"Shut up, Robert. You're drunk already."

"Hard to say. Too much blood."

———

SHE REGAINED CONSCIOUSNESS, the light of the distant stars reminding her that she was lying on muddy ground. She tried to stand, but fell back down. She succeeded in getting up on her elbows. She was too weak to cry for help. Who would hear? Who would care? The whole city was crying for help. With a tremendous effort, she finally rose, staggering. Her knees trembled; her feet were like lead. Now the stars grew in intensity, rolling in the sky, and she had to look away, nauseated by the sight. She reeled and each step caused her wounds to throb. She wiped her mouth where blood still flowed. She followed the sound of beating drums and chanting voices.

Hands outstretched, she felt her way through the darkness. She toppled into a ditch. She clawed at the thistles and weeds with her fingernails. She felt the clammy touch of the dead. The harsh smell of lime filled her nostrils. It dawned on her that she had fallen into another mass grave, this one on the bayou's edge. Desperate, she managed to pull herself out, but she couldn't find the strength to stand. She vomited something thick, clotted, and her legs went numb. The path wavered before her like a stream in the moonlight. There was so much blood, perhaps there *was* a stream. A stream of her own blood running into the void ahead. Her blood had turned to water. She wept and prayed. But what good are prayers when the last hour has arrived? A dog approached and licked her face with its rough tongue before vanishing into the trees. She crawled on her belly, dragging her dead legs.

The drums were loud now, the singing fierce. When she reached the clearing, black faces huddled around her.

"Who is this?" someone said.

"It's the Zombi," said another.

"No," said the Sorceress. "Her name is Josephine."

They carried her to the altar and examined her by torchlight. They washed and bandaged her wounds and lit a white candle at her head and another at her feet. She could feel the old woman's bony hand in her own. Someone was applying dirt to her face. Someone else placed a heavy instrument in her other hand—a machete? Somewhere nearby, a hen cackled.

She breathed with shallow gulps, trying hard to shut out the noises around her, the words spoken so fast and loudly until they were garbled, until they buzzed against her chest like giant insects, but it was no use. The ceremonial words triggered a thing that had been inside her all along, a monster that had known her ever since she'd come to the city to live with the Good Doctor. It was larger than anything, larger than the darkness that had enveloped her, forever removing her from the solace of light. She would not get better, and she would never return. If she returned, it would be as something unrecognizable to her. So she said to those gathered around her: "Conjure me."

After Tallant left to dispose of Celeste's corpse, the Good Doctor threw away the vase of jasmine that his slave had placed on the mantel. He knew little of voodoo, but he understood that a charm like the one placed under his wife's bed was evil. It was meant to cause serious harm. His slave had betrayed him. No doubt she had worsened Celeste's condition. Perhaps the girl had even tortured his wife during her final days. Where had Josephine gone? If she returned, he would sell her. Put her back on the auction block.

In the silence of the library, he sat with his arms hanging off the chair. He drew in a breath. A mosquito buzzed his ear. He swatted it; blood spotted his palm. If I could die now, he thought. Peacefully, gently, without a tremor or a crying out. If I could be with her. If I could believe I would be with her. His fingers tightened slowly and his head sank forward on his chest. He sprang suddenly forward and grabbed the gun, putting it into his mouth. The taste was vile.

Celeste. Take me where you are.

He stared at the portrait of his mother, a beautiful Spaniard, whose long red hair flowed over her milk-white bosom.

He had no idea how long he'd been there. After a while, though, his deepest sorrow faltered. The most penetrating despair of his life lost its edge. The flagellant's curse, he thought, to grow accustomed to the whip. He straightened up and stood. Still alive. His heart pumped senselessly, his blood churned without purpose. Bones and muscles and tissue—all functioning, but for what? He looked at the gun on his desk. He picked it up again, put it back down. Then he turned away with a sigh and left, closing the door behind him quietly. He was on his way to the Charity Hospital, where he would do his best to placate the dying. He would do his job and hope to find some meaning in it.

———————

ON HIS WAY HOME, Tallant smashed the bottle against the wheel of an incinerated carriage. New Orleans smelled of death and useless remedies and, above all else, naked fear. For the first time since the epidemic began, Tallant felt at one with the city. He remembered the night, years ago, when the sky was lit by the fires of a slave revolt. An angry crowd had ignited ten thousand bales of cotton on the levee. Ships were cut from their moorings and sent floating down the river in flames.

Warehouses were raided, and molasses and sugar were poured onto the burning cotton. Great clouds of black smoke shut out the warm spring sunlight. A night of complete terror. It was the same kind of pleasure he felt now, an exhilaration in the promise of further unrest and suffering. Only now, the gutters ran with blood and decomposing animals. Indeed, he felt at peace in a doomed world.

At his front door, he stomped the crud from his boots before taking them off. Inside, the house was quiet and, socks on his feet, he entered. Miles away in the bayou, the Sorceress and her followers continued to practice their heathen religion. Tallant heard the drums; the ceremony was reaching its climax. Raising the dead. Sacrificing the goat. Fondling the snake called Zombi. Tallant laughed, shook his head, took a light from the kitchen, and proceeded upstairs into his dark bedroom.

The lantern seemed to dim; was the kerosene low? He fumbled in his pockets for a match, but there was none. He would have to go back downstairs to get more kerosene and some matches. He stumbled in an effort to locate the bedside lamp. Beneath the sound of the drums, he heard a floorboard creak. He stood stock still for a moment, then swung his fading lantern left and right. The sound of something sharp whistled through the air. He turned toward the sound and saw, fleetingly, the perpetrator of his own murder, an avenging Zombi.

He felt the blade catch him in the neck.

CIGAR CITY SATAN

I t was another toothsome meal at Arlo Dankworth's cabin, tucked beneath mossy oaks and the bridge at Columbus Drive along the Hillsborough River. It was customary for Dankworth to treat us to smoked mullet and dandelion bread after he'd had wrapped up an unsettling investigation, and once we finished dinner, he regaled us with a story that spurred our hunger for a glimpse of worlds beyond our own, where entities and ghosts sought to ruin mankind.

Back then, Tampa was a sleepy backwater of 100,000 souls, its humid doldrums punctuated by bursts of colorful tragedy thanks to an escalating conflict between the union representing migrant cigar factory employees—Cubans, Spaniards, Italians—and Depression-strapped manufacturers. We read up on the violence in the *Tampa Daily Times*; up to this point, Dankworth had never mentioned sleuthing in such an environment. However, this evening, we noticed that he opened a box of Vicente cigars, a brand produced in a factory located mere blocks away.

After we lit our tobacco and enjoyed a few blissful puffs, Dankworth began to speak.

"When I revealed to my New York friends my decision to set up shop in Tampa, they looked at me as someone who wears his socks on the outside of his shoes. They don't understand how spirit-rich the swamps and brackish waters can be. I will now relate an example.

"Weeks ago, I received an unusual note from *El Centro Asturiano de Tampa*, which you likely recognize as the social club and mutual-aid society for people arriving from the province of Asturias in northern Spain. Many anarchists are in their ranks; they are warm witty people and I find myself at complete ease while drinking *café con leche* with them and discussing a range of subjects—political, philosophical, technological. An Asturian waiter in the Columbia restaurant brought me the message, written on the back of my tab for lunch: "*Por favor*—help us. Plant Park bandshell, 7 p.m. tonight."

"I looked up at my waiter, who was at this point standing at the bar to fetch a drink for another table. Crisply tuxedoed, he looked at me docilely and nodded. I nodded back, paid up, and left.

"Later that afternoon, here in my cabin, I cleaned and sharpened the stiletto glove I'd inherited from my comrade, the one who was for a time an attaché for Prime Minister Baldwin; I've mentioned him in the past, so you know he is sorely missed. I steeled myself with a capture of Beethoven's *Ninth* on the chronograph and the latest issue of *Gentleman Boxer*. Too nervous for supper, I took a shot of bootleg before hopping on my quadrotor and heading toward the park.

"A well-dressed top-hatted gentleman waited for me in the bandshell. He was seated and reading the paper, looking unruffled. His aristocratic demeanor and fashion suggested he was European, educated, sophisticated. I leaned my equipment against a lamppost and entered the amphitheater, hands in my coat, where my knife-shooting leather mitt could be easily pulled. Seeing me approach, he folded up his paper and stood to greet me with a smile empty of malice.

"I reached out my hand to shake, which he obliged. 'Mr. Dankworth, my name is Spurgeon. I regret calling you at this hour and under these circumstances, but my organization feels desperate and your assistance is required.'

"'And what *is* your organization?'

"'The International Cigar Makers' Union, and we are under siege from, well, sinister forces.'

"'Describe these forces, if you will, Mr. Spurgeon.'

"He nodded and said, 'Fire routinely erupts in the curing room of the factory on Seventeenth, next to El Segunda Bakery. The damage, which occurs in the night, is blamed on the employees, and while the union does its best to protect our own, the evidence, thin as it is, is difficult to refute. We are *not* saboteurs, Mr. Dankworth.'

"'I know the structure,' I said, omitting that I lived within a stone's throw. 'People walking in and out at all hours. Anyone could be igniting the fires. By the same token, there should be plenty of observers to this phenomenon.'

"'Management placed a security officer outside the room, which we agreed to, despite our contract. The fires continue, with security rushing into the room to find none of our employees inside, even as flames rip through the dried leaf fillings. It is almost as if a paranormal force triggers a conflagration. Many of the workers are Catholic, believing in demons. They say the room requires a cleansing.'

"I didn't scoff at this, given my profession. Mr. Spurgeon shook his head as if to scold his own surrender to such an otherworldly possibility and continued. 'So we summoned a priest, who blessed and purified the area with holy water. It made things worse; the fires increased. The police are now involved and our chapter is in danger of having our charter revoked by the national in New York.'

"'You want me to investigate,'" I confirmed. 'You suspect supernatural pyro.'

"Spurgeon lowered his head and crossed his arms, the universal gesture of the defeat of rational intellect when confronted with the uncanny. He looked up at me: 'Can you help? We will pay for your services, of course.'

"I shooed away the suggestion, fascinated enough by the prospects of such a bizarre case. 'I will offer you a reasonable invoice at the end of my investigation. For the moment, let us plan on my arrival tomorrow, preferably before the factory opens for production.'

"'How does three in the morning sound?' said Spurgeon.

"'Honestly, it is a repugnant hour, one that I hope can be salvaged with a cup of *café con leche*.'

"Spurgeon grinned. 'We will have plenty of *café* on hand to help you complete your investigation, Mr. Dankworth. All we ask is that you please refrain from alerting anyone else to our present troubles.'

"I assured him I would show the utmost discretion with this case, as I do with all my investigations.

"Before we parted, he offered another piece of information. 'One more thing I must tell you, Mr. Dankworth. Loud voices precede the fires. Unearthly gutturalisms.'

"I assured him that my sounding wouldn't be thwarted by such rude antics and that the cause, explainable or extraordinary, would be discovered. We shook hands again, and I returned here, feeling silly for having brought a weapon."

At this point in the telling, Dankworth took a moment to clear phlegm from his throat, then asked the group if we were comfortable and to make sure the mosquitoes weren't nipping us unduly.

We assured him we were fine and to carry on with the story.

"The sky was pitch-dark when I collected enough fireflies sufficient to power my Amulet of Distortion, which I last used in the case of the skunk ape in Sara-sota, to life-saving effect. If a demon haunted the cigar factory, I would be able, with a bit of luck, to twist its powers against itself, sending it back to its spawning ground.

"Arriving at the factory, I chained my quadrotor to an oak tree, the odor of tobacco leaves hanging thick in the dewy air. I walked a few steps on the red-brick road to watch several workers file in, wearing khaki pants and white dress shirts, sleeves already rolled up for a graveyard shift, their faces moist with perspiration. Despite the strange phenomenon of tobacco catching fire, they seemed happy, even ebullient, in their chatter with one another, laughing and affectionate.

"A security officer stationed outside the main entrance noticed my presence in the streetlamp's glow and glared at me, so I circled behind the rear of the building where I saw the silhouette of Spurgeon finishing a cigarette. As I drew closer, I noticed a straw picnic basket on the ground, on top of it a thermos and two ceramic cups of steaming milky coffee.

"'Thanks for meeting so early,' he said. 'I'll take you through the loading dock where the tobacco is brought into the factory. This way you'll see how it all ends up in the preparation bins. First, though, coffee.' He extended one of the cups, along with a piece of Cuban bread in wax paper.

"I took a bite of bread and a sip of the *café con leche*. 'Delicious,' I said, by way of thanks.

"Spurgeon raised his mug in a small toast, I did the same, and we sipped a little more coffee and chewed a little more bread. 'You studied at Oxford?' I asked.

"'Cambridge,' he said. 'My father is a Londoner, my mother from Gijon, *en España*. I don't miss the weather in England, but the camaraderie was special.' He offered a cigarette, which I declined. He put his own smoke away and when we were done with the refreshments, he said, 'I'll show you where it happens.'

"'The haunting, you mean.'

"'Yes, the fires begin in the curing room and our members manage to put them out almost immediately.'

"'Using what?' Methyl bromide?'

"'Carbon dioxide extinguisher,' Spurgeon said, turning away from me and toward the factory, walking. 'The cleanest agent on hand; it doesn't damage the leaves. Still, an odd fungus seems to grow on them.' He shrugged at this.

"I followed him inside, walking up a small stairway, through black wrought-iron gates flecked with rust, and into a single-story ancillary structure wedged against the main building. Giant leaves of tobacco cured here, hanging from hemp ropes strung between metal poles planted in the dirt floor, mounted gas lamps imbuing the room with a sacred radiance. Leaves were fastened to the lines with large metal clips and the powerful smell of raw nicotine spiked my bloodstream. The space was vast, though line of sight was extremely limited. If someone was in there with you, it would be difficult to notice.

"Let me secure a spot to observe," I said, indicating an elevated lectern, like a lifeguard's shoreline perch, against the far wall. If you've never been inside a cigar factory, lectors read aloud from newspapers using bull-horn-cone speakers, so employees can hear of world events while rolling cigars. In any case, Spurgeon nodded at my request, so I pulled a notepad and roto-pen from my coat and made my way to the stakeout position.

"'The curing staff will be here soon to treat the leaves,' said Spurgeon. 'In the meantime, the factory owner has assigned security officers to the building.'

"I looked up to confirm their presence, one at each of the two entrances to the room, neckless musclemen brandishing the same uniform that the guard outside the factory had been wearing.

"'They will not interfere with your investigation and they are armed only with batons.'

"'Fine,' I said, removing my coat and folding it over my arm. I touched the amulet underneath my guayabera shirt to make sure it was primed and ready for use. 'How many employees typically handle the curing?'

"Spurgeon insisted only four workers would be in the room at one time, so I waited for them to appear. When they did, they took stock of my position in the lector's seat, but then quickly went to work, stringing the leaves with machetes before hanging them to cure. In a half-hour's time, they were done with their tasks and exited.

"Spurgeon left the room, too, along with the guards —to let the owner know I was on the premises and in the process of conducting an investigation. I had a good view of the curing room from my vantage point, but the humidity got the better of me within a few minutes, undermining the caffeine I'd ingested earlier, and drowsiness overtook me. I could hear nothing but the sound of the same factory workers returning to open the bales, slicing the tobacco leaves, and securing them along the lengths of ropes. Again, they finished and left.

"Everything seemed to be moving along nicely, when suddenly I was startled by a diabolical noise, like the grunting of a woeful predator ready to pounce upon its prey. Hearing the disturbing peal, my fatigue instantly vanished.

"I looked out into the area whence I imagined the din was emanating and saw nothing. Then I spied just the slightest bit of movement at the room's farthest end, as if someone were tickling the hanging leaves while lying on the dirt floor.

"I stepped down from the lector's perch, hand firmly grasping my Amulet of Distortion. I relied on its luminosity to move very carefully into the maze of tobacco and as I navigated its haphazard configuration, the darkness seemed to gather strength, nurturing its potential for surprise and, yes, violence.

"As if on cue, when I transitioned from one row of leaves into another, there was a blur of movement on the ground and a frightful hissing. I directed my amulet at the noise, illuminating something I hadn't suspected, a demonic entity whose name I had long meant to learn, but never had the time to adequately research.

"With the upper body of an indecent plague-ravaged harlot and the lower extremities, including the tail, of a swamp-roaming alligator, the creature was known as the daughter of Abzyou, a female demon from the Coptic texts that took pleasure from inducing miscarriages and cradle death. The saline estuaries of Tampa provided an ideal environment for this miscreant.

"As I brought the amulet to its grotesque face with my right hand, I used the other to cover my nostrils so as to mute the rank odor, which rivaled the dregs of an outhouse. The demon slithered forward, raising its head and nude torso in a yogic pose, red eyes glistening with vertical-slit pupils, long hair like seaweed, an elongated tongue unspooling from a mouth of fangs and cracked lips, rasping with tubercular ferocity.

"Then it inhaled mightily, arching its spine backward, and I knew in an instant that I had to leap away or risk immediate incineration.

"I didn't see it dead-on, due to being in frantic motion, but the heat and flash of a fireball erupted and I felt the hellish blast singe the hairs on my neck. I rolled with the impact of my clumsy tumbling, but before I could wield my amulet as a weapon against the beast, she slithered away with a wall of flame forming behind me, leaves igniting and an inferno beginning to take shape.

"Coughing from the smoke, I kicked at the burning tobacco with my shoe and succeeded in knocking it from its tether. I stomped on the mess, now enkindled upon the ground, like a child in the throes of a tantrum. It was to little effect, though, and I could perceive in the flickering light the soles of my shoes charring. I also felt my ankles aching from the burns I was no doubt giving myself. I'd left my jacket at the lector's chair and just as I was about to sprint to retrieve it, a burst of carbon dioxide engulfed me.

"It was Spurgeon, grasping an extinguisher. His expression was determined and he said nothing until the fire was completely snuffed. He was so thorough that he took a long moment to saturate my shoes.

"Finally, he said, 'You will be reimbursed, Mr. Dankworth. I hope you are not seriously injured.'

"I brushed debris and ash from my shirt. 'A close call, but I remain mostly unscathed. Your *ex machina* is sincerely appreciated.'

"'What did you see?' he asked with urgency. 'Who is the culprit here? Guards are stationed at each of the two doors and no one has entered or departed from this room. In which direction did he pass? We can grab him now.'

"'It is not mortal, Mr. Spurgeon,' I replied. 'I regret to inform you that this factory and your employees are in terrible danger. A lower-level demoness lurks here, vomited up from the depths of hell and undoubtedly nested somewhere in this area. We must pinpoint her location and eradicate her from this realm.'

"With a look of concern on his visage, he repeated, 'Nesting demoness. Well, throw me into a pit!'

"'A pit,' I said, 'is exactly where we shall find her.'

"Spurgeon rubbed his waxed mustache in contemplation. 'Leaves contaminated with the strange fungus —or bacteria—are thrown into the mulching pile, a six-foot hole sheltered in the smaller structure adjacent to us. There are often rats, which we poison with arsenic and copper sulfate.'

"'Then *that* is where we will corner the demon," I said. "I must ask you for an additional weapon, however, before we wage our battle.'

"'What is that?' he asked.

"'Ethylene glycol,' I insisted. 'It's the only way to counter the flames.'

"'You mean, of course,' he said, 'an antifreezing agent.'

"I nodded. 'I will need a significant amount of it if I'm to wrangle this demoness and send her back to the underworld.'"

Dankworth paused to ask us if we required more whiskey. On the edge of our seats, we replied in the negative, encouraging him to continue the telling. He gave a mischievous smile, which I think showed an appreciation of how much we were enjoying his story.

He went on. "Spurgeon was poised to take me through one of the doors of the room to reach the mulching pile, but I tapped him on the shoulder to halt his progress. 'Which wall of the curing room connects to where you are taking me?'

"He indicated the southern side of the room, so I headed in that direction to inspect. Sure enough, a stench was emanating from a loose patch of dirt there at the baseboard. 'Let me guess," I said. 'The pile is directly on the other side.'

"Spurgeon confirmed this. I instructed that we should immediately recruit a small construction crew and have them pour a concrete foundation into this area, to keep the demoness from escaping into this room once we invaded her burrow.

"Then we made our way to the mulching pit, which required a handkerchief over our noses to keep the fetor from bringing us to our knees. It was a large, dark, and vegetative trench and I could instantly appreciate why Abzyou's daughter had selected this spot for her lair. What I had difficulty comprehending was *why* she was intent on burning the tobacco with her incendiary exhalations.

"'She is inside the bowels of this trough,' I said to Spurgeon. 'Here is the plan. We will seal the other side of this wall with concrete, then pour the ethylene glycol into *this* hole, which will force her out and give me an opportunity to shove her through a dimensional doorway.'

"'You mean, you'll use the charm around your neck?' Spurgeon clarified for himself. 'Is it dangerous to us? To the non-demonic, I mean?'

"'I cannot use it to banish you to another realm with the demon,' I said, calming his fears. 'The Amulet of Distortion affects only supernatural bodies, not terrestrial organisms.'

"He seemed satisfied with this answer. 'Then let's go forward with the operation,' he agreed. 'There is a concrete mixer on the premises and the antifreeze is in the garage. We should be ready to launch our assault before dawn.'

"True to his word, Spurgeon had a pressed-steel mixer spewing paste and aggregates as the sun began to tinge the sky a pinkish orange. One of the security guards, Juan, delivered three child-sized drums of ethylene glycol to the mulching barn. I prepared a vulcanized hose, fifteen yards long, attached to a lamp-lighter's pole of equal length, with pressure from the factory's standpipe. The guard assisted me in shooting coolant into the monster's nest, but only after we had nearly depleted the third drum did we hear the wretched grunting again.

"The evil noise sounded like an undead personage striving to devour its own rotten entrails, then howling through a mouthful of offal.

"'Get ready, Juan,' I warned. 'We have stirred the creature and she will be angry.'

"She was, indeed, incensed and in utter agony. Emitting a soul-wrenching shriek, she scratched and clawed her way up through the maw of the pit, then exploded into the air, having wrenched the nozzle from the pole, clutching it in her maw as it continued to issue antifreeze as she landed upright, balancing perversely on her alligator-like hind legs. Blinded by coolant, Juan fell to his knees, screaming for relief. But there was none; ingesting just a tablespoon of the stuff can result in death. With my accomplice neutralized, I had to move quickly and efficiently.

"The skin of the demoness was blue and cracked with ice and when she raised herself upright like a hooded cobra to bare her fangs and growl at me, the compound had run out. She lunged, but I saw it coming and skull-cracked her with an empty metal drum, which silenced her momentarily.

"She shook off the blow and narrowed her eyes, tracking me for another go. She drew in her breath as if to fireball me. The effort of it seemed to rack her chest with pain, thus I knew that the coolant had penetrated her lungs and incendiary glands, making it impossible for her to set me ablaze for the time being.

"I pressed my advantage, tossing the can at her, which she easily dodged, but at the cost of retreating slightly. I took that moment to raise the Amulet of Distortion and bathe Abzyou's daughter in a Ray of Disfigurement, a spell used by ancient wizards to render flesh into dust and dust into flesh. Stories of this jewel go all the way back to Egypt, where some say it fell into the possession of Moses, who used it to part waters and summon locusts. In the hands of a clumsier magician, such as myself, it could be wielded for more primitive and deadly results.

"And wield it I did, transmuting the demon's physical form into granular dross and oily grime.

"But before I could completely disassemble the demon from our world, I felt someone behind me clench my arms, pinning them to my side, the amulet's effects dissipating. I struggled to free myself, stomping my assailant's feet with drenched shoes and trying to tip us both over, so I'd have a chance to wrestle free on the ground. But his grip was unbreakable and the demoness was reconstituting herself, the icicles on her body melting away, the antifreeze wearing off.

"'Let me go!' I screamed. 'Idiot! You're giving her time to recover!'

"There was an impact, the dull thud of something smashing into my assailant, and I was suddenly liberated. Without turning to thank my savior or see who had restrained me, I once again trained the amulet upon the demoness. She hissed and screeched in the excruciating light of my returning enchantment, the particles of corporeal form rising up like bubbles and disappearing, and within moments every part of her revolting form was rendered into imperceptible subatomics.

"Satisfied that I had successfully banished the creature, I looked back to see Spurgeon lying unconscious on the ground, with Juan standing before me, flushing his coolant-flecked eyes with water from a thermos he'd picked up somewhere.

"'He grabbed you,' he said, indicating Spurgeon. 'I yelled at him to stop, but he seemed driven, as if someone or something was controlling him, manipulating him like a puppet.'

"'Any idea why?'

"Juan shook his head.

"'Well, I said, 'thank you, Juan, for coming to my aid. If you had waited any longer, the demoness would have gained power and come after us in a fit of homicidal rage.'

"'*No hay problema*,' he said, in a Cuban-accented Spanish. 'The water is helping me. I was worried I might be permanently blinded.'

"'Well, that's good news. When you're feeling better, let's move Spurgeon into his office and question him.'

"We did as much and when Spurgeon gained consciousness, we interrogated him over hot coffee and warm Cuban bread slathered in butter. He insisted he had no memory of attempting to thwart my efforts to expel the demoness and I believed him, so honest and disoriented were his responses. He seemed rehabilitated, like the Spurgeon I had originally met, who loved English camaraderie, a cigarette, and a cup of *café con leche*.

"And so we destroyed the creature's nest and inspected the rest of the factory to make sure no other spectral forces were at work there. When we were satisfied, we assured the factory owner that there would be no more acts of arson on the property and we sent a telegram to union headquarters in New York, notifying them that the problem had been resolved. In lieu of money, I was paid in boxes of Vicente cigars, which we are now enjoying together at this moment."

We had questions, of course. Perhaps too quickly, I posed one. "Why *did* the monster torch the tobacco? And how can you be so confident that Spurgeon was hypnotized by the demoness when he bear-hugged you into submission?"

Dankworth answered, "Arson wasn't the creature's aim. Spurgeon's brief enslavement, upon closer examination, seemed to be linked to the discarded tobacco he used to roll his own cigarettes, singed leaves that had been rejected by the factory for being contaminated during recent fires. I borrowed a microscope from Doctor Frye, who as you may know treats impoverished patients at her clinic in Tampa Heights, the bacteria growing on these leaves looked highly unusual similar to a Haitian strain she had encountered years earlier, which seemed to instill brief bouts of catatonic schizophrenia. Her opinion, which I shared, was to administer antibiotics to poor Spurgeon. For the last few days, he hasn't suffered another episode."

"Wait," I said. "You mean, a creature from hell sought to conquer mankind with diseased cigar tobacco cured in the city of Tampa, tobacco that induced mind control and savagery and would be distributed around the world?"

We all paused mid-puff and simultaneously examined our cigars before putting them out in the ashtrays Dankworth had placed for our benefit around the sitting room.

"Look at the time!" said Dankworth with a glance at his watch. He continued to fearlessly puff away on his own stogie. "It's nearly midnight and I have another interesting case in the morning. Off you go!"

And off we went, our hunger sated, though at the same time hoping we weren't destined to become slaves of the Cigar City Satan.

GIANT CATS OF THE PHARAOH

R yder Thorne was a talented young writer, albeit a hack living in Las Vegas. Ryder had a flair for language, but was completely deadline-challenged. His efforts to support himself as a freelancer, a literary gun for hire, among the many Strip-focused media outlets had come to nothing. He was perpetually broke and owed the government a few hundred dollars every April, the cruelest month. Thus, he ended up working in the human-resources department of the Pharaoh Hotel-Casino, scribbling propaganda in a dingy cubicle farm.

The Pharaoh paid him to write and edit an employee newsletter, *The Tablet*, the title of which suggested someone prominent in the marketing or HR department had heard of ancient Canaan. But for all the creativity allowed Ryder, he might as well have wielded a hammer and chisel to crack cuneiform script into chunks of clay. He accepted the job under the illusion that he would spend his days interviewing chefs on how to prepare the perfect soufflé, probing showgirls on the usefulness of classical ballet instruction, and discussing the philosophy of Sun Tzu's *The Art of War* with executives. Instead, Ryder toiled endlessly on pointless memos designed to make middle managers sound like brilliant pharaohs and everyone else sound like eager slaves.

And now the entertainment director, Craig, had emailed Ryder's supervisor one of the most humiliating assignments in the history of the hotel's internal PR department: a front-page story on the new filtration system designed to remove the strongest odors in the jungle-like environs of White Lion Lair, a new big-tiger sanctuary constructed inside the casino.

"*Please* don't make me write about animal-poop purifiers," Ryder pleaded with his boss, Eileen, in her office. "Why can't I delve deeper into the myths and realities of white lions, instead? Did you know that they're considered divine in South Africa—"

Eileen cut him off with a dramatic sigh. "Remember when you wrote that epic piece on the history of jazz? You barely mentioned the lounge here!"

"The lounge is called Love Supreme, Eileen. After the John Coltrane album?"

"That's *not* why they named it that. And take the camera for pictures."

"I've got to shoot the story, too? Fine, I'll photograph some lion butt."

"You would. Seriously, don't let your writing get all scholarly."

"Well, I *do* have an MFA."

"Which stands for what? *Mother*—"

"Stop, Eileen."

"The trainer's name is Alvin Powers, by the way.

And call him before you waltz in there. Don't interrupt him. Powers is working with a famous biologist on lengthening the life span of our white lions."

"Saw it on Channel Eight last night."

"Watching TV, Mr. I'm-So-Literate?"

Ryder, twenty-three, had to chuckle. He was more than a little in love with his thirty-five-year-old boss, a divorced MILF with an ex-dancer's still-toned body who cursed like a sailor. None of it, however, mitigated the genuine dread that filled his heart at the prospect of composing an article about ridding White Lion Lair of the odor of cat feces.

"I'll call Alvin now," he said.

She shook her blond-highlighted head but with a naughty smile. "Get out there and make me proud, young Ryder. Do a good job, and I'll buy you drinks after work."

———

DR. ALEJANDRO ARAGON sat at a table in Starbucks on Maryland Parkway across from the University of Nevada Las Vegas, sending a birthday e-card to a fellow geneticist in Oslo, Norway, and sipping greedily from a nonfat cappuccino. Afterward, he planned on replying to a number of email interview requests from prominent European science journalists, all wanting his expert opinion on the recent discovery of giant sea creatures in Antarctic waters. Turns out a breed of starfish is five feet in diameter.

Since he didn't have the organism in front of him or in his laboratory, he didn't have much to say, except that the existence of kraken was always something he believed possible, given the right set of environmental conditions. What he wouldn't reveal, of course, was that he'd already achieved incredible results with terrestrial mammals.

The lavish funding for his dream project came from a world-renowned lion trainer and occasional environmental activist named Alvin Powers, whose awesome jungle cats had long dominated Hollywood, several Florida theme parks and hotels, and now Las Vegas. Aragon knew that Powers, in the course of his entertainment career, had amassed a significant fortune, but the last check had bounced and, although the famous trainer assured him that the mistake had occurred on the bank's end and that the money would be forthcoming, the scientist hadn't seen a penny of it so far. Annoying, because Aragon had just bought a new jet-black Hummer.

As he sipped his hot drink, another priority email popped into his inbox with the subject line: "On the record?"

Aragon put aside the e-card and opened the message. In it, a reporter, whom Aragon knew from the glory days of the now-defunct *Omni*, revealed that he'd been contacted by a publicist claiming to represent Powers and that the key to unlocking the life-expansion secrets of white lions would soon be revealed in a major academic paper. And since Aragon obviously served as Powers' lead researcher, could the reporter acquire an exclusive interview—no later than today?

Aragon felt his face getting hot. He rose from the table and dumped his still-warm cappuccino in the trash. He didn't want the caffeine to escalate his heart rate any further. Fuming, he sat back down and began striking the keypad of his laptop and dashed off a 500-word screed to Powers. Reading it through again, he tweaked a few words for added vitriol and raised his hand to slam the return key...then thought better of it.

Instead, he deleted the email and took a deep breath.

Rubbing his temples, he asked himself why Powers had put them in such a wretched position. Alerting the media was tantamount to suicide for a project that hadn't been vetted through any university or federal grant. Was Powers purposely sabotaging things? And if so, for what absurd reason? If he'd gone bankrupt, why not be on the level about it? Why risk having the results fall apart and tempt a scientist to take his research elsewhere? True, Aragon had had the test results independently confirmed in Oslo, but...

Suddenly a password-protection alert arrived, flashing its high-priority warning. Answers to the scientist's question were sitting in front of him now: Powers had somehow broken the code, downloading files from Aragon's lab computer.

In his haste, Aragon ripped the power supply cord from the coffee shop wall socket and slammed shut his Air too forcefully, angering a neighboring Mac fan, white earbuds in.

"Shame!" said the skinny hipster college kid, without looking up from his MacBook.

"Yes," Aragon admitted sadly. "Shame on me for trusting that fucking trainer." He grabbed his keys and made for the exit.

WITHOUT EVEN CHECKING to see if a memory card was in the camera, Ryder strapped it over his shoulder, stepped out onto the smoky casino floor, and headed in the direction of White Lion Lair. He'd also left behind his notepad and digital audio recorder, but didn't care. Employees were rarely quotable and Ryder would end up fabricating them anyway. Why bother with the empty theatrics of in-house journalism? The Police's "Truth Hits Everybody" played on the sound system as Ryder weaved through the throng of gamblers.

He'd done his homework. The beasts in question originated from a private game reserve in South Africa's Eastern Cape. Brought to the States in the early 1970s, they lacked many of the inbreeding afflictions suffered by captive lions. Extinct in the wild, white lions numbered only about 300 in the world, at least a dozen of which were cared for by Powers right here in Las Vegas. He bred them for a number of theme parks and enjoyed a reputation for well-trained good-natured cats.

Ryder arrived at the lair at the end of a feeding. Powers, inside with the gorgeous animals themselves, placed some kind of raw hamburger-like patty directly into the maw of one of the lions. Ryder knew this meant he'd have to wait for the cats to get sleepy before Powers would exit the lair and head toward the gift shop, crammed with stuffed animals and T-shirts. So the young scrivener gave the tourists room to gawk and passed time by chatting with a couple from—

"Albuquerque," the man said.

"Enjoying the Pharaoh?" Ryder asked.

"Humph," said the woman, on the dowdy side, unimpressed with anything.

"Well, we *were* having a great time," explained the man. "Until that trashy hooker over there asked my wife if she was interested in a three-way."

Ryder snorted. "Man, don't they have security in these places?"

"Security needs to help that lion tamer," said the woman.

Ryder turned. The same cat Powers had fed reared up on its hind legs and swatted at the trainer's brow as if his head were a ball of string. The crowd gasped. Powers fell to the ground. A fellow trainer came to his aid, and another clapped to draw the lion's attention.

The lion then yawned as if nothing had happened.

Gradually, Powers, leaning on his fellow trainer with what looked like a sprained ankle, exited the lair as a purple-jacketed security officer approached him.

Ryder edged closer.

"We need to fill out a report," the officer insisted.

"In the gift shop," said Powers, voice hoarse, the superficial scratch on his forehead bleeding slightly.

Ryder hung back for a moment and watched the trainers direct the aggressive lion into the dark recesses of the lair, probably to the loading dock. Would she be caged with a scarlet placard around her neck that read BEWARE OF LION? Ryder entered the gift shop just as an employee was printing up a piece of paper for Powers. The old man pulled a pen from his shirt pocket and clicked it. Ryder noticed his hands were shaking and his face was ashen.

"Frisky cat," said Ryder. "Was that Baby? I thought she was a lioness of advanced age."

"Yes, Baby's a senior," said Powers, refusing to look up from the paper, but not writing anything, either.

"Name's Ryder. I'm with *The Tablet*," he said, extending his hand. "Been giving Baby steroids?"

Powers coughed once, looked up, and squinted at Ryder without shaking his mitt. "You guys misspelled one of my employee's names in the last issue."

"Oops, you mean Phuk." Ryder hated it when people pointed out his newsletter's copious errors. "Sorry about that. Vietnamese is tricky."

"You spelled it with an F," said Powers, dabbing his forehead with a handkerchief. "And with a C and a K."

"Yes, well, it seemed correct at the time."

"Here for a story on the new filtration system, I'm told."

"You got it."

"Sorry, not installed yet. You're early, I'm afraid. The usual ventilation fans are running now."

"Huh. It's just that we got an email from Craig with marching orders."

"Craig doesn't understand that my cats need time to adjust to the sound."

Ryder furrowed his brow. "I thought the filters were silent."

"They are, which is why they spook my cats. I've been introducing the filters to them back at my ranch."

Ryder recalled reading somewhere that Powers rotated lions every twenty-four hours, with three in the lair most days and the rest at his compound at the western edge of Las Vegas Valley. Ryder remembered something else. "Hey, you know, *The Tablet* has never published photos of the ranch. Think I could drive out there this weekend?"

Powers turned back to the document, cleared his throat. "For the newsletter?"

"Well, maybe I could profile you in a magazine like *Florida Monthly*."

Powers directed his gaze at Ryder for the first time and appeared to consider the idea. "You write for *real* magazines, too?"

"When I need extra coin." Ryder raised the camera. "Should I photo-document your wounds?"

"Prefer you didn't."

"No problem."

"Tomorrow might be a good time to talk more about my research with Dr. Aragon," said Powers, finally writing his name and address at the top of the accident report. He tore off a scrap and handed it to Ryder. Now he was smiling. "Two o'clock?"

"Sure. May want to clean and bandage that," Ryder added, indicating the cut on Powers's forehead.

The trainer shrugged. "I assure you my cats are free of scratch fever."

"Good to know," said Ryder. "See you tomorrow."

He returned to the office and brought Eileen up to speed—except for the *Florida Monthly* article. She didn't seem convinced Powers was in his right mind.

"What's he up to? As far as Craig knows, the installation is complete. How long does it take getting lions accustomed to *less* noise?"

"No idea. How about those drinks?"

"Take a rain check? My son is sick again and I'm off to daycare."

"You should sell your kids for, like, money."

"Not until eBay says it's legal. Speaking of, you have my permission to use the company camera tomorrow."

"Great. You'll get tons of cat butt, I promise."

THE NEXT DAY WAS WINDY. It took Ryder thirty minutes to reach the ranch, the journey completely caking his Hyundai in dust. He pulled up to a gate that said NO TRESPASSING and searched his jeans for the scrap of paper Powers had handed him, hoping for a cell number.

But Powers was already limping his way to the gate from a trailer twenty yards away, the wind threatening to let fly the Golden Knights baseball cap barely covering a swath of gauze.

Ryder poked his head out the driver's side window. "Am I early or late?"

"Early," said Powers. "Come in anyway." He unwrapped chains from the gate, pushing it open.

Ryder parked next to the trailer and got out of the car. He took a moment to survey things. Aside from the trailer and Powers's pickup, there was a rectangular warehouse with what looked like giant Plexiglass windows on the roof. "Sort of a greenhouse you got here," Ryder said to Powers. "Is there vegetation?"

"Lots," said Powers. "It's called a habitat. Helps them more psychologically than anything."

"Lead the way, Mr. Powers."

Despite the sprained ankle, Powers led him to the habitat and paused before opening the door. "A flash may confuse them, so allow the lions time to adjust to your presence."

"You bet."

Then Powers opened the door, and all hell broke loose.

An eardrum-bursting roar and an odor of rot were

followed by the sight of the habitat exploding in a hail-storm of particleboard smithereens and shards of fiber-glass. Ryder instinctively ducked, grinding the company camera into the ground, cracking the lens. The impact of Powers' body thrown against him by the blast knocked the breath from the writer's lungs.

Gasping for air, he crawled out from under Powers and crouched low, feeling vulnerable and monkey-like as he swiveled around to catch sight of whatever had charged them. What he saw made him scramble back-ward and he gouged his skull on a piece of the half-demolished habitat. His hand shot to his head and came away full of blood.

"Nice kitty?"

Had a concussion distorted his eyesight? He hoped so, because one of the white lions had somehow grown to be the size of a school bus. It raised its massive paw in the air like a guillotine and a shadow fell over Ryder. Despite that initial roar and charge, though, the cat's expression was now serene. It gazed blankly at Ryder Who, in his fear and haste, had somehow tripped the flash. The paw dropped to the ground, the cat curious about the source of light.

Suddenly there was a sharp crack and the lion flinched. It got low to the ground and roared again, this time with more fear and pain than hot anger. Without another sound, it blinked several times, turned, and trotted off toward the parking lot, stumbling into Ryder's car and crushing the passenger side with a drugged misstep. Ryder watched in amazement as the lion gradually lay down on its side and fell still. The animal's chest rose and fell, which meant it was still breathing.

"Thank God," said Ryder, his legs shaking too much to stand.

"Not God," said a man in a lab coat. His baldness, white beard, and thick glasses were the only normal things about him, especially after Ryder noticed the smoking tube of PVC resting on his shoulder like a rocket launcher. "I'm Alec Aragon. You'd better come along."

Ryder saw a black Hummer, door swung wide, parked next to his own car by the trailer. "Not unless you're headed for the hospital. Alvin here is—" The writer recoiled from the dark blood pooling under Powers. Nausea gripped his throat.

"Dead." Aragon pushed at the center of his glasses. "As will be many people in the Pharaoh if we don't hurry."

"White Lion Lair," said Ryder.

"Powers shipped one of the test cats there this morning."

"Test cats? What the hell was he testing?"

"Something with which he had no business. Mainly my unpublished notes." Aragon fitted a metallic projectile into his homemade PVC blaster and aimed it at the drowsy lion.

"Wait, what are you doing?" said Ryder, now able to stand.

"Get in the truck."

"Man, all I wanted to do was write a magazine article."

"Plenty to write about now."

ARAGON PATCHED the gash in Ryder's skull using a first-aid kit he kept in the Hummer. Then, Ryder reached Eileen on his cell. "Eileen! You need to call Craig's department," he told her, "and you need to do it now!"

"What? Wait. Slow down, Ryder. Call Craig's department? And tell them what?"

"Tell them to quarantine a lion named—"

"Lio*ness*!" barked Aragon, gunning the engine.

"Sorry, a *lioness* named Baby. Under Dr. Aragon's orders."

"Ryder, it's Saturday morning. I'm with my son at the walk-in clinic."

"You outrank them, don't you? I'm telling you, they have to do what you say. And fast!"

"All right. But can you tell me what's happening?"

"I'm riding in Dr. Aragon's Hummer. We're on a mission to stop a mad lion, uh, lioness."

"How mad?"

"We're talking fifty feet of pissed-off puddytat!"

"Ryder, how many times have I told you to stop smoking pot in the morning!"

"Make the call, Eileen. You'll save the Pharoah a hefty hike in the liability insurance premiums. Oh, and some lives while you're at it."

Ryder hung up just as Aragon screeched onto the Las Vegas Boulevard turn-off, rubber tires burning gray smoke. Laying on the horn, the military scientist nearly flattened a motorcycle cop issuing a ticket with his bike parked before yanking the Hummer onto the sidewalk. A few pedestrians, already unnerved by an intensifying dust storm, ran in all directions. One screamed an epithet.

"Go back to Ohio!" Ryder screamed back, even as he death-gripped the truck's oh-shit handle. Finally, the Hummer got stopped by a backup waiting to get to the Pharoah's valet parking next to the *porte cochere.*

Ryder took the opportunity to ask, "Dr. Aragon, why did Powers delay the filtration system?"

"He thought it would hamper the oxygen levels and temperature controls he needed to grow the cats in the lair and habitat. Powers was rather clumsily—"

The traffic moved and the Hummer hit a steep Pharaoh entrance speed bump, then Aragon continued.

"—relying on principles outlined by those of us studying the growth rate of jungle animals," Aragon lectured as if at the front of a classroom, rather than running a casino slalom course, now at up to fifty miles an hour. "He told me he needed help extending the lifespan of his lions. I agreed, but then he kept taking strange experimental detours. I think he wanted to sell cat meat, judging by the contacts he made last month."

"Cat meat! To who?"

"Who knows? The Chinese, maybe."

"Weird. He had no idea, did he?"

"No, he didn't realize they'd grow so fantastically. Neither did I, really. Otherwise, I would've heeded my suspicions."

"How many monsters did Powers make?"

"He only had enough resources for two cats."

As they drove into the hotel parking lot, a roar could be heard from inside the structure.

Aragon looked at the writer. "Too late to park. We're going in."

"Going in? Oh—"

The Hummer careened into the crowded Pharaoh

entrance, swerving through the queued taxicabs, waiting airport shuttles, and luggage-grappling tourists, around the concrete barriers, scraping a limo with its metal grill and shooting off bright sparks. Valet attendants and hotel guests leaped for cover. Before Ryder could brace himself for impact, Aragon smashed the massive all-terrain vehicle headlong through the massive glass front doors. Face ricocheting off the dashboard, the sound of shattered glass crashing from all directions, Ryder touched his nose to make sure it hadn't been crushed or severed. Although Pharaoh security officers weren't armed, they were tough characters and he was almost as scared of them as he was of another giant white lion attack.

Lurching past the tiled lobby, Aragon got a back tire caught on a nest of slot machines and the Hummer did a doughnut right there on the casino carpet before slamming its front end against the short wall of the center bar. Aragon grabbed the PVC tube from under his seat and scrambled out of the truck, running for the lair.

Ryder barely squeezed between the passenger door and a splintered crap table, players scattering in all directions.

Apparently sensing an imminent collision, Aragon stopped dead in his tracks and—like a football lateral play—tossed the PVC tube at Ryder before getting slam-tackled by a burly security officer.

Ryder caught the PVC on the run. Looking at it in his hands, he squelched the terror in his heart.

Glasses crushed by the security officer's boots, arms wrenched behind his back, the scientist yelled at Ryder, "Take her out!"

Ryder hesitated a moment before the fear of being

similarly tackled and restrained got his legs pumping. He sprinted for the lair, parting the waves of patrons who likely deemed him either a thief or crazed terrorist. A few screamed, but mostly they scattered, giving Ryder a wide berth. An alarm began wailing. From the corner of his eye, he discerned security officers quickly making their way toward him, but he was already at the lair.

What he saw horrified him.

An enormous lioness, Baby, had already broken through the Plexiglass and was busy gnawing, with much enthusiasm, on a mangled thighbone in the now-empty poker room. The cat's golden eyes pierced Ryder's own as Baby ripped raw bloody flesh from the bones. Fumbling with the improvised weapon, Ryder tried to find the trigger.

A deep and deafening growl complicated Ryder's effort to determine which end of the barrel to point at the lioness. Unsure, he made an uneducated guess, praying that he wouldn't be launching a grenade at the officers no doubt gathering behind him. At least they weren't piling on top of him. They'd have more disastrous concerns if this didn't work.

Before he could draw an exact bead, Baby leaped into the casino, her weight causing the ground to quiver. Pursuing her, Ryder spotted a security golf cart and jumped in, slamming his foot into the electric pedal and lurching forward.

"Out of the way!" he yelled at a dazed cocktail waitress, who managed to balance a tray of drinks despite the mayhem.

Baby left a sudden and merciless trail of shattered roulette wheels and Three Card Poker tables in her wake. She even bowled over a candy-red sports car that had been perched atop a bank of slots, almost snuffing an old woman struggling to escape with her walker and oxygen tank. The thud of the car hitting the floor and the crack of the windshield sent shivers down Ryder's spine. How in the hell was he going to immobilize what must be a ten-ton animal? Worse, this was feeding time, which meant Baby was probably still hungry, despite the instant meal she'd made out of whomever that thigh bone had once belonged to. Christ, feeding time at a casino full of plump juicy tourists! They'd even rubbed themselves in delicious coconut tanning oil, the unsuspecting fools.

Naturally, then, Baby was headed for the pool. Once outside, there was no telling how much carnage the giant lioness might inflict. He caught up with her poolside as she licked a paw and rubbed it against her head, basking in the light. Sunbathers hurried back inside, most of them barefoot, but some tripping in their sandals, falling down, and all leaving behind their towels and bags.

To Ryder's complete dismay, a crying child on a raft gingerly floated into the center of the pool. Her mother stood at the edge, yelling and gesturing for the girl to swim away. *Shut up! You're going to draw—*

Sure enough, the frantic behavior caught Baby's attention. After snacking on a cowering therapy poodle, the lioness stood on all fours now. She reached out with a front paw to snag the girl's raft. The child screamed as the oversized paw descended, just as Ryder brought the cart to a halt by smashing it into a lifeguard stand, knocking it into the water. The carnage distracted Baby, and Ryder was once again face-to-face with giant feline death. Stepping out of the cart, legs shaking, hands sweating, he raised the PVC tube, squinted, and clenched his jaw.

"Heavenly creature," he said aloud, stunned for a moment by the cat's towering ivory beauty. "Forgive me for what I hope happens next."

Ryder pulled the spring-loaded trigger, launching whatever lethal rocket had been inside and leaving him engulfed in a thick cloud of acrid smoke. The projectile detonated against the head of the lioness with brutal force and Baby emitted such a long chilling shriek that Ryder felt compelled to drop to one knee and cross himself like a good panic-stricken Catholic.

He kneeled quiet for a while, waiting for his ears to stop ringing and the smoke to dissipate. They did, finally.

News helicopters began hovering over the scene like buzzing vultures. Metro officers had arrived—after all the fuss had ended, naturally—guns drawn, but they ignored Ryder. Instead, they slowly surrounded the inert lioness, inspecting for signs of life.

One of the cops prodded her burned and fractured jaw with the butt end of his flashlight. Baby stayed dead. Satisfied, the officer spoke into his shoulder radio, grabbed a spool of yellow police tape, and began sealing off the pool area.

Ryder tasted blood in his mouth. He wanted a cigarette, though he didn't smoke. He also wanted a gallon of vodka, though he was fonder of pot. Then he felt a hand on his shoulder. Looking up, he saw a divine sight: Eileen's face, her expression of horror included.

He remained on his knees, coming out of his daze. "How's your kid?" he asked, speaking first.

"Fever's down. He's with his dad. What about you?"

He laughed. "Writing an article on filtration doesn't sound so bad now."

"I bet. Let's go, Ryder."

"I think I love you," he said, giving her a hug and a peck on the cheek as they left.

Later that night, in bed and feeling like a panther, he whispered in Eileen's ear, "*Grrr.*"

————————

BY THE TIME Ryder had vouched for Aragon in a written statement and a tape-recorded interview, the scientist had already been booked, processed, and released after serving eighty-two minutes in the Clark County Detention Center. From a table at the Coffee Bean & Tea Leaf near campus, he answered a call letting him know all charges had been dropped. He was using a remote server to erase files from the mainframes in Powers' habitat. Soon he'd be taking his notes with him to Oslo, where he and a friend would get the project running again, this time with funding from an actual government zoo rather than a privately contracted, and very much glorified, zookeeper.

Testing the expansion serum on a couple of white lions would've been much easier had he known Powers planned on shipping one to the Pharaoh that morning. And the arrival of an amateur journalist, while ultimately very opportune, had certainly added another layer of complexity he couldn't have anticipated. Still, by and large, the whole thing had gone rather smoothly. A lioness had killed Powers as he hoped, and now

Aragon was released from contractual obligations and free to sell his discoveries to the highest bidder.

On the negative side, a trainer was eaten, the Hummer totaled. Private insurance in the States would be costly from now on. Fortunately, he worked for the government and rarely paid his own coverage. He'd rely on public transportation until his flight. The weather was getting warmer. Soon Las Vegas would be nearly inhospitable.

Moving to Southern Nevada last year, he had very much looked forward to working with and vigorously experimenting on white lions. Too bad Powers's hunger for publicity derailed the plan. Norway would be a much different story, however. Although there was an abundance of wildlife—bears, lynx, wolves—there were no unique creatures with which to test out and confirm new gene-mutating concoctions. He sipped coffee.

Or were they?

Aragon typed "Oslo, Norway wildlife" in the Google search bar and noticed a result marked "reindeer."

Ah, reindeer.

Aragon opened up a new message in Entourage, addressing it to his Oslo buddy. He mused on the subject line, before chuckling to himself and tapping out: "Next Xmas."

In the body of the email, he wrote: "Santa Claus better buckle up tight."

GHOSTS ON THE MOON

S tretching her arm out the driver-side window of her tangerine Prius, Evangeline Hart punched the access code on the metal keypad. As the gate slowly opened, she checked her appearance in the rearview, using her fingertips to even out her bangs. It was a nondescript apartment complex and she was only questioning a sketchy janitor, but she learned long ago of the value of setting the tone early in an interview. She needed to immediately project determination, strength. Empathy was useless at the start; later on, you could always pretend to identify with someone's feelings in order to acquire damning—or exculpatory—information.

Evangeline was the lead agent at Abraxas Investigations and the company assigned her the most arduous cases. She had an instinctive talent for unearthing texts and emails that confirmed or torpedoed allegations of inappropriate workplace behavior. She could gently coax a confession from the loudest, most lecherous, newspaper veteran or slyly shred a featherweight,

PhD-minted, harpy's bogus Title IX complaint in minutes.

The fact that the janitor residing here in Coyote Springs Villas hadn't hired an attorney made her believe she could file her report tonight and stay poolside at her hotel tomorrow until checking out and driving back to San Diego. Sure, an off-site interview could be tricky, especially if the case went to trial. But her notes were exhaustive; if she saw so much as a shot glass on the coffee table, she'd have him sewn up. Besides, the last time an accused employee had invited her to a sit-down at his place, he whipped out his sex toys to impress her, which the jury didn't appreciate, costing him severely in the end. And *that* guy had been a CEO, not some pervy toilet scrubber at a third-rate observatory beyond the light-polluted mountain range of Las Vegas.

When she pulled her car into a space in front of Villa 5, he was standing outside, smoking a cigarette and flicking the ashes into a concrete-mounted barbecue grill. He was tall, fit—and she was surprised to see—handsome in a black V-neck, dark jeans, and sunglasses. Clearly, he was an aspiring Strip entertainer toiling for a paycheck before his big break. The veins in his forearms made him look aggressive and she felt her pulse quicken.

"Hello," she said, getting out of her car and pulling the hem of her skirt. "You must be Jeremy."

"Evangeline," he said, walking up to shake her hand. "Thanks for agreeing to meet me."

"Actually, I called *you*." She couldn't read his eyes behind his Ray-Bans to determine if he was messing with her. "Starbucks would've been a more neutral location, but I understand how you might feel a little under siege at the moment."

Jeremy shrugged and removed his shades. "I made coffee. Care for some?"

God, those eyes. "That would be nice."

She followed him up the staircase to his condo, trying not to stare at his glutes. She'd expected his pad to smell like body spray and bong water, but the door was open, along with the windows, and a lavender-scented candle was going somewhere. Standard single-guy apartment—tidy, though, with a dark musical aesthetic. A framed poster of Billie Holliday, mouth open in song, hung next to a wall-mounted resonator guitar, its aluminum cone gleaming like a sad mask of Greek tragedy. Evangeline had dated a musician in college who adored of Roy Acuff, so she knew something about folk, country, and blues.

"That's a Dobro," she said.

"Yes," he said, passing her a cup, then gesturing that she should have a seat on the sofa. "I play guitar and sing in a band." He sat down in an upholstered armchair, out of place amid the other IKEA items.

She appreciated his lack of surprise at her recognizing the instrument. "You don't look like a country musician."

Grinning, he shook his head. "Rock. But I appreciate all music."

"Good place to start," said Evangeline, reaching for the legal pad covered in her notes. "It says here you initiated contact with Dr. Zwicky in October of last year by sending her a mix tape."

Jeremy sighed, rubbed his forehead, obviously flustered the interview was already underway. Somehow his response didn't make him look any less masculine. "Yes."

"And one of the tracks on the mix is—please tell me if I'm saying it correctly—W.A.S.P.'s 'Animal, F-word Like a Beast.'" She couldn't help but allow an edge of sarcasm.

"Look," he said. "That song was recorded forty years ago by a hair-metal group. Paige—I mean Dr. Zwicky—had mentioned in a company email it was her favorite Halloween song."

"Her favorite song? Or did she say W.A.S.P. was her favorite band?"

He didn't reply. He leaned forward in his chair, running his hand through his long black mane.

She clicked her pen once, a trick she used to get someone to respond truthfully, uncarefully.

He turned his gaze on her, steeling himself. "She's not human, you know."

"You're saying that Dr. Zwicky seemed cold to the prospect of going out with—"

"No," he said flatly. "I mean, Paige isn't a real human being."

It was Evangeline's turn to be silent. She studied Jeremy's eyes for signs of insanity. Finally, she said, "Jeremy, you don't have to answer this, but are you currently being treated by a doctor who has prescribed you psychotropic medication?"

"I'm not crazy," he said. "I'll show you exactly what I mean."

When he reached into his jeans, a twinge of fear spiked her nervous system. But it was only his cell phone; he had a video playing when he pushed the device across the coffee table.

The image was unsteady, blurry, dark, shot at a distance. It seemed to capture a foregrounded Zwicky taking part in a yoga class on the observatory rooftop with at least five other women—probably professors and graduate students from the nearby university. Evangeline recognized the distinctive hydraulic door that opened to reveal the telescope, plus she'd taken *hatha* classes since college. She saw that these women were starting in *balasana* pose, then moving into *simha garja*n, and finally settling a severe version of *marjarisanaa*. It was an unusual sequence in that particular form of yoga. But what was more extraordinary was the eerie sound.

They were howling, were collectively baying at the moon, a melancholy crater-pocked orb that hung behind them, silhouetting their feral postures.

And then, it seemed to Evangeline, Zwicky's body convulsed, expanded into something grotesque and frightful—

The hell?

Whoever had made the video had been stunned by what was occurring, which caused the recording to suddenly shake and shut off.

"Can I just?" she said to Jeremy.

He nodded, covering his mouth as if he, too, were watching this footage for the first time.

She used her index finger to rewind the video and pause at the moment of transformation. But it was all distorted shadows and vague menace and impossible to figure out precisely what was going on in Zwicky's contorted and rippling frame. And in the vibrating bodies of the others.

Sure, it was odd, spine-stiffening, but it had no bearing, really, on her interview.

"Well," she said, pushing the phone back to him, "this confirms Dr. Zwicky's suspicion."

"Suspicion? Of what?"

"She suspected you were secretly filming her evening *trataka* sessions at the observatory." Trataka was a meditation technique that involved gazing steadily at a still object so as to improve blurry eyesight, clear a cluttered mind, and even, yes, cultivate psychic abilities. Silly, but there was no harm in being silly. Even if you *were* a respected astronomer with a PhD from Georgetown.

"They're not out there doing yoga," said Jeremy, struggling to contain his voice. "Paige is trying to conjure some, some kind of—I don't know—*demon* or something."

"Fine," she said, clicking her pen to indicate she was going to write it down.

"Hey, you know, I don't care what you put in your report. My band just signed with Napalm Records, so I'm dropping this job to tour Europe for the next three months. We're playing festivals in Scandinavia and trust me, I want to put Las Vegas and that werewolf bitch behind me for the rest of my life. But my conscience needs to be clean. The reason I'm telling you this and showing you the video is because the cops here won't even listen to my story. They think I'm another rocker high on bath salts. But I googled you and saw what you did in Phoenix."

He was referring to her years-ago role as a whistle-blower for another investigations company. She'd been working for an outfit with an unacknowledged conflict of interest; when she brought it to her boss's attention, he ignored it. Desperate to avoid a stain on her rep, she went to *Fortune* magazine. The case involved an infamous yoga teacher who'd unsuccessfully litigated to copyright his poses, been accused of improprieties with students, and happened to be a hidden co-investor, along with Evangeline's boss, in a line of Hindu-themed cosmetics.

"When are you turning in your notice?"

"I emailed my manager this morning."

"Great! Our interview is over." She stood up to push the legal pad into her message bag.

"Hold on. No way. What about Paige and her lycanthropy ladies?"

"What about them?"

He stood, too, walking around the coffee table to block her exit. When he got up, his quads looked strong; he obviously didn't miss any leg days at the gym. "Tonight is the super-wolf blood moon. Let me be straight with you, because I know she hasn't: The event she's organizing? It's not a benefit for the observatory. If you don't believe me, take a look."

"Maybe I will," she said, pulling the bag strap over her shoulder. "I have a mat in my trunk."

"No, not as a participant." He touched her arm and even though it felt slightly menacing, it nearly melted her. His eyes were so dark and sexy. Was the head-banger out of his gourd or just mysteriously and wildly soulful? "Don't go near them when they begin doing their poses."

"I need to leave," she said forcefully, heart thumping in her chest.

For a moment, she didn't think he'd move aside. But he acquiesced, walking to his door to open it for her.

"Thanks," she said, walking out. "Good luck in Europe."

"We have a gig tomorrow, actually. A showcase at the Hard Rock. You should come."

"Sorry, I'll be home by then."

"Back in San Diego."

She didn't respond to this. "Goodbye, Jeremy."

"I have your email," he said, watching her walk down the stairs. "I'll send you a link."

———

IN HER CAR before setting off for the observatory, she used her phone to research "super-wolf blood moon." It was, according to HuffPo, a total lunar eclipse. For a few hours, sun and moon would be in alignment on opposite ends of the planet, the earth's shadow covering the moon with a reddish hue—thus, a *blood moon*. And because this was all occurring at the moon's perigee, when its orbit drew nearest to us, the lunar rock appeared bigger, brighter.

Maybe that's why I felt unhinged with Jeremy. A giant red moon about to pull me apart from inside my womb. He's a rock star, no doubt. Probably half the reason his band got a record deal.

When she arrived at the observatory, it wasn't yet noon, but already preparations were underway. From the parking lot, she could make out, on the dome's rooftop, a velvet-roped patio area with a DJ booth and black-clothed cocktail tables. The wealthy and elite of Las Vegas had RSVP'd and it looked to be a significant fundraiser for the observatory and the larger community. She half-considered asking Abraxas if she could attend, but the conflict would be enormous. Better to stay in the room and finish her report.

Once inside, she made her way to the observatory's administrative office and found Muriel, the woman who cut everyone's paychecks, handled their vacation and sick leave, and edited the employee newsletter announcing their awards and family births and deaths. She was the one who'd reached out to Abraxas after working for more than a decade with Dr. Zwicky; Zwicky was also godmother to Muriel's daughter. Also, since the observatory was funded, strangely enough, through a humanities grant, that made it difficult for the union to waste resources on Jeremy's creepy-voyeur issues with Dr. Zwicky. For the observatory, it had been a relative bargain to retain the services of Abraxas and Evangeline.

"Tell me," said Evangeline, "that Jeremy emailed you."

"He did!" said Muriel, swiveling away from her computer screen. "He tendered his resignation. I'm just waiting for the director to sign Jeremy's last check."

Evangeline wiped her brow with comic finality. "That's a relief. Still, I'd like to chat with Dr. Zwicky. For the sake of thoroughness."

Muriel made a face. "Probably unnecessary at this point. Anyhow, Paige is overwhelmed with planning the meditation fundraiser."

"It'll only be a few minutes," she insisted.

"Well, we've already paid Abraxas and your boss seems *very* pleased with the outcome."

Bitch. "Fine. Thanks again, Muriel. Please keep us in mind for any future issues."

"Absolutely. Let me know if you'd like to attend the event tonight." Muriel then turned her chair back to examine her screen, chock-full of photos of observatory astronomers and support staff taken at an outdoor gathering.

"I'm good." Evangeline was about to leave but then noticed an image of Zwicky in a long-sleeved shirt and denim capris winding up to throw a Frisbee at someone off-camera. "That looks like a blast," she said. "Last year's fundraiser?"

"Oh, it was *so* much fun," Muriel cheerfully reminisced. "The annual Autumnal Equinox picnic from September. I won Best Chili!"

Evangeline took out her pad to write down the words on Zwicky's shirt: *Occidere Solem. Lunam Amor.*

It had been a long time since she studied Latin in high school, but she translated it easily enough.

Kill the sun.

Revere the moon.

EVANGELINE SHIVERED poolside at the Excalibur in a white bathrobe and slippers with a few hotel towels draped over her legs, checking her emails. It was surprisingly chilly in Las Vegas, even for January, and she loathed spas filled with irritating children and old people with their wrinkled and saggy skin. Her drink order was taking forever. Everything about the afternoon was testing her patience and if that Baileys and coffee didn't arrive soon, she was going back to sit in her room, watch Netflix, and have a burger brought up.

I need to get laid.

She was about to put away her phone when her inbox pinged. A message from Jeremy and, as promised, a link. She clicked on a SoundCloud file of, she assumed, a tune by his band. She'd already researched his music, the lyrics of which exhibited aspects of misogyny that she planned to include in her report. This song, though, was ineloquently titled "Against the Forces of Darkness."

She put on her wireless headphones.

He didn't really sing so much as scream, but the Viking ferocity of his performance turned her on more than she could have anticipated. She could also tell that he was an exceptional, if overly technical, guitarist. He had fast expert fingers. For a moment—it was only a fleeting fantasy and not something she'd ever wish for in real life—she imagined his hand on her neck as he took her from behind.

"Irish coffee?" said the waiter, lifting the glass off his tray.

"Thanks," she said, taking the drink and hoping her face wasn't red from her blue reverie.

It tasted wonderful, hot and sweet, creamy and liquor-infused. *Another twenty minutes on the Stairmaster tonight as punishment for this sin.*

Then she noticed the song had an interlude, a moody Dobro breakdown that took everything in a different direction, into a space where Johnny Cash and Metallica might collaborate. It was intriguing and—to her ears—unique.

She read the email again: *11 p.m., Hard Rock.*

You're on the list. Good luck with the She-Wolves! He'd included his phone number.

She called him.

"Evangeline?"

What. "How did—"

"San Diego number," he explained. "What did Paige tell you?"

"I didn't get to speak with her. Your resignation made it unnecessary."

He groaned. "Can't you use your investigative powers to, like, *cancel* the event?"

"I'm not with the observatory, Jeremy. I'm a glorified third-party vendor."

"It's more than a bad feeling I have."

She didn't say anything for a beat. Then, "You can be my date."

He blew out a breath. "They'll call the police on me before I get through the door."

"No doors involved. I just need you to drive and wait for me in the parking lot."

"Um, okay. I expect you'll tell me more."

"Where are you now?"

"Guitar Center buying strings. You?"

"Excalibur. Come over."

He chuckled. "I'll be there in fifteen."

"Don't get any ideas. I want to show you Dr. Zwicky's dissertation."

"Academic reading is your idea of foreplay?"

He's almost funny. "Not quite. She did her field-work at Newgrange."

"In Ireland."

Not every metal head rocker would know that. "Yes, there's a Neolithic Passage Tomb there. She studied the effects of moonlight, specifically how it penetrates the tomb's roof box and travels along a passage and into what is, in essence, a light chamber. As the moon rises higher, the beam widens, so the entire room is bathed."

She explained the rest of Zwicky's theories over beers in one of the casino bars. She'd brought the wrong jeans to Las Vegas but still knew she had enough going on to keep Jeremy interested.

"So basically," he said, "she earned an astronomy doctorate based on a bunch of writings on ancient archaeology? That's like getting a performance degree for composing a bunch of pop jingles."

Ouch. Maybe he's not so smart after all. "Sure, but this part is really strange, don't you think?" She pointed to a section of the dissertation titled "The Quantifiable Impact of Lunar Irradiation on Female Aggressive Tendencies."

"Wow," said Jeremy, taking a sip of Corona. "I think I get it."

"Get what?"

"She's creating an army. An army of wolfwomen."

Evangeline snorted too loudly.

"No, listen, she's always talking about how the telescope is just a bunch of mirrors used to collect and focus light."

"Pillow talk?" she said, gently elbowing him. She was a little buzzed now.

"I didn't sleep with her," said Jeremy in a serious tone. "I mean, I certainly *wanted* to. That was before she tried to bite me."

Evangeline didn't know what to say. The revelation scared her; it suggested either Jeremy or Zwicky was bonkers. Maybe both. And that she might be joining them in their madness.

Her investigator instincts kicked in. "Why did she try to bite you, Jeremy?"

"Because, over steaks, I made the mistake of telling her that I had bought silver-plated guitar strings," he said. "You think I'm crazy, don't you."

There was at least one way to find out.

———————

THE OBSERVATORY WAS THRONGED with revelers, so the drive up the mountain took a solid twenty minutes before Jeremy even reached the parking lot, with a line of black Chevy Suburbans stalled on the approach up to valet.

"This is fine. I don't want to give them my car," she said. "Park somewhere down here. I'll text you after I've shut it down."

Jeremy nodded. He'd explained to her how to turn off the telescope. "You can't miss me in this bright orange roller skate."

"Hush," she said. "I love the color."

She stepped out of the Prius and began walking uphill—in heels, tight little black dress, and her Kate Spade purse. It was at least fifty degrees and she didn't have a sweater. *God, give me strength.* When she reached the observatory entrance, Muriel was checking in people at a table. "Ms. Hart, you decided to come after all."

Evangeline nodded. "My hotel is a tad boring this evening."

Muriel laughed and handed her a name tag. "We're

so glad you could make it. Don't forget there's a silent auction. And the yoga demonstration starts promptly at eight."

Evangeline made her way through the admission turnstiles, past the gift shop, and to the elevator that led to the rooftop. She'd temporarily fallen in with a cluster of blue-haired fundraising marks who were busy complimenting one another on their smart cruelty-free stoles. Engaged in their discussion, they didn't notice her as she slinked away into the dark recesses of the facility.

At the access door, she held the white plastic card Jeremy had given her, which belonged to his manager, who'd forgotten ever giving the musician an additional off-the-books key. The red light turned green, and she was in.

The telescope was hardly state-of-the-art, but it was a beautiful piece of 1990s-era scientific machinery. Evangeline had read up on it, learning that it was a multi-element optical interferometer that relied on aperture synthesis to observe stars with angular resolution, producing images with the highest resolution. It absorbed and intensified light from the stars—from other galaxies—with ease, making it the perfect chamber for...

For what exactly? For transforming yoga-panted moms into a werewolf army?

She walked over to the control station, looking for a lever marked SHUTDOWN. She was about to pull it when she heard a noise.

"You're the investigator from Abraxas," said Zwicky, outfitted in sky-high heels, a mesh top, and a pair of zebra-striped leggings. She looked ready to walk down a red carpet, not lead a fundraising yoga session. "We didn't get a chance to talk."

"Does *now* work for you?" said Evangeline, reaching for something in her sleek black Cameron Street Brennan.

Zwicky smiled. She looked lovely and lethal as she sauntered around the telescopic chamber's workstation to get closer. "I think it's too late to chat. You're here because you think you know something. Maybe Jeremy gave you information. Maybe you're sleeping with him."

"There's a better chance," said Evangeline, retreating until she bumped against the telescope, "that you believe in the power of a super-wolf blood moon to bring forth the Morrígan, the Queen of Phantoms, from her lunar prison. You mention her often in your dissertation."

"You're a thorough cunt, I'll give you that." Zwicky's beautiful form began to vibrate, her soft alluring features and limbs giving way to something bestial covered in dark stiff hair. Her canines became longer, sharper; they glistened with saliva. Her nose pushed forward, her nostrils melting until they became snout-like. Her voice shifted down an entire octave. "But you're not going to ruin tonight's summoning," she groan-slobbered. She squatted down on her haunches as if preparing to leap.

"I've undone a lot of awful people's horrible plans. What makes you different, dog-breath?"

The wolf-creature that had been Zwicky jumped at Evangeline. But the workplace investigator had already raised the silver-plated guitar string with both hands like a garrote, catching the she-wolf between the top and bottom rows of teeth, lacerating the inside corners of the mouth.

Zwicky's forward momentum impacted Evangeline, knocking the base of her skull against the telescope, hard. She almost laughed out loud at the irony of seeing stars, but was too focused on the werewolf reacting with terror and misery to the introduction of silver into its mouth.

At this moment, Muriel entered the room. "Ms. Hart, I didn't think to tell you that there are absolutely *no* therapy animals allowed at all in the observa—*oh my goodness*."

The creature suddenly turned to the older woman, its jaws foaming, howling in thunderous agony, poised to attack.

Evangeline was already charging at Zwicky and managed to loop the guitar string around her neck. There was a sound of sizzling flesh, followed by a shriek-yelp of anguish. But then Evangeline's ankle got caught in the caster wheels of an office chair and she went down, flat on her back.

Expecting Zwicky to tear her to shreds, she covered her face with her hands. But then she heard claws clacking against the concrete floor and when she opened her eyes, she saw that she and Muriel were alone. Screams from outside meant the werewolf had scurried its way out of the observatory and into the desert badlands of outer Vegas.

Evangeline stood up and brushed wolf hair from her dress. She used her most reprimanding voice. "I hope, Muriel," she said, "that I won't have to invoice you for the damage incurred by recruiting protected animals into your bizarre eco-fundraiser here in the middle of absolutely nowhere."

Muriel didn't seem to hear. She staggered, still in shock from the encounter, leaning against a desk for support.

"Um, Muriel? Are you okay?"

The old woman nodded.

"Should I call an ambulance?"

"No. I just need a minute."

"Great. Well, I'll need to get this DKNY dry-cleaned. Goodbye, Muriel."

Evangeline shut down the telescope and texted Jeremy. She took another door as curious onlookers began to push through into telescopic chamber's main entrance.

———

JEREMY'S SET at the Hard Rock was phenomenal. He nailed every solo and Evangeline worried she was going to have to clobber a few groupies to keep him at her side. Later, at Excalibur, he made her a bag of ice for her head and massaged her ankle in the tub. She wasn't that kind of girl, so she wore her one-piece bathing suit while he still had on his Tommy John's. "What if Paige comes after you?"

She shrugged and pursed her lips to blow at a froth of bubbles. "I'm not scared of her. I've had CEOs try to plant bombs under my car, HR managers hold knives to my neck. And what's she going to do, track me to San Diego? Plus, I've got my trusty guitar string—good thinking, by the way, making sure I had it with me."

His strong hands felt amazing pressing on her toes. She was glad she'd gotten a pedicure yesterday.

"Okay. So much for Paige. What about you—after you file your amended report, of course?"

She placed the ball of her foot against his muscular chest. "I was thinking of using my vacation time. Maybe see Europe. I hear there are some amazing rock festivals in—was it Scandinavia?"

He laughed. "How much time can you take?"

"Three months."

They continued relaxing in the warm water of the tub as the full moon of blood, hanging low and large, simmered in the night sky like an omen of forbidden lust.

HEVN

evn walked past Valgt, the record shop, mistaking it for a brothel.

The windows were blackened, and the neon girl's fanged mouth glowed like all the other red-light signage, making the shop inconspicuous on a block of massage parlors and peepshows. This was Oslo's lowest-rent neighborhood, where Pakistani immigrants sold kebabs from illegal charcoal grills. As he doubled back, they glared at him. Hevn scoffed to himself. Despite his blonde mane, he was six-foot-seven and had trained in boxing with the *Forsvaret*. He bore the flattened nose and cauliflower ears earned on a sun-blasted minesweeper deck in the Persian Gulf. It was only the threat of a dishonorable discharge that kept him from constant and brutal fighting.

There was an incendiary rage inside Hevn. A demon—an all-consuming fire spirit escaped from *Muspelheim*—roiled his heart, waiting for the right moment to be released. Or the wrong one. He'd not only learned to box on that minesweeper; he'd also developed the discipline to keep the beast contained.

Inside, Valgt lived up to its reputation. There were no customers. A gas-masked, Valkyrie-helmeted, female mannequin in white-lace lingerie stood across the aisles of vinyl albums. Candles flickered in skull-shaped sconces, and the walls were decorated with taxidermized animal heads. The shrieked vocals and frenzied blast beats of a band unfamiliar to Hevn only enhanced the morbid gloom. He liked what he was hearing spinning on the turntable, though he would have preferred it five levels louder.

"Good music," he said to the dark figure behind the register.

An orange ember glowed, and the man exhaled a plume of clove-scented smoke. "My previous black-metal project," he rasped, his voice like sandpaper dipped in hot tar.

"You're the singer?"

The man nodded. "Guitarist, too. Didrik." He extended his hand. "Welcome to Valgt."

Hevn shook hands, assessing Didrik's physicality. He was shorter, stockier. Young thirties in a black leather biker jacket and matching pants. Greasy, unkempt, dark hair. Weak jawline. Didrik didn't look violent. But, as Hevn well knew, the most lethal psychopaths treading the earth appear unassuming, normal.

"I'm Hevn. The drummer."

"Heard you were big," said Didrik. "But you're nearly a giant."

Hevn suppressed a scowl at being teased, and shrugged. "I'm big enough to lift my drums."

"What about carrying gasoline, eh?" It was still pretty dim, and his eyes hadn't fully adjusted, but Hevn could make out a smile on Didrik's face.

Hevn was grinning now, too, playing the game. "You heard about my trip through Lillehammer."

"Read about it in the newspaper here. And I know what Grimm says about you."

Grimm was Hevn's coworker in the rural town of Hokksund. They worked together in a cement plant, repairing worn-out equipment with power tools and welding torches. They'd bonded over lacerating black metal and fantasies of toppling Christianity with heathen rituals and church arson. A month ago, Hevn pushed the latter notion into reality, hopping a train into forested Oppland county and setting fire to a beautiful wooden congregation house built near the end of the Bubonic Plague that had decimated medieval Europe in the 1300s.

"What does he say?" asked Hevn.

"Says you're a real *rasshøl*. Grimm would know."

Hevn figured Didrik was referring to the murder. Grimm had done nine years for hammer-smashing a man, a complete stranger, to death in the woods after drinking with the victim for hours in a pub. Since it was deemed an "impulse killing," Grimm's sentence was reduced. Good behavior ensured he was released before his thirtieth birthday. Norwegians believed in rehabilitation.

"I'd toast Grimm with you," said Hevn, "but you haven't poured anything to drink."

Didrik guffawed and slapped his guest on the arm. He leaned over to open the mini-fridge on his side of the glass display case and finger-hooked a six-pack of

Ringnes. Hevn took a moment to look around the shop and spotted a crossbow leaning against a pile of records. He considered asking a question but thought better of it. Didrik yanked a can from its plastic yoke, handed it to Hevn, and cracked open one for himself.

"To Grimm," said Didrik.

"An unrivaled savage," Hevn added. "A student of lunacy."

"To lunacy," Didrik agreed. He tapped his can to Hevn's and slurped.

The record stopped. Hevn heard a muffled thump and what sounded like a human groan.

"You have a basement." Hevn raised his beer and arched his brow.

"I do indeed," said Didrik, lowering his head and meeting Hevn's gaze with hooded eyes. He mock-whispered with glee, "It's full of treasure."

"Do I get a tour?"

"Of course."

After turning off the OPEN sign and locking the entrance, Didrik led him past the blinking apocalypse mannequin, through the STAFF ONLY door, and down a set of stairs littered with cigarette butts. The cellar, spare yet spacious, was better lit than the shop above and smelled like an ashtray in a gym locker. There were a few booze-stained mattresses on the floor and a drum kit—a Super Pro GLX, favored by black-metal bands that loved its thunderous double-kick drum capability—surrounded by stacks of giant amplifiers, jet-black B.C. Rich guitars perched on stands, and a PA system for vocals.

"I love that kit," said Hevn.

"What drummer doesn't." It wasn't a question.

Hevn heard the groan again, louder this time. He walked over to the space behind the staircase whence the noise had emanated and peered into the shadows. There, chained to the wall with handcuffs and gagged with electrical tape, was a woman.

Her platinum hair was cropped, and she wore torn jeans and a ripped, blood-flecked shirt. She'd been corpse-painted, her face and neck a paler shade of undead, eyes shadowed, cheekbones darkened. On the black tape pressed to her mouth, someone had painted rows of broken teeth. She resembled a crazed, skeletal kabuki actress. For a moment, Hevn wondered if Didrik was pranking him.

The captive whimpered with fear, snot pouring from her nose, and he knew this was no practical joke; she was being held against her will. Hevn could feel the demon straining to break free. He counted down from ten to keep from losing control.

"We have a captive audience today." Didrik giggled, clapping his hands and rubbing them together. "Shall we get started?"

"Have you hurt her?"

"Only with my music. She's probably as deaf as we are at this point. The *real* fun begins tonight. In Borgund."

"You grabbed her when?"

"Day before yesterday. In the park. She mistook me for a weed dealer."

Hevn nodded, his gaze still lingering on her terror-ized loveliness.

"The Americans," Didrik continued, "torture their prisoners with heavy metal played at ear-splitting volume." He stroked the girl's painted features as she shook her head and sobbed.

The amps were already cranked. Didrik dimmed the lights and strapped on his guitar. He turned a knob to unleash a squall of feedback, then shut it off just as suddenly. "Volume," he said, "is something we have in abundance. Let's see what you can do, Mr. Hevn."

He went over to the kit and sat down on the drum throne, then adjusted its height and the angle of the mounted toms. He picked up the sticks vibrating on the snare when Didrik dug into a bludgeoning lurching riff.

Wincing, the woman shut her eyes, collapsed to her knees and, hands manacled behind her back, rested her forehead on the ground as if joining an Islamic prayer.

With only a measure to decide on a rhythm, Hevn spontaneously opted for a double-time intro beat before slowing to a heavier sludge groove for what he assumed was the verse. He planned on snare-and-floor-tom-rolling directly into the chorus, wherever that happened to land. But he played softly, for only himself—to soothe the beast. It felt wonderful to play the drums, but the girl was in enough agony, and Didrik was screaming a narrative of satanic majesty. His tobacco-stained teeth scraped against the head of the microphone, the impact sounding like a flaming 747 crashing in a fireball.

Every few measures, Hevn looked over at the woman, drowning in misery, unable to cover her ears from the maelstrom, sinking deeper. He watched as she curled into the fetal position.

NIGHT FELL. They scarfed falafel and loaded the rental van in the alley behind the strip mall. Didrik brought along the hunting crossbow. It was a four-hour highway drive to the stave church in Borgund, a gorgeous basilica structure with a ceiling held up by scissor beams and dragon heads carved into the gables of the tiered roofs. Hevn had visited the church once as a child during a family road trip. Those were happier times. His sister was still alive then, their parents together. Inside the space, he recalled the musty smell of old leather, the odd presence of several illuminated votive ships designed by seamen, and the massive and intricate wooden pipe organ that sounded like the voice of God.

That was a long time ago, however. God hadn't spoken to Hevn in years—only the beast. Now, though, he wasn't sure which one he was hearing.

In the cab of the truck, Didrik popped in a cassette demo by a Swedish death-metal trio. Chainsaw guitars, drums like rotting zombie flesh beaten with mallets, a guttural shriek so intimidating it bristled Hevn's neck hair. Hevn sensed that Didrik was keeping his own ogre on a leash, fighting the urge to floor the gas pedal, eager to douse the spruce-hewn sacristy in petrol and watch flames consume his victim.

"So," Didrik began, replacing the Swedes with a Finnish death-doom tape. "What was it like?"

"Better than drugs," said Hevn. "Better than sex."

"Did he speak to you from the flames?"

"You mean...Satan?"

"Yes," said Didrik.

Hven shook his head. "I wouldn't have listened anyway."

"Well, I follow the Lightbringer."

"Well, we have a common enemy," said Hevn.

Didrik nodded. "Christianity will die soon."

Thump thump

"She doesn't give up," said Hevn.

"I'm sick of it," said Didrik, jerking the steering wheel back and forth, causing the weight in the cargo hold to shift from side to side. There was a muted squeal of fright.

THUMP THUMP THUMP

"I hope she doesn't get drenched," said Didrik, laughing. They had chained her inside the back of the truck with several no-spill gas cans. He jammed down on the brake, then let up, jammed down and let up, bucking the van, rolling the contents of the hold forward and backward. Then he slid into neutral, straining to hear beyond the idling engine for any muffled crying.

"Go to sleep now," said Didrik, and he began singing a Norwegian lullaby in an eerie baritone, even though she couldn't hear him.

> *Now, our little one shall sleep sweetly*
> *The cradle is made up for the baby*
> *There it will lie tenderly, softly*
> *Our baby will sleep safely*
> *Quiet, quiet, sleep sweetly*
> *That baby will sleep safely*

Hevn nearly said to him, "When you're not yelling into a mic, you have a pleasant voice." But he refrained. Instead, he said, "Look," pointing at the eyes of an animal glowing in the middle of the road.

"Told you there were reindeer," said Didrik, braking to stop the truck. He picked up the crossbow from the floorboard, opened the driver's door, and stepped out.

Paralyzed by the headlights, the reindeer stood stock still as Didrik took aim and fired an arrow into the creature's chest—a perfect kill shot. Blood spurted as the deer stumbled drunkenly, hooves clicking against the asphalt. It tried to run, then trotted in a circle and collapsed, twitching briefly before becoming still.

"Hoo!" yelped Didrik. "Venison." He put the crossbow back in the cab and made his way to the dead animal, no doubt to drag its carcass to the truck.

Hevn got out to open the cargo door. Didrik hauled the carcass by its hind legs, arrow still jutting out, leaving a trail of gore in the road.

Together, they wrapped the deer in a plastic tarp and swung it into the hold. Aghast with this development, the woman tried to scream, shaking her head and flailing at the bleeding meat with her manacled legs.

Hevn slammed the door shut and watched Didrik light a cigarette. They opened beers.

A sedan with a family inside it cruised slowly by, the mother's brow furrowing as if searching her memory for recognition of the two long-haired metal heads who had stopped their truck in the road for mysterious and likely illicit reasons. The dad kept the vehicle moving, speeding up when they passed the car.

"Kidnapping," said Didrik.

"Arson," said Hevn.

"Hunting protected animals."

"Drinking bad Norwegian beer."

They laughed together loudly in the cold air.

A few minutes later, back in the truck and driving down the highway again, Didrik said, "Hail, Santa!" He laughed again.

A single white snowflake fell from the sky to rest on the windshield.

THEY PULLED into a darkened parking lot carved out of the wilderness. The stave loomed in the clearing like a giant monster anchored in shadow, scales like swooping bat wings waiting to be stirred into action. They'd passed by a security booth the size of an outhouse. The light was on, but no one was inside. Didrik parked in the handicapped spot closest to the church entrance then stepped out of the truck. He put his crossbow on the sidewalk, stepped into the foot stirrup, re-hooked the rope to cock the crossbow, and loaded the arrow.

"This thing," he said, "is awesome."

Hevn yanked the cargo door open with a clang. The woman was whimpering, pressing herself against the front of the hold, not wanting to be led out to whatever doom awaited her.

"Don't make him come in there," warned Hevn.

For the first time, her eyes met his. Her brows lifted a little, and he held her gaze. Then, with a grunt, she inch-wormed her shackled body toward him, getting some of the deer blood that had leaked from the tarp on her skin and clothes. He helped her out of the hold and to her feet, stooping to loosen her leg manacles so she could at least walk, if awkwardly, haltingly.

As the three walked to the front of the truck, Hevn

grabbed the bolt cutters from the cab, so he could bust the chain locking the church doors.

But Didrik had other plans. He was bent over, fumbling to find a throwable rock. He picked up a decent-sized stone and smashed a hole through the stained glass. Using his crossbow, he punched out the remaining shards.

"You first," he instructed the woman, dragging her in front of them with the chain and booting her in the spine.

They made their way through the rectory and into the worship space.

As THEY CHAINED the woman to the altar, she struggled wildly, manacles clanking, the horrific realization dawning that they intended to burn her alive.

Only when he had her pinned down for Didrik to fasten the locks did Hevn notice her crucifix necklace.

"The witch is afraid," said Didrik, standing now at the chancel's edge. "This moment will haunt Norway for centuries."

"Yes," said Hevn. "It will."

Didrik unscrewed the cap of one of the gas cans and hefted it, holding it out to Hevn. "Want the honor?"

Hevn shook his head. "This is your first. The honor should be yours."

Gag still in her mouth, the woman gargled what sounded like a prayer.

Didrik laughed at her misery. Giddy with the effort, he began dousing the place in gasoline. "Wretched stink!" he exclaimed. "Better than sulfur!"

He flick-ignited a match and began, "Bringer of light—" But before he could say more, Hevn smashed the back of his head with the bolt cutters. "Odin is the *only* light," he hissed. "You're a sad dilettante, thinking I'd turn you into a serial killer or help you wreck civilization."

Didrik staggered forward, facing his assailant. "Pagan bastard!" He pulled the crossbow from his shoulders and fired instinctively, without aiming.

The arrow struck Hevn in the neck, just missing his vocal cords.

"You're really good with that," he wheezed, calmly approaching Didrik. He snapped off the arrow's end and pushed it all the way through. Blood poured down his chest, soaking his shirt and leather jacket. The demon was free now, unleashed. The sensation was indescribable. He wielded the arrow like a dagger, its tip glistening with gore.

Didrik had no chance to reload. He collapsed against the communion railing and could only scream as Hevn skewered him through the eye.

———————

A YEAR LATER, after the TV news interviews and the book was published and she became the leading spokesperson for victims of the widespread satanic church-burning epidemic that was plaguing Norway at that moment in history, Agnora married an investment banker and adopted a child from Syria. She made her husband promise never to reveal the details of that night in Borgund, when she was nearly sacrificed inside a stave church for the perverse pleasure of a twisted musician.

When she saw a picture of the other man in the newspaper in a profile of an up-and-coming Oslo metal band, she gasped. Law enforcement had never success-fully identified him. He was using a different name. She read the article many times, remembering the man with the pugilistic face and blood all over his neck and torso breaking her chains, carrying her out of the church, and singing her a lullaby.

Right there in her sunlit kitchen in her apartment in Aker Brygge, she kneeled down, touched the crucifix on her necklace, and said a prayer for the man she knew only as Hevn.

COMIC BOOK HELL

What Bentley Flood read stunned him.

He was sitting at a table in the concession area, holding a yellow mustard-soaked hot dog in one hand, with the other flipping through the convention events guide. In ten minutes, Dr. Mortimer Spanuth from Gonzaga University was scheduled to present a paper on *Nekro*, a late-sixties one-shot produced by an honest-to-goodness satanic cult with vague connections to the Manson family. Flood had overheard the story behind this comic book at an informal Charlton Comics staff party in Dover years ago, but only three copies had been mimeographed at a youth hostel in Amsterdam, according to legend anyway, so he never dreamed he would see a copy himself, much less at an academic conference tacked onto the biggest comics-industry gathering in the world. He scarfed the wiener and went in search of Room 16A.

In the years before the internet forever changed the

game, Flood had pursued obscure and unusual comic books by hook or by crook. He was a large sluggish man with bifocals, too-tight and sauce-stained T-shirts, and prominent paunch. He owned and operated a pizza shop in Las Vegas and rented a nearby house whose only serious amenities were a kick-ass stereo system (he loved to blast Journey and Styx) and a walnut-paneled den crammed, of course, with box upon box of comics. From Monday to Thursday, when business was slower, he escaped the hassles of food service, ranging the continent, sniffing for the pages of forgotten curiosities. His travels led him to places like Slapout, Alabama; Crested Butte, Colorado; Friendly, Maryland. He scoured not just specialty stores, but flea markets, junk shops, yard sales, and estate auctions. He hunted for the unfamiliar promotional (*Kernel Corn Trains a Champ!*), the scarce anti-drug giveaway (*Four-Color Tales of Junkies*), and with each new find, his addiction intensified, his anticipation grew. But the joys of discovering pristine copies of rare comics had lessened over time. Lately, he'd sought the world's strangest comics and made no secret that he was the best at finding them—in mint condition.

His obsession brought him, not for the first time, to San Diego for Comic-Con International, the biggest annual gathering. As a collector, Flood had no interest in the industry's self-congratulatory hype; men in tights did nothing for him. But he'd heard rumors of an anonymously published "horse-breeding primer" comic, as well as an anthology of pre-WW II aviation-adventure strips reprinted by a mom-and-pop outfit somewhere in North Dakota. Having exhausted his fellow collector connections, BBS leads, and fanzine-ad tips, he hoped to uncover these oddities at the Comic-Con. But now the satanic comic took precedence.

He threaded the exhibition hall, a gauntlet of dealers, row after row, each with a folding table to display his (they were almost always men) comics. He felt smug in his superiority to these pushy scum, particularly the speculators, that awful breed of hipster collector. Indeed, today's urban professionals made it difficult for Flood to relax in a comic book store. They picked the shelves clean like vultures on a corpse, buying everything from *The Astonishers* to *Zebra Force*, spending upwards of $200 in a single visit, beaming tides of joy over their "investments." Flood knew for a fact that these guys drove home and immediately shoved the comics into polyurethane bags on the chance of a market upswing. What, he wondered, was the ultimate goal? To finance their kids' college educations? On comic books? How sad.

The convention center was a madhouse. Earlier in the day, he'd served as a human speed bump for a stampede of baseball-capped baggy-jeaned teenagers, the zippers on their book bags abrading his arms, their bulky footwear scuffing his penny loafers. Now he dodged and weaved, maintaining a steady brisk pace, confident in his maneuvers. It felt good to move quickly through the crowd, so good that he surrendered to impulse and goosed a young woman wearing a fake animal pelt who was passing out promo stickers for some negligible series. When she squealed, he broke into something resembling a jog and never looked back. Winded, he rode an escalator to the mezzanine.

The atmosphere in Room 16A was markedly differ-

ent, charged with intellectual rather than puerile energies. Seated in the audience were a dozen or so acade-
mics, men and women his age, all of whom appeared to
share his serious regard for comics. They were a
composed bunch, talking quietly, yet intently, with one
another in groups of two or three. It was all very religious in comparison with the unchecked consumerism
raging outside. Priests in a whorehouse, thought Flood.
He wanted very much to be a part of a network of
comics scholars. If only he'd graduated from college. Or
even high school.

He sat down next to an attractive young woman, no
doubt a graduate student, with milky-white skin,
another corn-fed doll from Nebraska. She wore the kind
of skirt that, to Flood's mind, suggested both strict
professionalism and reckless carnality. Like Lois Lane
drawn by, say, Frank Thorne. She was inspecting her
face in a compact mirror.

A lifelong bachelor and hard-core nerd, Flood tried
to engage her in high-minded conversation.

"Batman and Robin," he said. "Gay lovers or just
good friends?"

She turned to the collector and greeted him with a
look of inebriated eagerness. "Is there a reception
tonight?"

"Are you a collector?"

"No. I'm a hooker." She turned back to her
compact.

Flood felt his face go hot. Christ, he thought. This
really *is* a whorehouse.

"See that old guy there?" she went on. "With the
bow tie? That's my john."

Flood's eyes followed to where she was pointing at the front of the room. "Is he a professor?"

"Yep. A smart one."

"He looks drunk."

"And more. He's about to recite a paper he wrote."

"On what?"

"A *freaky* little thing. It's got S&M and death."

"Ah. So that's Dr. Mortimer Spanuth."

"You don't know Mortie?"

"Nope. But I know the comic he's going to discuss. I've always dreamed of owning it. I'm a collector, you see."

"Huh," she said, wrinkling her nose in distaste. "Well, this comic doesn't do much for me. If you're into that satanic stuff, though, I can find you a girl."

"No thanks. I just want to see how it looks on the page."

She glanced at him in an uneasy fashion that made him wish he'd held his tongue. Then she snapped her compact shut and said, "So why are you here? To buy the comic from Mortie? He's got it, in his hotel room, you know. Made me scan his presentation slides at the hotel business center. So lazy."

"I don't think he'll part with *Nekro*. It's a very rare piece."

"How rare?"

"Enough that I'd give him five thousand dollars for it."

She whistled. "For a little more, I'll steal that comic book for you, no problem."

Flood's heart fluttered at the prospect. A thieving hooker sent down from heaven to make him the single most important figure in comics collecting and funny-book scholarship. "Call me B," he said, a nickname he'd always wanted for himself.

She shook his hand once, softly, and said demurely, "You can find me in the personals under Veronica."

STONED OUT OF HIS MIND, Mort made his way to the front of the room. The introduction was heartfelt, the applause considerate. In the blurred faces of the audience, he sensed cordiality and patience. It fortified him. Most likely, this would be the last presentation of his academic career. "The horror," he mumbled to himself before stepping up to the mike.

His bid for tenure had been disastrous. The jackals had torn him apart, leaving him with nothing. They'd hired him to establish an Institute on Popular Culture Studies and he'd done just that. True, the faculty affiliates were long in responding to the provision for a credit-transfer plan, the newsletter never really got off the ground, and the women's-studies program jumped all over his back for neglecting to include their core faculty. But how in the hell was he expected to seamlessly create an institute out of thin air on such a meager grant line when he was teaching three auditorium-sized undergraduate classes per semester without so much as a teaching assistant? Hadn't he, after all, orchestrated a conference last year that brought to campus such luminaries as German psycho-Marxist and pornographic comics historian Klaus Scheindunger? And hadn't he managed to serially publish the bulk of his dissertation in this country's most vital comics fanzine, *The Pulp Fancier*? None of it mattered; no one cared. Last month, his colleagues had betrayed him, bestowing on him the Judas kiss. Suspicious of his proposed honors seminar on the notorious Tijuana bibles of the thirties, they voted in favor of his tenure—but with reservations! And that was all the dean needed to send Dr. Mortimer Spanuth packing. Once named a leading American scholar in pop culture by *Chap* magazine, Spanuth's chances at age fifty of landing another tenure-track position in his specialized field were slim.

It was an unjust world. But yesterday, he'd pledged to drink and drug and screw the world away with the help of his new friend, Veronica, whom he met in the hotel lounge and with whom he shared a deep affinity for televised drag racing and pro wrestling at high volume. After four brain-mulching martinis each, they became mirthful and were finally cut off and kicked out of the lounge for commandeering the TV and cranking ABC's "Wide World of Sports." Veronica escorted Mort to his room, where he paid her to perform acts of lowbrow wantonness that bordered on the violent and involved a convincingly detailed Batgirl costume, after which they smoked some of the exquisite reefer a dread-locked student had handed in, along with his final paper, as an end-of-the-semester gift. Mort loved the stuff; it made him feel manly, unbeatable. Without any prompting, Veronica sang the reefer's praises, too, and when she turned on the TV, he sat beside her in bed, watched her pull the sheets up above her breasts and stare stupidly at the screen, mouth slightly open, big brown eyes glazed behind her Batgirl cowl.

He wondered if he was half in love with her.

Indeed, Mort saw in Veronica those qualities he prized in the best comic books. She was garish, muscular, thoughtless. He relished her irony-proof mind. He saw in her things that made him gasp in awe and shake his head in abject embarrassment. One moment he was infinitely bored, the next he was throbbing with romantic passion. Hit or miss, all or nothing, that's the way he preferred it. Naturally, such an approach to life never did him a bit of good, yet there it was and he couldn't be expected to change now, not at his age. Besides, the peaks were genuinely ecstatic, offsetting the dull lapses. Yes, he would either dispose of this gap-toothed harlot by tomorrow morning or stand by her side until the fucking bombs started falling.

Now he looked out at the crowd and took a deep breath. He'd been too embarrassed to wear his reading glasses, the frames of which had been accidentally deformed under Veronica's ample haunches in the course of their naked antics. So he leaned forward—the lectern was solid enough—and squinted at his notes.

"Esteemed colleagues," he began. "Fellow enthusiasts."

Feedback sliced through the room and people groaned for mercy. As Mort turned his head to clear his whiskey-burned throat, someone managed to fix the problem. He began.

"The underground comic book movement was born in February 1968 with the publication of *Zap Comix* Number One. The creators printed, stapled, and sold an estimated five thousand copies on the corners of Haight Street. In less than a year, after the underground network of head shops and counterculture stores began distributing their comics, the creators were famous. Within that same year, the Manson family's brutal murders shocked the nation. Satanism, psychedelics, and the criminal element were already thriving in San Francisco by 1965, around the time Manson—then a newly released ex-con—showed up to preach his special brand of love and hate. His message reached the LA Satanists and one cult in particular, calling themselves the White Knives, combined some of Manson's ideas about hypnosis and mind control with the do-it-yourself creative impulse of the Haight district and came up with its own unique and legendary comic book, *Nekro*. They completed the comic in less than a week, thanks in large part to drug-binging and their total lack of aesthetic standards. However, the printer they hired alerted authorities and before the cult could find so much as a ditto machine, they were forcibly disbanded by Hoover's G-men. Obscenity charges and continued heat from the feds drove core members to Amsterdam, where the comic was printed on stolen equipment, even while the group was under intense surveillance from European authorities intent on stamping out any burgeoning Hitler-like activity. So they went underground and were never heard from again. And now, for the first time in the US, the infamous comic book produced by expatriate Satanists will be shown and elucidated. Warning: Many of the following images are so badly drawn as to be unrecognizable and so vulgar many would not consider them art. Can somebody hit the lights, please? Thanks."

Mort reached for the slide remote. "And away we go."

For reasons he couldn't articulate, Flood felt deeply threatened by Dr. Spanuth's presentation. How had a college professor managed to track down a copy of *Nekro*? And for what scholarly purpose? As satanic images slid by on the screen, Flood saw that the comic was, in terms of artistry, a piece of junk. It was full of crudely rendered bikers and pirates and sadistic lesbians and all kinds of unsavory demonic freaks shooting and slicing and sexually torturing one another for no apparent reason, other than the creators' ghastly kicks. Why would Dr. Spanuth waste his skills—honed after years of professional training—on such a historical obscurity? The professor was treading dangerously close to Flood's hallowed terrain and the collector wondered if justifiably neglected comics represented the future of academic pursuits. If so, he should probably sell his restaurant and get a PhD himself. He knew a great deal more about comics than this silly fellow in the tweed jacket, jacked up on God knew what, that was for sure.

As Dr. Spanuth continued, now tracing the influence of the satanic comic on later artists, Flood turned to Veronica and whispered, "You're right, it's hideous. But I need it, okay?"

"Yeah," she said, brow furrowed, distracted by the slides. "I mean, who the fuck would do that to a dog?"

"God only knows."

"Ten grand."

"That's double what I'm offering."

"Why don't you see if your way works?" She laughed.

He looked at Dr. Spanuth, then focused his gaze back on Veronica. "Half now, the other on delivery." He pulled an envelope of cash from his fanny pack and stuffed it into her hand.

She nodded. "This afternoon. We're staying at the Sheraton. Meet me in the bar at three."

He did his best to calmly exit the room, then headed toward the payphones over by the Christian Comic Arts Society. He called his friend Tarp Wurtzel, Conservator of Ephemera and an unrivaled expert in comics restoration. With the greasy receiver pressed to his head, Flood fumbled with his checkbook to figure his current balance and waited for the connection. Over the din of a performance-art rendition of Herbie Mann's "Superman," in which superhero-costumed dancers "interpreted" the pre-recorded disco music, he asked, "Have you ever handled an actual copy of *Nekro*?"

"Completely and totally impossible," said Wurtzel. "Everybody knows that only three copies were made and the police destroyed them before they could be distributed. I've personally seen a little-known photograph of the cover. Back in eighty-one, some wealthy old turd with links to Crowley's daughter offered me a dickload of money to do a forgery, but I didn't want to get involved. Believe me, if there was a copy in existence, this guy would've owned it."

"I've just walked out of this douchey academic's presentation on *Nekro*. The slides look totally legit."

"Well, then I'm telling you. It's bullshit."

"Maybe," said Flood. "But I don't think so. The slides are photographs and the pages, you know, the way they're yellowed with age—"

Tarp cut him off. "Remember when you paid fifty bucks for the educational comic that explained the stock market? If you'd called the Treasury Department's toll-free number, they would've mailed you hundreds of copies for free!"

"If this thing is real, it could put me over the top. I'm thinking it'll at least earn me the cover of, what's that magazine called again, *The Pulp Fancier*?" Guilt mixed with ambition and confusion sloshing in his hot dog-bombed guts, Flood switched the receiver to his other ear and said, "Tarp, I'm going to need you to wire me some cash. It's just a small loan, you understand."

HOURS LATER AT THE SHERATON, Albert Plastino, better known in the underground satanic community as Chokebore, was sitting on a bed, dabbing his forearm with some cotton balls he'd found among the professor's personal effects. His succubus tattoo was still weeping blood. It itched, too, and the aspiring devil-worshipper fought the temptation to scratch. There was no pus, but gangrene wouldn't have surprised him. He'd been negligent. The night before, after his brother—his *real* brother, as well as an already-active member of the White Church of Satan—playfully mashed a Taco Bell bean burrito against his Chokebore tattoo, Chokebore, in his drunken logic, improvised beer as a cleansing agent shortly before passing out on his mother's couch, the frenzied sounds of his brother's Nintendo NES lulling him to sleep. He hadn't showered since and he didn't have time to wash now. He needed the comic book. If necessary, he'd beat the shit out of the college professor. Or even scalp him.

"Come on, Dr. Dumbass," he whispered.

Bribing the maid to let him into the room had been easy. Mexican maids loved speed and so did Chokebore. Secretly, he liked dark-skinned women, though Belcher had often warned him of their impurities. He stood up from the bed, threw the bloodied cotton balls on the floor, and reached for the smoldering joint in the ashtray. He was impressed with the professor's grass. The speed he'd ingested earlier was beginning to amp up the electricity sparking through his veins and the grass was strong enough to take the edge off. Another freak-out episode was the last thing he needed right now.

Indeed, his initiation mission, stealing a comic book, made him fearful, because of its unexpectedness. He'd envisioned getting branded in the small of his back with the red-hot pentagram-shaped tip of a wire coat hanger or maybe chanting in unison with other initiates their solemn vows of allegiance to the Goat Lord, or even having group sex with some of those young nubile women Belcher kept promising, but never delivered. Instead, Chokebore had been given a peculiar objective: steal a comic book. Belcher was big into history and tradition this year, or so his brother told him, and saw the acquisition of the world's first satanic comic as a cornerstone in the construction of his new White Church of Satan.

Whatever happened to stockpiling weapons? Kidnapping heiresses? What was he—Chokebore, a.k.a. the Prince of Brutal Offerings—doing at a convention swarming with thousands of geeks? Did such a mission reflect poorly on Belcher?

Recently, Chokebore had begun to notice imperfections in the church's members. In his estimation, many were mentally deficient or physically deformed; some were even non-White. Despite media coverage and concerns expressed by the Southern Poverty Law Center, the Anti-Defamation League, and other enemy groups about the appeal of Belcher's recruiting efforts, the church seemed to be little more than a loser's way station. But because he'd made a formal commitment and the church refrigerator was always stocked with beer and frozen burritos, Chokebore was going to see this thing through to the end.

He wanted badly to turn on the TV, watch *MacGyver* or *Roseanne* or something with bite to it, but he worried that he'd get too engrossed and be unprepared when the professor returned to the room. He wasn't worried that Dr. Dumbass might overpower him; Chokebore was a tall twenty-two-year-old bruiser who by many people's assessment excelled at inflicting bodily harm. He'd put many a hardened punk rocker into the hospital with his savage mosh pit behavior. Whenever a mosh pit failed to achieve critical mass, Chokebore would grow bored and shatter a beer bottle against a Mohawked head. Then he'd start cutting. For that and other merciless antics, he'd been arrested several times and served a total of six months in prison. The only constant in his life had been a propensity for unchanneled violence—until he met Belcher. Since then, Chokebore saw himself as a reformed punk-rock burnout. He had plans to cultivate his spiritual side under the auspices of Belcher's White Church of Satan before going on to write songs in the vein of his favorite band, Corrosive Angel. Already, he was playing rudimentary guitar chords with the church band, whose repertoire included such hate-folk anthems as "We Are the True Minority" and "Tainted Black," as well as a few Manson covers. Chokebore envisioned his future self breaking away from Belcher and starting his own cult-cum-rock group. He had a name in mind: The Tides of Woe. If no one liked it, he'd cut them.

Hearing the card being inserted into the lock, Chokebore sprang into action. He reached the door just as it opened and yanked Dr. Spanuth into the room by his tie.

The professor's hands flew to his throat, and he struggled to keep from being strangled.

"The comic book," Chokebore demanded.

"*Nekro?*"

With his free hand, Chokebore flicked open his butterfly. "As a doctor, you know that flesh is a relatively easy thing to remove, right?" Then he pushed his prey deeper into the room.

Spanuth frantically looked around, then fell to his hands and knees to check under the bed. "There was a briefcase here. It's gone."

"I don't care about your briefcase," said Chokebore, angrily kicking the professor in the ass, knocking him into a lamp.

"Ow!"

"I want the comic. Then I'm gone."

"Say, who are you anyway?" Spanuth wanted to know as he regained his balance.

"The Prince of Brutal Offerings."

Dr. Spanuth scrambled around the room helplessly, still searching in vain. "I swear to God! There was a briefcase!"

Chokebore began to think that the professor was telling the truth. Had someone beaten him to the punch? The maid? Is that why she let him in so cheaply? He scratched his shaved head. Who else had he seen in the hall? Just some dumbass Lois Lane-looka-like hooker he'd sold some speed to.

VERONICA SAT at the bar of the Sheraton reading a three-page letter one of her regular johns had written in preparation for their next appointment. The pathetic letter described what he wanted her to do to him.

> *After our glamorous photo session, order me to crawl into the bathroom where the real humiliation will start. Once in the bathroom, order me to stick my face in the toilet. With my face in the toilet, flush the toilet, telling me what a no-good slave I am. Make me lick the toilet with my tongue. I am your toilet cleaner.*

She sighed and neatly folded the letter before returning it to her purse. The dom routine was getting old. Men today were all developing the same silly fetishes. She put the blame squarely on the flourishing underground S&M magazine scene and something called the "computer Bulletin Board System." She longed for the days when all a john needed was a straight fuck with her wearing a Wonder Woman tiara. Now they wanted to do everything *except* the deed, which wasn't what annoyed her. What annoyed her was that she had once been the kinkiest person she knew.

As it happened, on the TV above the bar, two professional wrestlers—one wearing a mask, the other some kind of Celtic skirt or kilt—grappled with each other. What a coincidence, she mused. A televised wrestling match had, in fact, become the gateway to her current profession as a call girl/dominatrix/submissive serving the particular needs of the comics community.

She was twelve years old and in a motel room on vacation with her family when she first encountered such sweaty theatrics and she couldn't tear her eyes away from the screen. Inside a canvas ring, one wrestler lay defeated on his back while another kneeled beside him to inflict repeated blows to the face and head. He then rose to grind a heel into his prone opponent's groin.

She recalled asking her brother, "Is that allowed?"

"It's all an act," he answered. "Staged and scripted."

"Turn off that miserable trash!" her mother yelled from her bed. She was smoking a cigarette with one hand and holding a fresh drink in the other, eyeing their father passed out on the other bed.

It wasn't the combat that Veronica had found so riveting; her father liked to watch boxing, and she was familiar enough with the blood of sporting men in conflict, their twisted grimaces of pain. But *this*. This was something different.

She'd never seen anything like it. Yet it was as if it had always been there, on the edges of her imagination; it really hadn't startled her as much as she was pretending. She seemed to understand this spectacle with a secret and unspeakable knowledge. She saw what her brother didn't: the urge to take part in a perverse drama, to deliver punishment in a public game of humiliation. She was hooked.

Throughout her teens, she enjoyed watching reruns

of the old Adam West "Batman" series. The show's goofy sense of humor and wacky costumes appealed to the depraved side of her, the part that longed to whip with, and be whipped by, purring Eartha Kitt's cat-o'-nine-tails. She picked up the habit of reading comics every week and soon learned to distinguish between the two major universes of DC and Marvel (the Big Two, as they'd been called since the mid-sixties). She found her first real john at age seventeen at the musty back-issue bins of a comics shop in Mission Bay. He was a slightly chubby graduate student in English at San Diego University. After seducing him through her feigned appreciation of the Valkyrie comics character, she made quick work of him—Neil was his name, wasn't it?—by pushing him toward anger and a state of sexual volatility. She purposefully lost his treasured copy of *Fantastic Four* issue 48 (the debut of Silver Surfer), infuriating him enough that he roughly stripped her naked, tied her to a chair, and flogged her into multiple orgasms with a plastic spatula in his mom's house. She returned the favor by costuming herself as Hawkgirl, complete with giant wings and beak mask, then luring him into his mom's garage and binding him to the engine block of his restored, hard-top, jet-black AMC Javelin, where she ball-gagged him and massaged his prostate with a good old-fashioned grease-stained monkey wrench. That was fun. When she finally cut him off, he got so desperate for her that he offered to pay with anything for another encounter—cash, food, his leather jacket, and eventually, yes, his Javelin.

A year later, she learned of Comic-Con, an annual gathering of thousands of comics geeks and potential clients who, in their heart of hard-ons, realized that they loved to dress up and be dominated by superheroines and supervillainesses. Veronica's superpower was the ability to sexually arouse nerds with her obscure comics knowledge and crafty wardrobing. Soon, she gained notoriety in convention circles all over the west coast and picked up the nickname Scarlet Witch. She didn't mind it. In fact, she thought it suited her

Someone tapped her shoulder, pulling her out of her wrestling-induced reverie.

"Relax," said Flood, even though Veronica hadn't flinched. He perched himself on a stool. "It's just me."

"Got the money?" she asked.

Flood handed over the entire Western Union envelope.

She counted the bills and said, "Open that menu in front of you."

He did as he was told and inside the menu was the comic book, Mylar-bagged with a cardboard backing.

"It's a beauty," he said. As he held it in his hands, the comic book touched the deepest part of him. The kind of religious ecstasy a nun feels, he thought.

"Eye of the beholder," said Veronica. "Now how about a BJ?"

"No thanks. I don't want anything to interfere with my high."

Veronica snorted. "Suit yourself." She hopped off her stool and made her way out of the bar in search of the young beefy guy with the tattoo of two hands around a faceless head sporting a Mohawk. She needed more speed.

Flood had expected to experience a private high in owning *Nekro*, but the moment slowly grew empty, his body filling with the sense that the desire to own this comic book was greater than the satisfaction of owning it. It seemed, somehow, unfair. Still, he lay down on his hotel room bed and gave himself over to *Nekro*, examining its odd images. Around seven, he could have sworn he heard someone twist the door handle on his room. Out of habit, he'd chained it. When he got out of bed and opened the door, the long bright hallway was empty. On the carpet, he saw a swath of what appeared to be human skin. He looked at it for a long moment before deciding it was prank by horror-comics fanboys.

An hour later, he was celebrating his forthcoming ascent into the comics-scholarship firmament at a waterfront bar with some fellow collectors. He brought *Nekro* with him, planning to show it off. Whatever it was that had been left on the carpet was now gone. At the bar in the company of other obsessive personalities, he lost the desire to brag about his latest acquisition. They seemed to be all talking about superheroes, constantly; everything they said was predictable. He was bored, distracted, for the entire evening. His beer tasted flat. There were no hot dogs on the menu. So he announced a headache coming on and left. When he returned, he found his hotel room torn up, completely trashed, clothes strewn.

Paranoia oozed its black liquid into his brain. Satanists! They were real and they were after him and his comic book, the key to his future and an escape from pizza-slinging. He carefully removed the comic book from his briefcase and placed it on the nightstand. He chained the door, pushed the furniture against it, and watched bad cable.

After a sleepless night, Flood padded to the bathroom, brushed, showered, and dried himself. It was a short flight home, but he didn't want to damage the comic book. So he shaved his back and, using thin medical gauze, delicately wrapped *Nekro* between his shoulder blades. He filled his briefcase with near-worthless reprint copies of *The Cross and the Switchblade*. He dressed, finished packing, and went downstairs to buy a seat on the shuttle.

At the airport, he entered the main terminal and checked his suitcase. Through the shifting throng, he caught sight of an electric shoe polisher over by the car-rental booths. Flood placed his right leg into the machine and deposited some coins, allowing the spastic cloth to nudge his shoe leather. He took the opportunity to scan for threatening behavior, but in San Diego International, everyone seemed swarthy and disreputable. Afterward, humorless security guards X-rayed his briefcase and detected his body for metal objects. The concourse was a gauntlet of newsstands, fast-food eateries, coffee shops. Passengers hurried to their departures and he had to dodge a frantic senior citizen trailing a cart of golf clubs. When Flood reached his gate, he found a line in front of the ticket counter. With the comic taped to him, he was hesitant to sit; he'd be sitting plenty on the plane. So he positioned himself near a slanted tarmac window, alert and ready for hints of trouble. His departure time was an hour away.

"So far so good," he said to himself.

Ten minutes passed and he had to pee. He sighed, disappointed at his puny bladder, and threaded his way to the restroom. The place was emptying, with some guys splattering the urinals, neglecting to flush, and walking right past the sinks. *Disgusting*, thought Flood. *My stoned teenage employees do better*.

To get as far away from unclean humanity as possible, he was pushing in the door of the last stall when something clipped the base of his skull.

He yelped and lurched forward, bouncing off the tile wall. In a series of swift evil movements, the assailant gripped his thinning scalp, head-locked him, and pressed what seemed to be the sharpened end of a toothbrush to the bridge of his nose. From the periphery of his vision, Flood saw a skinhead with facial piercings. The man hissed in his ear, "What's a kike without a nose? You know what I want. Give it."

Choking, Flood offered his briefcase. When the man took it and released his hold, Flood collapsed, splashing his arm into the toilet. He spun around, ready for the deathblow, but whoever had attacked him was gone.

For a few seconds, he fought back nausea, then struggled to compose himself in the mirror. Once the pierced punk realized that he didn't have the comic, he'd come back to kill Flood. But the collector wouldn't be ambushed like that again. He needed to disappear into a crowd. He washed his hands and exited the restroom.

In the busy brightly lit airport bar, he commandeered a stool. He groped in his pockets, found ten dollars, bought a hot dog and a Coors, and somehow the sight of these two ordinary things was reassuring. There was also something heartening about the drinkers around him, the sports programming, the cigarette smoke and grease. Twice, Flood thought he heard someone in the bar calling his name. For a while, he listened for his flight number. But then he sipped his beer and ate his hot dog, ignoring the TV, concentrating instead on the entrance to the bar. Dazed with food and paranoia, he lost track of time.

Eventually, he asked the bartender if the plane to Las Vegas was boarding yet.

"Flight announcements aren't made in the bar, sir. There's a big sign right there saying so. And it's on all the menus."

"What you don't understand," said Flood, "is that I'm under attack."

The bartender raised an eyebrow but continued to towel a mug. "You're right. I *don't* understand."

Flood hastened toward his gate, but the plane had taken off. Fortunately, the ticket agent was sunny and compassionate, her teeth chalk white. "I've got you a seat on the next flight. Straight shot to Las Vegas, but it's boarding now. Last gate. That way," she said, pointing.

He rushed to the end of the concourse. Heart pumping, lungs burning, legs aching, he was finally at the center of things, a comic book hunter in the adventure of a lifetime. Let the scholars laugh at him now. His work was so important that people wanted him dead, or at least severely wounded. He, Bentley Flood, was a heroic figure on a journey of mystery and madness, while the smug professors were relegated to the sidelines, ignorant and hapless observers, powerless in their academic shackles.

He boarded the plane just as the engines fired. He felt safe, for now.

This is what he'd always wanted, to feel the pinprick of danger, to sense dark eyes watching him. He was a man with a valuable artifact, one he needed to keep safe, even as men in dark clothes would kill for it. The world around him had changed. The gaze of Satan beamed warm light upon his treasure-laden back. The truth was now upon him. He had never wanted to own comic books; instead, he wanted his life to resemble the drama and easy moral absolutes found in the pages of four-color funnies.

The plane leveled and the seat belt sign went off. Hungry for another hot dog, thirsty for another cold beer, he pressed the flight attendant call button above his head.

WHEN HE LANDED at McCarran International, no one was waiting for him, thank God. He carefully made his way to the long-term parking area, checked the back seat of, and underneath, his brand-new Nissan Sentra, then drove straight to his downtown shop. It was a Monday in the middle of lunch hour and Pizzamaster Pizzeria was doing brisk business, ideally situated as it was a block from the courthouse, where lawyers and judges, plaintiffs and defendants, stenographers and CPAs all longed for the cheese and bread and pepperoni necessary to fill the void of their existences.

When Flood walked in, the acne-plagued teenagers behind the counter barely registered his arrival. Finally, one kid, all silver braces and wearing a bright-red paper Pizzamaster hat, paused mid-dough toss and said, "There's a guy here to see you."

Flood froze, slowly turning 360 degrees to determine where the threat was perched. The kid gave him a concerned look and added, "He's already in your office. I let him in. Carrying a longbox of comics, for some reason."

Tarp Wurtzel, old buddy, best and most overweight pal. "Thanks," said Flood.

He opened his office door and there was Tarp, sitting in Flood's chair in front of a leaning tower of comics, intensely preoccupied with taping a bagged and boarded issue of—what the hell was that anyhow, *Alpha Flight*? "You owe me big time," he said without bothering to look up, glasses angled at the very end of his nose.

Flood sighed, acknowledging the debt. "I'm sorry. Look, I had to move quickly. I was never going to have a chance like that again."

"So. Where is it? Not *on* you, I hope."

"Yes."

Flood pulled his shirt over his head until it was wrapped around his forearms, then he turned his back to Tarp to reveal *Nekro*.

Tarp struggled against his own girth to stand up from the chair and examine the artifact. "Oh, Antichrist," he said softly, as he carefully began to remove the tape.

"Ouch." Flood jerked. "Too slow. Just rip it off quickly and be done with it."

"Can't do that. No way I'll risk damaging the comic."

Flood knew his friend was right. He shoved his shirt-tethered hands into his jeans back pocket, removed his wallet, and placed it between his teeth. "Guh fuh ipp!"

"Okay, then," replied Tarp, and began peeling the comic loose.

After a few minutes of intense hair-being-slowly-ripped-from-the-back pain, Flood and Tarp both scruti-nized *Nekro* under horrific fluorescent light, each holding a different part of the comic with rubber-gloved hands. Flood had the urge to tell his collector buddy about his near-fatal experience in San Diego International but thought better of it. He didn't know whom he could trust. It had dawned on him that perhaps the prostitute had sold him the comic, then sold his name and hotel room number to the satanic assassin who wanted the book for his cult or whatever. He could probably benefit from buying a handgun at some point. He wasn't going to part with *Nekro* easily. The Dark Ones would have to pry it from his cold dead hands! Well, actually, no, but maybe he could sell it to them for more than what he paid? First, he needed to figure out exactly what he had in his possession.

"You're holding it way too closely," scolded Flood. "It's mine, you know."

"Except that I brokered the deal."

"Tarp, I made it clear I was asking for a friendly loan. Not a home mortgage."

"Speaking of, let's take it back to my place and deacidify it."

Deacidification was a laborious process wherein restoration experts like Tarp spent hours spraying each page of a rare and valuable comic with an alkaline reserve meant to neutralize oxidation and fungi. In the dry desert climate of Las Vegas, this was overkill, in

Flood's opinion. Still, San Diego had felt especially humid. Killing off any lurking crud was a safe bet.

"Okay," said Flood. "But don't even think about asking me to leave the comic at your house overnight. It can air out in *my* apartment, thank you."

"Deal."

Flood followed Tarp in his own car, *Nekro* absurdly seat-belted in the front seat beside him like a silent well-behaved toddler. When they pulled into the cul-de-sac in front of Tarp's house, Flood noticed a large black-clothed figure leaning against the hood of a beat-up Taurus across the way and a creeping dread entered his heart.

Though he'd never laid eyes directly on his attacker, Flood suddenly recognized him.

He stomped on the brakes and laid on the horn.

Confused and thinking Flood wanted him to hurry up, Tarp leaped out of the car, looked at Flood, then opened his mouth and raised his arms as if to say, "What's your problem?"

Flood's problem was now behind Tarp. The man put his thick succubus-tatted arms around the unsuspecting comics-restorationist's neck and head, almost but not quite lifting the three-hundred-pounder off the ground. Flood recognized a sleeper hold when he saw it. Such rear naked chokes were often dangerous and Flood's instinct was to flee. But he fought off the fear running amok inside his chest and stepped on the gas, heading right at them. As he reached about twenty miles per hour, the Nazi punk tossed Tarp headfirst onto the car's windshield, shattering it. Tarp's face now wore a mask of blood, as he ricocheted ragdoll-like onto his own front lawn of xeriscaped pebbles. Flood managed to clip Chokebore's leg and the cruel cultist fell to his knees, grimacing in anguish, but the car continued on and smashed into the driver's side of Tarp's Mazda.

Newfangled airbags, front and side, exploded on impact, fracturing Flood's nose. His face gushed crimson, the hot gas and chemicals blinding him, burning his lungs.

Trapped, he coughed up something wet and tried unsuccessfully to scream. He heard a loud pop and then a flatulent hissing sound and observed helplessly as the bags began to deflate. Soon he was face-to-face with the skinhead and his Mexican pigsticker.

The attacker roughly reached his arm past Flood's mutilated face to grab *Nekro*, stuffing it carelessly down the front of his jeans. "Last words?" he asked Flood.

"Only. Wanted. To own. Something. Rare," Flood blubbered, pinned behind the wheel like a doomed insect, gasping for breath, choking on blood.

"You did," said Chokebore, laughing for a moment with the blade up against the pizza-parlorist's fat throat. "Congratulations."

Before the man could slit his throat, Flood heard what sounded like the dull impact of an aluminum bat connecting with a skull.

The face suddenly fell away from the door window and there, replacing the malevolent stare, was the cowl of Batgirl. It was Veronica, a hooker with a heart of gold and the swing of Babe Ruth. She was in love with Flood. She had to be.

"Asshole tried to rip me off," she said, pulling her cowl away to reveal her beautiful features. "And he cut off a pound of Mortie's flesh."

Flood's eyes went wide. "He's not—"

"Dead? No. In intensive care. I found him in time."

She pulled Flood from his shattered vehicle and *Nekro* from the crotch of the unconscious Satanist lying on the ground. "But *this* guy had to learn the hard way: You do *not* fuck with Batgirl."

"Should we. Call the. Police?" He could hear Tarp moaning in the grass. "Ambulance?"

She shot Flood an intense look and he quickly understood that the blood on his lips intrigued her.

"First," she said, "kiss me."

THE BALLAD OF THE
SKUNK APE

Rawlings cursed the buttonbush growing along the bank. Using shears, she'd easily trimmed back the young palms and wax myrtles, but to get the shot she wanted required extra effort. She removed her sneakers, completely inadequate for the terrain anyway, and stepped into the warm Myakka River.

She lopped off the sprouts still in front of her, which tinkled as they landed in the water, much like the sound a deer would make as it entered the vegetation for a drink or something to eat. She felt a breeze pass through a shady grove of twisted oaks behind her—a ribbon of air that made the hairs on her neck bristle. Then she experienced the sensation of being watched.

She quickly jumped back to the shoreline, scanning in both directions. Not a gator in sight. *Dumbshit. Take your precious nature photo and move on.*

She grabbed each shrub after cutting it, throwing it on shore instead of letting it fall in the water. She'd already dispatched eight shrubs and was leaning forward to cut the farthest one when the snout of a fifteen-foot reptile appeared between her feet and her heart iced over.

Only his massive bony head was visible in the shallow water. Judging by what she saw, he was an absolute monster. His eyes were like two jaundiced marbles. She recalled the advice a crusty poacher had offered back when she freelanced for newspapers. "Whatever you do, don't scream—especially in a high voice. Animals in distress make that noise. And distressed animals are what gators love to eat."

So she bit her fist hard, nearly drawing blood, and raised her dead mother's pruning shears with the other hand, trying to make herself look as big and imposing as possible. Deepening her voice, she bellowed as loudly as she could. "Fuck off!"

The horrible face turned away and the creature lunged underwater, its form replaced by foam and spray. But she could see a massive shadow gliding through the murk. Eventually, the gator's head floated serenely twenty yards off, like a piece of driftwood. Calm after a near-fatal storm.

Rawlings dabbed sweat from her brow with a bandanna and struggled to process what had just happened. Quickly and silently sneaking up on prey is what alligators do, how they feed, and this beast was no doubt just as surprised as she was. Tall grass and plants ensured he couldn't see her until he ended up, well, between her legs. He simply reacted to what he'd heard: buttonbush hitting the water. It was natural behavior, not an evil desire to kill her.

Maybe she'd have been better off killed by a gator. Here she was in the middle of Myakka River State Park, hoping to find artistic inspiration or, at the very least, motivation and direction at a time in her life when she had nothing—no man, no job, not even family in Florida. Just the minimum credentials necessary to convince herself she enjoyed a career in fine-art photography. But she hadn't done a new show in more than three years.

As she began to rehydrate with a bad-tasting vitamin-water product, she noticed a figure walking behind the shrubs on the other side of the river. As her perspective sharpened, she realized that whatever was moving over there was at least eight feet tall. It took long strides that, although on two feet, had little resemblance to a human gait. She tried to register it as a bear until she realized a bear walks on four legs, not upright. And it was much bigger and hairier than her friend Bob Dye, whom she was expecting.

"Skunk ape?" she said under her breath, fumbling for her Canon 5D MKII. As she clicked the shutter, she knew she was capturing mostly dense marshland, but maybe a break in the foliage would allow for a brief line of sight.

Gone.

She exhaled, stood stock still for a moment, and strained to locate noise in the distance. Nothing. Maybe the distant honk of a moorhen. She rifled through the camera viewer. One image revealed a small black blur smeared across the top of tall aquatic plants. She had no desire to give chase for fear of stepping on another gator. Besides, if she cornered a skunk ape, what then? She had no weapon or net. Just pruning shears. She rechecked the images but came away disappointed.

Rawlings recalled how for years, the skunk ape had

been said to inhabit the South, Florida in particular. In 2000, supposed photos of a Myakka skunk ape were sent anonymously to the Sarasota Sheriff's Department. She recalled seeing them online a few years ago; they struck her as being grainy images of an escaped orangutan. Now she was less skeptical. Whatever she'd just spotted walked like a hairy beast—like Bigfoot. She hadn't smelled anything skunky or foul, though. Christ, what the hell was it?

She looked to the wading birds around her for emotional solace. A green heron sat hunched on the branch of a silver-gray oak skeleton. He splayed his gorgeous feathers and squawked angrily before taking flight. Nothing for the soul there. She could still feel the blood pounding in her temples.

But here came someone beautiful enough to help her forget what had just transpired: park ranger Bob Dye. Body of a Chippendale dancer. Brain of a Chip 'n' Dale cartoon character. He looked amazing, even in his beige state-issued shirt, shorts, and wading boots. For some reason, though, he was carrying a bag of hot dog buns.

She tried hard to be glib, even though her hands continued trembling. "Firing up the grill soon, Bob?" She pushed her blond hair behind her ears, hoping he'd notice her eyes. People often found them haunting. Or so they told her.

He stopped and brought the bag to his handsomely chiseled face, as if inspecting the contents for the first time. "I confiscated these from a family. They were about to throw 'em to a gator a bit downstream."

Rawlings knew Bob took such violations of campground policy seriously. A fed alligator grew bold and approached people at every opportunity. Then the animal had to be "removed." To feed a gator was to condemn it to death. "I wish they wouldn't do that," she commiserated.

Bob continued to approach her, but now his attention was focused on the massive head floating several yards off. "That there's a big one," he noted. "Five hundred pounds, at least. Thought it was Old Bill for a second. But he don't have no scar."

"He came between my legs," she said, instantly regretting it.

"Did he, now?" Bob acknowledged the double entendre with a quick smile, then asked, genuinely concerned, "Did he bite you?"

She shook her head. "I scared him off with my death-metal voice."

"Good thing it ain't mating season. He'd have ripped you in half."

"Shit, you know, I didn't even think of that." Sometimes she wondered if Bob was a bit of a douche. He seemed to take an unusual amount of pleasure in finding women in the marsh and giving them advice and warnings.

"Nice shears. The park's?"

"No, my mom's. I need them to take photos."

Bob had to mull that one over for a moment. Then he said, "Ah, I can see why. You're right up against the wilderness preserve. That's Deep Hole just over there. So how'd the photos come out?"

"Actually, I was interrupted by Godzilla," she said, indicating the gator. "And then I saw what I'm pretty sure was a skunk ape walk by."

Bob snorted.

"Seriously. I have something, but it's not much." She picked up the camera and moved close to Bob so he could see the viewer. He smelled good, like coconut sunblock with a hint of dude sweat. Eventually, he grabbed the Canon and studied the blur.

He handed back the camera. "Don't call CNN just yet."

"Thanks for the advice."

"Hey, I got something to ask you." He kicked once at the dirt, like a bashful child. "A favor, really."

"Okay." She could feel her lust for Bob overtaking her adrenaline. Or was it just her stomach growling? She hadn't eaten anything yet today. "Do you want to talk about it over lunch? I'm starving."

Bob glanced at the watch on his thick manly wrist. A wrist Rawlings dreamed would hold her down as he fucked her brains out.

"Sounds great," he said. "Let's throw your canoe in the back of my truck, though."

———

THEY LUNCHED AT SNOOK HAVEN, a fish camp and restaurant engulfed by oaks and palms at the east end of Venice Avenue. Sitting on the patio in the shade of an umbrella, they sipped sweetened iced tea and ate chicken Caesar salads and watched as orange-vested canoeists deposited themselves from the boat ramp into the Lower Myakka. A giant green fly buzzed Rawlings's face repeatedly until she swatted it dead with a rolled-up copy of *Aperture* magazine. She scraped it clean using the side of their wooden picnic table and finished her salad.

"Ever hear of repellent?" said Bob.

"Yes, it's why I let you hang around."

"Ouch."

She toothpicked her teeth and squinted at him, recalling a time, much like this one, when they were having a casual lunch and she'd articulated her carnal feelings for him. He didn't go for it and, she had to admit, it had damaged her self-esteem. Though perhaps he only required more encouragement. "So what do you need?"

"Park brochure. Photos in it are from before the *first* Bush was in office. Needs to be updated. They put me in charge of the project."

"Doesn't the park have a PR team?"

He shrugged. "Cutbacks."

"I don't shoot for free," she warned. "I appreciate the access you give me, Bob, but I've also done a lot to bring attention to Myakka. That show I did—"

"I know, I know." He held up his hands. "I was at the opening and the press you got us was awesome. Look, we can't afford to hire you to shoot a whole catalog or anything like that, but we'd like to at least get a shot of the new outpost."

"New outpost? Just saw it this morning. Nothing new about it."

"Not the gift shop. We're opening a concession in Clay Gully."

"Why? The north gate isn't even open during the week."

"On weekends, we have people on their bicycles accessing through there. We had three hundred on Saturday and not all of them can live on energy bars alone."

"Says who?"

"Grumpy moms. Their fat lazy kids need juice boxes to pedal harder or whatever. Look, I only have a measly grand to play with, but I really just need a few photos."

"Deadline?"

"How about next month?"

Rawlings thought about it while Bob carried away their plastic trays and dumped their plastic plates into a plastic bear-proof trashcan. She lit a cigarette and French inhaled, staring at his ass intently. Then she thought about what she'd seen in the marsh and how it might figure into her next book.

It had seemed so easy to stumble across the skunk ape. Who was to say it couldn't happen as easily again? Okay, it sounded ridiculous, but what better way to jump-start her going-nowhere-fast career than by delving into cryptozoology with real-life photos of a mysterious Florida monster? Oh God, she was losing it. She was horny, in a professional slump, and in dire need of a rock-solid agent. But the last one had ripped her off to the tune of $100,000 and she was hesitant to commit to what might be further abuse. Still, a photographer friend had done incredibly well in New York with a show devoted to tracking what might or might not have been a chupacabra near San Antonio. If you asked Rawlings, it resembled a hairless jackal.

When Bob returned, she said, "Let me meditate on it."

He opened his eyes wide. "Absolutely. Hope I didn't offend. Just ain't no budget."

"Not at all. You know what helps me meditate, Bob? Beer."

He chuckled. "All right. Where can I treat you?"

"Horsefeathers."

"Love that place!" he said. "My shift ends in four hours. Meet you there at nine."

———

SHE DIDN'T LEAVE the park. Instead, after dropping him off at HQ, she borrowed Bob's truck, headed back into the 7,600-acre wilderness preserve and toward Deep Hole, and put in at the park bridge, then paddled to the expansive marsh that bordered Lower Myakka. This was her favorite spot to photograph, full of gnarly oaks and graceful palms that leaned over the river. Turtles basked in the sun and herons posed like frozen, feathered runway models. She watched as a kingfisher crisscrossed the river, intersecting with a grackle skating across the water's surface. A sleepy limpkin emerged near the bow of the canoe as if to jump in for a ride. Rawlings laughed amid so much natural beauty.

Eventually, she skidded her canoe ashore, near the steel radio tower at the south end of the lake, where a peninsula of land supported a couple of palm trees that jutted out into the water. A small gator sunned itself at the base of the tower. She ignored it and pushed on. She had a career to reignite.

She entered the remote dilapidated birdwalk, built sometime in the 1940s and located along the shore between the lower river and Deep Hole. The latter was a giant sinkhole that a robotic camera had recently shown extended a half mile to the bottom. There was a tranquil yet blood-red sunset ebbing in the sky and as soon as her bare feet touched the wooden walkway, she felt a sense of peace, even amid the cacophony around her. She adjusted her ears to make sense of each noise—the hyena-like laugh of a coot, the rustling wings of a vulture passing overhead.

She popped two quarters into the lone, rusted, spotting scope and directed it toward a shallow lake a hundred yards away. She then trained her view on the length of green veldt that stretched from the walkway to the waterline, noticing how the green was occasionally scarred with small patches of rooted-up black mud where feral hogs had gone digging for mushrooms and water lilies and moccasin eggs.

Suddenly, what looked like someone dressed as a dark-brown hairy caveman creature stood up from the grass, his giant brow and stupid red eyes staring straight at Rawlings, piercing her. She felt her left leg quiver and turn gelatinous with fear.

"The fuck's going on *here*?" she said aloud, pulling away from the scope and looking around. "No one else see this?" She moved her head to the side to see around the faulty scope and observed the now-distant caveman standing a second longer before ducking back into the grass. She returned to the scope to see if the monster might still be there somehow, but it wasn't, and she felt adrenalized and fearful that whatever it was would hide in the grass until reaching the walkway.

She scanned for a sharp stick, an exit, a park employee, but of course nothing and nobody was around. The ranger station was a mile east. Was the skunk ape stalking her, following her around this entire park? What were the chances of her catching sight—twice in the same day, no less—of a mythical creature that law enforcement, journalists, and cryptozoologists had spent a lot of time and money unsuccessfully tracking down? For a second, she thought it might be Bob fucking with her, messing with her head, but there was no chance. This prank required brains he lacked. Besides, what could possibly be his motivation?

She forced herself to be bold. She unslung her Canon and softly padded to the edge of the birdwalk, closest to the green expanse. She grabbed a fallen oak branch in her non-shooting hand, waiting for the monster to raise his head again so she could Whac-A-Mole his Neanderthal skull. If that happened, she would take a photo of him unconscious, bleeding, before the scientists took him away for an autopsy or taxidermy in preparation for a high-profile museum unveiling.

Or maybe the photo would be of her final moments, the creature tearing her to shreds in the seconds that followed, destroying her beyond even dental recognition.

To her relief, or dismay, nothing happened. The birds continued their crazed babbling and movements, having never stopped even when the creature walked in their midst. Clearly, this was no guy in a rubber suit. He would have startled the fauna, causing them to go mute. Whatever the monster was, he belonged to the swamp; he was part of it. (Or was it a *she*?) This frightened Rawlings more. It meant the only way to get close would be to immerse herself completely in Myakka's mucky embrace. But she was hooked. She felt compelled to track the monster, snap its image, and make millions. It was the only way to succeed in a sensationalized media landscape that had far outstripped the headlines of the old *National Enquirer*.

Indeed, that was where she was headed: into the heart of tabloid darkness. *Bring it,* she thought, as the sun died on the horizon's line and mosquitoes began to bite her legs silly. *I want to get up close to this crazy action.*

But getting close to a skunk ape would require assistance. It was time to return the truck. She had a long canoe trip back in darkness.

———

AT FIRST, Rawlings was a tad embarrassed for suggesting Horsefeathers. It was her favorite Sarasota watering hole, but looking at it through the eyes of a younger late-twenties man like Bob, she recognized it as a cougar concentration camp, where MILFs and single older ladies prowled for young bucks eager to offer their services. Well, Bob did say he loved this place and his reasons were obvious. Perhaps she could work this to her advantage. Beer would make her plan easier to accomplish.

They grabbed a table in the lounge. Onstage, a guy with an acoustic guitar was singing what sounded mostly like Buffett covers. She and Bob drank from a seemingly bottomless pitcher of Coors. It wasn't long before she had her bare foot, toenails freshly painted fuck-me-hard red, on his crotch.

"You're hyper tonight," he said, wary. "What's up?"

She pouted. "I'm only trying to get *you* up."

So as not to create a scene, he oh so subtly pushed himself away from the table and her pretty toes. "You want something. I don't think it's me. At least not entirely."

She downed the last of her beer and lit a cigarette.

"I want you to take me into Deep Hole in Lower Myakka. I'm looking for photos for a new show."

"Why do you need me? I already work there, you know. And I don't have much time to babysit, actually. Besides, you're too tough for any babysitter to handle."

"It's not that. Look, I saw the skunk ape agai—*stop* shaking your head at me!"

"Okay, I won't." He chuckled.

"Seriously. That really fucking pisses me off. I know what I saw, Bob."

"I'm sorry. Where did you see it the second time?"

"At the edge of the old birdwalk. Fucker is *huge*. It's *not* some asshole in a gorilla costume, either. If that was the case, the idiot would've suffocated in, like, thirty seconds."

"Well, how long were you looking at it?"

"A minute tops. But I saw him in the middle of all that grass between the walkway and the lake. He popped in and out. But there's no way some guy could last out there, especially at dusk. It's remote. The bugs are lethal."

"Look, don't worry. I'll take you, Rawlings. It's not that I *don't* believe you. Plenty of folks have seen this damn skunk—" He cut himself off. "Hey. You see this guy singing? He saw a skunk ape once. Wrote a song about it. They played it on local radio a few times."

Rawlings raised her eyebrows and flicked ash into her empty mug.

"Hold on." Bob got up from the table and approached the stage as the Hawaiian-shirted singer was wrapping up "Mandolin Rain." Bob dropped a twenty into the tip jar and said something that made the performer smile and nod. Bob returned and told her to prepare for "The Ballad of the Skunk Ape."

"Who wrote it?" she asked.

"What do you mean? I told you, *this* guy. Name's Loren. Claims he ran into a skunk ape in Deep Hole ten years ago and the thing nearly killed him. It was in all the papers."

"Do you believe him?"

Bob sighed. "I don't know. It's a good tune. But man, the lyrics are weird!"

Loren cleared his throat and said into the microphone, "Some of you may remember this song," he announced. "It's one I'll keep with me to my grave." Then he began to strum a few major chords, a plodding country groove.

> *Deep in the Myakka*
> *Where Tarzan gators roam*
> *There's a bipedal mammal*
> *Who calls the swamp home*
> *At least 500 pounds*
> *Stands seven feet tall*
> *Hate to think if someone*
> *Set him loose in a mall*
> *A smelly end to your life*
> *A death worse than fate*
> *Listen now as I sing*
> *The Ballad of the Skunk Ape*

"Christ," Rawlings muttered, rubbing the bridge of her nose. She stubbed out her cigarette in her fries. "You're so right, Bob. This song is incredible. Was there a music video?"

"There's one on the YouTube. But listen! Right here's my favorite part."

> *U.S. Army scientists*
> *Had kept it alive*
> *Till it broke concrete walls*
> *Escaped into the wild*

"Bob."

"Yeah?"

"Please get me out of here. Like, now."

"You bet. I can drive. Not even buzzed."

"Great. I need supplies. Let's hit Walmart."

———

SHE SPENT the entire next day in Deep Hole, chasing her tail, pursuing shadows of shadows, while Bob managed a nearby controlled burn on a small island in the river. She caught the end of the burn and it was disturbing. She'd always considered gators to be dumb. But now from her canoe, she watched three of them congregating at the edge of the island. She wondered why they were there. Fire burned slowly across a strip of parched land. Finally, it reached the corner where the gators loitered and several rabbits suddenly leaped into the water, trying to escape the flames. Each reptile snatched dinner, dragging it underwater for a minute or two before coming up again and gradually moving away from the smoking island.

She shot scores of photos, capturing the visual essence of the skunk ape's habitat. (She also shot the new concession at Clay Gully.) Gators, birds, turtles, lichens—basic stuff. She had plenty of these images already, but she found herself shooting them differently, using light in a new way that accentuated the innate danger. Often, she let the sun silhouette and throw a pall over the subject, whether a limb-dangling snake or hanging clump of Spanish moss evoking a Southern lynching. The close encounter with the gator and her creepy skunk ape sighting had changed the way she looked at Myakka and she tried to explore a more ominous perspective. Why not? If her skunk ape show was to be a project of calculated sensationalism, everything else would need to fall in line, too. Still, she felt frustrated. Now that she was finally onto something big, she was ready for the climactic images.

Darkness came and a bounty of stars illuminated the sky. Glow-in-the-dark spiders and luminescent mushrooms peppered the ground, evoking Halloween. The night air came alive with animal sounds. Nocturnal creatures awoke from their slumber and shuffled about in search of water, food, each other. Rawlings grew tired, however, having not slept much the night before due to being impaled on Bob's cock. After buying camping supplies, she'd let him defile her in new and exciting ways. Young guys these days watched a lot of porn, it seemed, and she found herself doing things in bed she never would have considered ten years ago, before the internet. In any case, she'd been happy to oblige, even if her pussy was a little sore and she worried about getting a bad yeast infection after a couple days spent trekking a humid swamp in search of a mythical quagmire yeti.

Back at the campsite now, she popped a Tylenol, cracked open a Red Bull, and began working on a fire to set the mood with Bob, who, despite not being on the clock, promised he'd return after being radioed to deal with a coral-snake sighting in a cabin restroom.

She'd brought her own firewood. After wadding up a large piece of newspaper, she covered it with dry palm fronds. She stacked finger-size twigs in the shape of a teepee around the fronds, then built a larger teepee around the twigs with dry thumb-size branches. She lit the middle with a drip torch and as the fire blazed, she continued to add larger pieces of dry wood, enlarging the teepee's exterior. The flames were now bright orange and fierce and she was just about to start skewering a marshmallow when what sounded like a child screaming ripped open the air.

She grabbed the flashlight and her cell and sprinted in the direction of the cries. She sliced her shin on a sabal palmetto but gritted her teeth and pushed on, hoping it wouldn't leave too bad a scar. She had nice legs for a forty-year-old and she didn't want to damage them, even if a lost tyke in the marsh required rescuing.

But it wasn't a kid. The closer she drew to the sound, the more she recognized it as a peacock or some other bird. Her pulse had begun to slow by the time she reached the place near the trailhead where she imagined the scream had emanated. And then her heart seized up as she shone the light on a figure towering silently before her, a dead heron hanging from its shoulder like a white shirt.

The beast's red eyes glared at her, large yellow teeth exposed. She smelled the thing—if she could only capture the sickening odor of rotten meat on film! It permeated her senses and filled her with dread and nausea. The skunk ape emitted a guttural noise, but didn't move, perhaps momentarily hypnotized by the light. Then its facial expression suggested it could almost discern Rawlings behind the brightness.

Too close, too personal. She took off, running for her life. Branches of saplings and plants slapped and cut her face. Out of breath, she speed-dialed Bob and made it back to the campfire in less than a minute, sorting through the options for a weapon. Bob picked up just as she reached into her backpack for the small drip torch.

"It's here! At the campsite! Move your ass and save me!"

"What?! Okay! Wait right there!"

Shoving the phone into her cargo pocket, she raised the torch and quickly triggered the igniter, causing fire to pour out from the nozzle in an orange flood. She loosened the fuel tank so that it came out hot and heavy.

But it was too late.

She'd never heard so much as a foot-crunch, but the beast already stood in front of her. She screamed. It backhanded the torch from her hands, spilling scorching flames and gas everywhere. Yet it was to her advantage. The creature's arm caught fire, and it staggered backward. The stench of burning hair hit Rawlings's nostrils. She almost fell backward into the campfire, but recovered her balance and reached for the snub-nosed flare pistol in her bedroll.

She fired it off in the monster's general vicinity, but the cascading 12-gauge bore only ricocheted harmlessly off a palm tree and sizzled stupidly in the dirt. Still, it was enough to alarm the creature, which stumbled in retreat, holding its charred arm like any human would.

Headlights swung across the campsite. Leaving the

motor running and the lights on, Bob opened the driver's door and leaned out.

"Rawlings!" His voice cracked. "Get in! Now!"

But she was already snapping away with her Canon. The hellish fires and harsh truck lights created a vivid action sequence that would turn out spectacular, especially after some minor Photoshop tweaking. She even moved forward, shutter clicking, this time with the flash. It was too much, though, and the monster, terrified or angered, or just plain freaked out, charged at Rawlings, knocking her over into a tangle of tiger lilies. Then it grabbed her violently by the hair and dragged her into the darkness, leaving a trail of broken camera pieces behind. Legs flailing, hands scratching at the beast's mitt, she could only manage a hoarse cry.

Settling back behind the wheel, Bob revved the engine hard and released the parking brake, catapulting the truck beyond the campsite. It glanced off a massive oak trunk, cracking the radiator, but Bob saw them for a split second in the flash of a headlight beam before the glass shattered.

He smelled gasoline—had the tank ruptured?—and abandoned the truck in pursuit of a deadly monster and a woman with whom he was seriously in lust. To his horror, he could see nothing in the murk. Then there were screams, the sound of blows, shrill cries. He heard gurgling, blood filling a throat and mouth. It punished Bob's ears. He knew she was being killed just yards away. But goddamn it! Where?

"Rawlings!" he shrieked insanely.

Suddenly, the truck detonated behind him, not wildly like in a Hollywood movie, but sadly, like a cracked metal dumpster full of expired bottle rockets.

The heat was intense, though, boiling at his back, and in the orange light he could see Rawlings, blank-eyed, hair missing from her pale scalp, standing over a giant form crumpled against a clump of cypress.

What looked like pruning shears were plunged deep into its neck and black blood spurted like a cartoon geyser from the side of its ear.

She laughed for a few seconds, then squatted in front of the now-dead thing. She put her hand to its old-looking face, where a tooth protruded up from its bottom lip. There were tears in her eyes. Tears of relief, Bob thought. Though for a moment, he wondered if they were tears of pity for a creature of a kind they would never see again.

The sheriff and paramedics arrived a half-hour later. As Rawlings was being loaded into the ambulance on a gurney, Bob swore he heard her singing.

Deep in the Myakka
Where Tarzan gators roam

ISAAK

Someone was killing the sheep, two or three every night. In the morning, their stiffened but still-warm bodies lay in the barren ravine on the desert's edge, their throats cut. The herdsmen searched for clues and found nothing; strong winds and a careful culprit erased away any tracks. It was bad enough the animals were disease-ridden and preyed upon by thieves. Now, the sheep were being sacrificed without the use of an altar. This was a grave offense against the Creator. He who did not fear the Creator posed a threat to Abraham's tribe.

The people tried everything to discourage this threat. They lit incense at the outskirts of the village to ward off evil. The men hid quietly among the sheep, knives drawn. The women huddled together in their black wool shawls and drank strong tea and sang prayers. Isaak himself took to standing watch. Under the stars, he scanned the valley, waiting in vain for the approach of a cunning enemy. Despite the tribe's efforts, the sheep continued to be slaughtered.

One night, Isaak went out to count the flock, but Canaan was vast. Before he could finish, dawn arrived and with it, more dead sheep. Exhausted, he returned to endure the incessant howling of his father's peacocks. They strutted about in the yard outside his window, lavishly dressed and vacuous, mocking his fear and kindling his anger. They carried on until he pelted them with rocks. He slept for a few hours and when his tent became like an oven, he summoned the shepherds, but they had no news. Their helplessness increased his own. After haranguing them with all manner of threatens, he dismissed them.

He went back to his tent, where a baby lamb lay on its side, panting in the dirt. Its mother's teats had dried up. Isaak snatched corn and milk from the peacock pen and placed the bowls in front of the lamb. He stroked its soft short hair and gazed into its yellow eyes. Afterward, he took a bucket-bath and cleaned the lamb's teeth with a stick of acacia. When he was done brewing tea, he set off to see Hagar, his father's favorite concubine. Walking through the village, the air was dust and the horizon promised nothing else. The sun was poisonously hot. Wind blew under the tarpaulins, spraying grit into eyes and ears.

Despite a climate that grew harsher with each passing day, the village maintained its routine. Hampered by heavy jewelry, the young wives cooked, crouched over fires. The older women ground wheat on huge round stones and kneaded dough. Others carried head-bundles of leaves for the goats penned behind Abraham's mud-brick house in the center of the village. The children climbed trees to pick parched figs and dates with their nimble fingers.

Beneath the regular activity, however, Isaak sensed a palpable anxiety. It was evident in the way they looked at him, as if they were unjustly condemned to a cage that he designed. They looked at him plaintively, expectantly. Their plaintiff expectant expressions were pleas for release from the desert of Canaan, once a place of bountiful riches, now an infinite landscape of sun-blasted pain and humiliation. A plea for protection against the infidel who worsened a drought that had been plaguing them for three years, making the people frail and sickly and scared.

The sheep, of course, were crucial to the tribe's survival. They could be sold and traded for food. Killing off the sheep would plunge the tribe into famine and they could not suffer it much longer without surrendering to the deepest despair. Indeed, the infidel's fury was another sign that it was time to leave.

For months, the elders had urged Abraham to move his people farther north, but he refused, insisting that the Creator had not yet given them permission. Isaak himself had begun to doubt his father's wisdom and now sided with the villagers. He knew that to save the tribe, Abraham must allow them to migrate. He also knew that the tribe desperately wished him to confront his father, a task he was hesitant to perform. To challenge Abraham's judgment was to challenge the Creator.

Hagar was sitting behind a thorn bush windbreak outside her tent, clipping a sheep, constantly sharpening the shears with a chunk of waterstone. The drought had caused this year's wool to be short and coarse. Covered in sores, the animal seemed barely conscious; lines of green mucus hung from its nose.

"Isaak," Hagar said, "help me weigh this." She indicated a pile of wool.

No one except Hagar could get away with talking to the son of Abraham in this manner. However, Isaak lusted after her and because she recognized this, she gave him orders. He placed the wool on a huge balance hanging from a branch and scratched a number on the bale.

Finally, he said, "Did you lie down with my father last night?"

She nodded.

"What did he say?"

She stopped shearing and wiped her brow with her fingers. Then she looked straight into the young man's eyes. "He claims a messenger speaks to him."

"Does the messenger tell him to move the tribe north? Or to let us die here like fools?"

"Isaak, the path I once walked to reach your father's heart is barred. I am now a scorpion. Your mother has convinced him of this. He comes to me only for what is between my legs." She stood up and tossed the shears to the ground. The sheep bleated in protest and wandered into the miserly shade of a eucalyptus tree. Hagar's long black hair was undone. She was nearly as tall as he was and he blushed at her awesome beauty.

"My mother," he said, "is a silly old woman. She causes minor problems compared to what threatens us. Hagar, we lost more animals last night. I waited on the hill until sunrise and saw nothing. I'm not sure—"

He broke off, noting her inattention. She was staring at the sky.

He looked up, where hundreds of white cranes flew in loose formations, soaring bravely against luminous yellow clouds. Birds. It had been weeks since he last saw them. *Birds understand that a lifeless place must be abandoned. Only the vultures remain. And the peacocks, pampered by my father's servants.*

When the cranes faded from view, she said, "He is touched by madness. He tells me horrible things, Isaak, and he scares me."

Isaak shook his head. "The old man is melancholy. What about the tribe? Who stands with him?"

"He doesn't say."

"Get him to talk, Hagar. Soon I'll be forced into action. We have to know what he's thinking. Or if he's thinking at all."

Hagar looked hurt and unhappy.

"The longer he keeps us here," Isaak continued, "the more dangerous Canaan grows. I need you on my side." He grasped her shoulders to reassure her.

The shock of his request registered on her carefully composed face, the same face she wore when Sarah banished her to the desert for having birthed Ishmael, Isaac's half brother. When Hagar's expression turned to stone, it was best to avoid her. Once, as an adolescent, she disemboweled a nomad who had tried to rape her.

He left her there in the sun and when he glanced back, she was looking up again, watching the rainless clouds smear their unearthly colors across the heavens. He went over to the rough pastures to monitor the grazing.

Gradually, the day's mirages were forming, making it seem as if Canaan was surrounded by cool water. A herd of goats appeared and crossed the flats, heading for little islands of grass. The thousands of legs looked like the legs of one creature—a monstrous millipede—

followed by a lone goatherd. Isaak walked out to greet him, cautiously at first, until he was sure that he'd been watching a mirage and not a vengeful angel.

NIGHT FELL, the animals and men came in, and the chores were completed. They separated the lambs from their mothers and tied them to ropes, brought the newborns to the proper camps, caught and tethered the goats, lit incense, dispensed medicine, and mended equipment. At last, the shepherds could relax with their families. After dinner, they recounted the day's events and exchanged heated whispers about the son of Abraham. When would Isaak step forward? Clearly, the tribe was on the verge of famine. For years, the old man had seemed blessed by the Creator; he'd been a cherished leader, a true prophet. These last few months, however, he revealed himself to be a stubborn old fool, solely responsible for the tribe's decline and impending death. He should step down from his position or else allow the migration. Lately, people had begun to doubt the soundness of Abraham's mind. Rumor had it that he was going out alone into the desert at night to hunt down the infidel, the old man's bones creaking across dunes in worthless pursuit of the unseen, subsisting on nothing but locusts and honey, sometimes constructing an altar by himself, upon which he intended to sacrifice a ram to the Creator. Another rumor had it that Abraham himself was the infidel. The older shepherds, the tribal elders, finished their paltry meals, kissed their wives and children, and headed in the direction of Abraham's house.

With his mother's help, Isaak had arranged a meeting, the fifth this year, and he did not look forward to it. Tonight, he expected the elders to be desperate and direct, his father to be confused and defensive.

They sat around the fire in silence and sipped hot tea, anxious for things to get underway. When Abraham entered wearing his silk chieftain's coat, the men rose in unison and recited a litany to the power and glory of the Creator. The old man's face was withered, menacing and deranged. Using a cane, he hobbled over to the fire, sprinkled dust into the flames, and mumbled a prayer. Slowly, he raised his spotted hand to signal that the meeting had started.

Reuben spoke first. "Father Abraham, the riverbeds are dried up. After our well is emptied, there will be no water."

Then Azriel, "The animals have chewed this country into dust. Only a handful of pastures are left to graze."

Migdal said, "Please, Father Abraham, let us move to the north where we can prosper once again."

The old man stamped his cane on the dirt floor. "It is not yet time. The Creator has further use for us in Canaan."

"What use to Him can we possibly be when we are dead?" interrupted Enoch and the others bellowed in assent until Isaak was forced to quiet them.

"My brothers," Abraham continued, "I don't believe we will die here. We will live long, but only if we listen to the Creator."

Now Isaak spoke. "We *are* listening. But does He still cherish us enough to talk? Our sheep are being killed without the purifying fire. Surely the Creator has taken offense and will punish us for letting our animals die this way."

"No," said Abraham. "The Creator will punish the one responsible. The one who is among us now, posing as good and righteous."

Eyes shifted and people shuffled.

"Do you know," said Isaak, "the name of the infidel?"

Abraham turned to his son and said, "His name is Isaak."

Stunned, the elders were rendered mute, immobile.

Isaak could only muster the strength to say, voice cracking, "Crazy old man."

"Because you are my son," replied Abraham, "I forgive you. And I will spare your life. In two days, you will go out into the desert with me. Together we will offer a sacrifice to the Creator, so that He also may forgive you—and cleanse your soul." Then Abraham hobbled from the room, the sound of his cane retreating, leaving his dazed son to absorb the wounded stares and distrustful questions of the elders.

"What will you do now?" someone asked.

Shuddering with rage, Isaak spat on the ground. "I'll catch the infidel." But even as he spoke these words, he felt hollow. He suspected his father had accused him in front of the elders for just this reason. To prove his innocence and avoid shame, he had no other choice but to bring down the sheep-killer. A grown man, he was still being manipulated by his father.

His father. A savior and a prophet. But he was also a cruel monster who had done evil things to Isaak as a child. Nightmares plagued Isaak and they helped to forge an unbreakable bond of hatred between father and son. Not even death, Isaak acknowledged, would be enough to shatter the chains.

He stormed out of his father's house and returned to his tent, where, in the torchlight, he found the peacocks feasting on the corpse of the baby lamb, the first casualty of the oncoming famine. The spoiled peacocks had had their food rationed, and they were hungry enough to kill.

Isaak's blood pounded in his ears.

He plunged into the circle and grabbed the biggest bird by its brilliant feathers. As it hopped in retreat, he caught hold of its wing and yanked it back. The free wing smashed his face with sharp club-like blows, but he didn't let go. Sharp claws fastened on his leg and scratched his face. Isaak groped blindly until he found the neck of the struggling bird. The blue eyes looked at him without fear. Then the gore-slicked beak opened and vomited a stream of putrid fluid. Isaak placed his knee on the bird, pinning its neck to the ground with one hand while his other fumbled for a stone. The first blow crushed the beak and greasy blood spurted. Blue eyes stared at him, unfazed. He struck again and again until the peacock was dead, its feathers in grotesque disarray. He was still smashing the bird when Hagar pulled him off.

Rage spent, he buried himself in her arms and wept.

INSIDE HAGAR's TENT, Isaak woke up in the bed of his father's concubine. It was too hot for clothing and she lay naked beside him, the rhythm of her breathing sending him into a reverie in which he seemed apart from himself. He was watching them lying together in her bed. The smoothness of her skin, the curves of her thighs. What force was urging him to reach out and caress her breasts? He suspected it came from the Creator, but he would never be permitted to speak this truth aloud. And what part of the force impelled Isaak to choke the life from the innocent peacock and his father's ancient body? That came from somewhere else, some dark and unfamiliar place inside him, a place he wasn't yet ready to accept.

With his fingertips, he stroked Hagar's stomach, and she jerked awake.

"I'm sorry," he said. "I'm sorry I cried like a child."

She got up and fetched her robe. "The tribe's respect for your father has lessened these last few months, but his word is still considered faultless. Many believe you're the infidel."

"I might as well join my brother in the desert." The desert was the refuge of outlaws, the haunt of brigands, the home of demons and wild beasts, Abraham had banished Ishmael.

Isaac saw the corners of Hagar's mouth tighten at the mention of her son. "No," she said. "That cannot happen." She sat down on the edge of the bed and placed her soft hands on his shoulders. "I talked with the elders and none has chosen sides. The time is right for you to take your father's place. But first you must deal with the infidel."

"I don't think I can stop him," he said, miserable with his own failure.

"Patience," she said.

THE WORLD WAS quiet beneath a gauze of moonlight. Sheep bells tinkled in the warm breeze. Isaak was walking through a wilderness of sand. *It is a strange and terrible thing to have a single motive burning in your skull. It is like a heightened form of prayer, at the end of which you have either reached a state of blessedness or gone completely crazy. Has Abraham driven me into a deeper madness than his own?*

It was clear to Isaak that the pressures had changed him. Again and again, he returned to the rage that had assailed him after the meeting—and the fear of that rage. The words "Kill the infidel" did not fit with the man Isaak considered himself to be. Yet the statement echoed in his head. Everything angered him, but what enraged him most was his sense of powerlessness, that whatever he did to change things would be crushed by the vast weight of the desert and its monsters. You could not fight Canaan, and you could not fight the Creator. They taught you passivity, or they broke you.

He went to the nearest flock and, in an attempt to soothe his torment, he scooped a lamb into his arms and carried it to the hilltop. He tickled its lips and blew in its nostrils, then lay for a long time listening to the other animals chewing and coughing and crying and giving birth in the valley below. There was a time when Isaak had wanted the sheep as far away from him as possible. He recalled his childhood, having to constantly fend them off with kicks and punches. All night they spent jumping on his tent, rubbing their noses and rumps on it, pissing on it. They singed their faces on the fire, got in the way of things, and generally caused havoc. Now

Isaak wanted them all gathered at his feet, where he could watch over them and save them from harm; he wished them to seek out his affection. When the lamb in his arms grew restless, he let it go and watched it run down the hill in search of its mother.

Observing the lamb's progress, he glimpsed a spark of flint near the ravine. The infidel had made the mistake of sharpening his blade.

He smeared dirt on his face and limbs to blend with the darkness and made his way quickly and quietly down the hill. When he reached the ravine, he saw a figure standing there, a black ghost silhouetted against the stars. Isaak was breathing heavily, and drawing his knife, he struggled to control his gasps. But the figure had already sensed him and in the short distance between the two adversaries, a dying sheep silently kicked its legs, its life ebbing away. The figure coiled his body, ready to run.

"Move," said Isaak, "and I'll put your head on a spear."

There was no reply. The figure remained motionless.

Suddenly, the dogs went berserk. Barking, kicking up dust and rubble, they surrounded the figure and to Isaak's horror, they immediately charged. He heard the nauseating sound of metal striking flesh and bone, and a dog yelped, then howled in agony. The rest retreated, growling at the infidel, keeping their distance, but waiting for him to drop his guard.

"Dogs can't help you."

"Ishmael?" Isaak knew the voice, though it had changed somehow, deepened.

"It is I. I've been watching you for a while."

"Watching me?"

"I see things. I see that the tribe puts too much faith in you, Isaak. Can you really play Cain?"

"I'm not going to kill you, brother, but I do want to whip you senseless."

Ishmael stepped into the moonlight. "Just as Father Abraham whipped us when we were children. You think too much of vengeance."

"Why are you doing this?" said Isaak. "This is still my tribe."

Like a wolf, Ishmael looked harmless and quiet and blank in the eyes, but he was not like that at all. He survived by his wits, just like a wolf, and when he fought, he fought like one too. One man, Isaak knew, if pushed, could fight off ten.

Ishmael said, "Famine is here and the people should move north. Killing their sheep will force them out of Canaan."

"Our Father banished you and the people did nothing to stop him. You bear them no love. You mean to destroy Abraham."

A dog growled. Ishmael smiled and squatted in the dust and folded his arms, still clenching his knife. "You watch the animals for his sake? Once his victim, now his protector."

"Tonight, I am his protector. Tomorrow his assassin." Isaak surprised himself with his own announcement and knew it was true the instant he said it. There was no other way. There never was.

Astonishment took hold of Ishmael's voice. "Brother, if you kill Abraham, you will become something worse than Cain."

"Yes, that's right," said Isaak. "I don't want to be the

son. I don't want to be the sacrificial lamb. I want to be ugly. Ugly in the eyes of the Creator."

Ishmael jabbed his knife angrily into the dirt and let his head hang down.

Isaak said, "I'll do what you've been too afraid to do." At first, he thought his words courageous. And then the coldness, the flatness, of what he'd said began to scrape against his heart. He was confident he could slay the old man quickly and without hesitation. It was the Creator's retribution that worried him. *Better to die on one's feet. Better to be punished by God than suffer the scourge of a man.*

"Does Hagar know your plans?"

"Ishmael, you're a sheep-killer and a coward. Get out of my sight."

"Let me help you, brother."

"No," said Isaak. "It is too late for that."

ISAAK WAS WATCHING from the thorn bush. Hagar sat outside her tent, rubbing her hair with olive oil. She filled a basin with water and some buttermilk, then took off her blouse and skirt and poured the mixture through her hair and over her back. She washed the upper part of her body, then her legs and feet. Afterward, she combed out long black curls, which turned into ringlets in the morning light. When Isaak approached, she lifted her towel to cover herself casually, a mere gesture to form.

He ripped the towel from her wet body, and in response, she kissed him forcefully and led him into her tent. She sat on the edge of the bed, spine curved, and loosened the knot on his belt. He pushed her gently by the shoulders until she lay on her back, arms above her head. He gripped her waist just above the hips. Her legs opened to him, he could smell the sharp scent of her arousal.

Her eyes were open, her teeth pinning her lower lip. Isaak wondered what she saw.

He raised her knees and guided himself into her.

When it was done, they lay without moving, her head resting on his chest. After a time, she rolled onto her back and said, "The angel has ordered Abraham to sacrifice you."

Isaak couldn't help but laugh at this. His small act of revenge against his brother and father had satisfied him and he felt invincible. Yet he was grateful for her disclosure.

"Let him try," he said.

———————

EARLY THE NEXT MORNING, Isaak was awakened by his father.

"Sinful boy," said the old man, disgusted. "Black demon." He began to shake his son's leg, though this was unnecessary. Isaak had heard his father's approach for some time, the knocking of his cane, the creaking of his bones.

"I am ready." He looked into the old man's eyes, searching for signs of murderous intent. What Isaak perceived was tiredness and confusion, and for a moment, he doubted Hagar's tongue. But this was not the time for indecision. He arose, splashed water on his face, and strapped on his knife in plain view.

Together they walked past the peacock pen. Isaak expected his father to notice a bird was missing, but the old man said nothing. They escaped the dim firelights of the village and proceeded into the darkness of the hill, Abraham's bony legs wobbling with every misplaced step. Isaak reached out to steady him.

"Don't touch me," said Abraham. He made an attempt to swat his son's hand.

Pity wormed into Isaak's chest. The old man's mind was probably gone. Killing him would be like putting a wounded creature, a sick lamb, out of its misery. Isaak couldn't let his father win like that, so he pushed away the softness and resolved to cut out Abraham's heart.

They threaded their way amid heaps of rubble along the incline: rock, rotted wood, fragments of bone. A dark green snake as big around as a man's arm slithered across Isaak's path. He stopped to let it pass, cursing it the way his father had cursed him. "Stupid creature, always crawling on your slimy belly."

When they finally reached the peak, Isaak could barely make out an altar in the clearing, a haphazard pile of rocks and sticks not big enough to sacrifice a dog, much less the grown son of Abraham. The old man staggered to the altar. *Father Abraham, you're a sad priest. By what mad reasoning did the Creator choose you as his seer?*

Then Isaak noticed the slight figure standing beside the thorn bushes on the edge of the hill. He wore the soiled clothes of a nomad, though his pale skin seemed to glow in the darkness. He was as handsome as a prince, his hair long and lustrous. He stood perfectly still; though ramrod straight, his posture seemed relaxed, fearless. His eyes were a cold bright blue.

Isaak's head began to throb with the awareness that this man was a messenger.

"Are you here to slay me?" asked Isaak, pulling out his knife.

Weaponless, the angel said nothing, staring calmly.

Abraham dropped his cane and struggled to unsheath his dagger. "Evil thing," he said to his son.

Isaak closed the distance between himself and the blue-eyed angel. If Isaak was going to die, he wanted it over and done.

It had come to this. A doomed fight against the Creator's own foot soldier. All along, Abraham's help-lessness had masked an invisible and unfathomable power. Isaak had proven his father correct; he was a bad seed, a contemptible son, ignorant and fearful.

He was prepared to slash out with his knife when the angel made a sound like a cry, sharp and bestial.

"What?" asked Isaak, suddenly unsure of his actions.

Then he realized that the sound hadn't emanated from the angel. It had come instead from the thorn bush, where a young ram lay ensnared, its white body bleeding from numerous small cuts brought on by its struggle to escape.

Not recognizing the animal, Isaak said, "Is it yours? Speak, damn you."

The angel then turned to the ram and pulled it free. The ram followed the angel to the altar. Abraham, meanwhile, had fallen, causing the poorly built struc-ture to fall apart. Isaak saw his father's body sprawled on the ground and moved toward him, the old man still hurling curses, but before the son could reach out his hand, the angel said, "Choose your sacrifice, Isaak." The angel had picked up the exhausted ram and was now holding it in his pale arms.

"Is this a test?"

"Yes," said the angel, with just the hint of a smile.

Isaak nodded and opened his arms to receive the sacrifice. The angel stepped forward, and as he proffered the ram with both hands, Isaak struck him mightily across his handsome face.

The angel dropped the ram, threw back his head, puckered his quivering lips, and issued a shrill keening. The angel was singing a song of destruction, a prayer to rid Canaan of the pestilence known as Isaak. Before it was finished, Isaak struck again, but the angel made no effort to defend himself. Isaak grabbed his head, plunged his knife into the eye socket, and twisted the handle. There was no blood; the angel collapsed, the life rushing out of him in a single immense breath.

Isaak turned to Abraham, who had started weeping, still lying helpless on the ground. He struggled into something of a sitting position and raised a weak hand to his forehead. "You are the son of my nightmares," the old man said. "You have killed the Creator's messenger. Betrayed your own people. Your soul will surely burn."

"Yes," said Isaak. *Now I know what true sin is. Sin is to discard your own life and the lives of others.* But Isaak had made his choice and he vowed to show no outward sign of regret or remorse. He could not wait for time to slay his father. He stooped to clean his blade in the dirt, though there was no gore on it.

"Suffer eternal damnation," said Abraham, tossing his cane weakly at Isaak.

"Yes," said Isaak. "I think that's possible."

The clouds gathered and darkened, lightning

etching their shape against the sky's fading blue, promising wrath and retribution. Isaak stood, closed his eyes, and shivered as the first cool drops of rain touched his angry skin. He walked over to Abraham and kicked him in the face, then grabbed the nearly unconscious old man by his hair, pulling his head back to expose his wrinkled neck.

But before Isaak could finish it, he felt a divine presence behind him.

He turned to see four more messengers, standing together, and as lightning lit up the sky, they seemed like things of wax, ready to melt. Their faces and the flesh of their hands took on a bloodless corpselike appearance. He heard their screeching, then they swarmed him, and he was pinned by their strong pallid arms. They dragged him to the altar and when he realized their intent, he looked to his father, who had managed to regain his footing, his tattered beard fluttering in the wind. After recovering his blade, he joined the angels in binding the sacrifice.

"Abraham," said Isaak.

And then the old man took the stance of a weary father, still willing to step in on his son's behalf. Abraham seemed on the verge of speaking, but the wailing of the angels increased and the thunder crashed and the wind roared, and Isaak knew it would be a long time before the noises subsided and the dark curtains of rain parted to allow the light of heaven.

TOMB OF THE SPHERIANS

He examined himself in the locker room mirror, his nude body, a satchel of bones. His clavicle protruded sharply; his hips were skeletal. He had shaved his head when he began losing patches, but the stubble remained dark. Oddly, his pubic tuft had gone completely white. And he'd lost a front tooth, creating a hideous gap. His eyes, once blue, had faded into urine-hazel, his sockets sunken and shadowed. He grimaced at his reflection.

I'm a ghost. A phantom stalking a doomed paradise littered with masochists.

He wrapped a towel around his waist, sat down heavily on a bench, and wept into his hands as he recalled the morning. He'd woken with no energy, yet he felt compelled to break free from his exhaustion. When he stumbled into the kitchen, he saw Blair, naked under an apron and picking through a clump of mite-ravaged produce. She was attaching the hose of a CO_2 charger to a glass bottle in order to make club soda, while humming a pop song by a singer who might still be famous on the outside. Drinking carbonated water filled her stomach with gas and reduced her hunger pangs.

He laughed aloud at that moment. Before being sealed, a *High Times* magazine article had pondered the sexual dynamics of Eden2; the story went viral. But there was no erotic grandeur once the airlock closed. Just exhaustion. Deprivation. The accretion of defeat. Countless hours spent stooped over sweet potatoes, trying to blow off bugs with flimsy solar-powered hairdryers to salvage a mouthful of food. Hard labor and malnutrition had trumped their sexual energies, broken their spirits.

"What's funny?" Blair turned to gaze wanly at him, picking up a knife to cut some desiccated vegetables.

"I was thinking," he said, "that maybe they pumped too much oxygen in here."

Her face fell and she drowsily pointed the blade at him. "I love you, Lem."

"Then you love a corpse."

"We're not dead yet."

"Close enough. The seed stock is nearly gone." Indeed, Eden2's inhabitants had eaten it. There was nothing to plant.

"Mission Control won't change the rules. All they can give us is air."

"The rules are ridiculous," he slurred. Temper flaring, he worried his rage might cause him to faint. "Allowing nothing in or out? Stupid! We should be doing the most creative work of our lives." He was too tired to add: *Instead, we want to kill each other*.

"Lem," she said, touching his face. "If I get pregnant, we can leave Eden and have our baby in the world. In a clean hospital with white sheets. Where it smells like disinfectant instead of humid rot."

"What about our work?"

"This was a mistake. We're not God. We're not even good scientists. Just drained men and women."

"We're about to be something worse," he said. "The coffin key is gone. Shovels are missing and I can't find the blowtorch."

Blair didn't say anything. She blinked rapidly, what she did now when she couldn't process the unthinkable. "Since when?"

"This morning. I checked the desert grounds and everything is untouched. They'll start digging tonight, I imagine."

"We have to stop them, Lem," she said. "It would be evil to let them go ahead with it." An atheist before being locked in Eden2, Blair embraced Christianity after reading Dante in the library while ingesting less than five hundred calories a day. As she explained it to Lem, she saw, in the Italian poet's vision of hell, parallels to their own predicament.

"If they go through with it," he said, "it's all we'll ever be known for."

She kissed him in the garden of earthly deterioration. She tasted like decay.

Lem sat on the locker room bench and replayed this encounter. It pained him, but not because of Blair's sweetness or the idea of them dying together in Eden2. He cried because his mind was so famine-racked that he thought Blair looked lovely with her cheekbones razoring through the skin of her face. And because of a discolored lesion growing out of a mole on the side of his torso.

I know a piece of my humanity is lost.

He got up and, still wearing the towel, slipped on his shower shoes. He went to his second locker, turned the combination, and removed the case that held the 9mm he'd sneaked into the sphere in case of just this type of emergency.

———

ON CLOSURE DAY, the four men and four women had gathered on a patch of green lawn that stretched beneath the glass windows of the coral reef habitat. Surrounding them was the noise of camera shutters and news helicopters and a Lakota Indian elder in a feathered headdress reciting a prayer. Lem watched a movie star striving to foster an environmentalist image vomit into a recycling bin, suffering from the summer heat at the base of the Catalinas outside Tucson. In matching canary-yellow jumpsuits, six sweating spherians stepped to the microphone and uttered brief platitudes about the future of the human race. Lem was seventh to recite his lines.

It was all rehearsed, of course, except when Augustine, the rainforest manager and last to speak, jokingly referenced the Donner Party, the ill-fated group of pioneers who, snowbound in the Sierra, resorted to eating their dead. Augustine's comment wasn't widely quoted and Lem didn't remember it until Blair reminded him after Kane's funeral the day before. A spherian dying was a contingency for which Mission Control had planned, hence the plastic tomb complete with padlock. The key was provided in the likelihood of an infestation of coffin flies, in which case the body required cremation. But the key was missing, which most likely meant that Augustine planned to unearth the crypt, cook Kane's flesh with acetylene, and eat it before it spoiled.

Lem and Blair understood that cannibalism was possible; they were the nutritionist couple. They knew how to properly consume the deceased, but were against it. The taboo was absolute, the shame eternal. They sided with another couple, Kane and Monika, in prioritizing research over closed-system purity. The others, however, believed in the secondary objective: surviving inside an artificial Earth. Augustine led that group and Lem wanted to bust his skull. Or, he thought, retrieving the pistol, put a bullet in it.

Lem met Blair in the glass library tower where they could see anyone approaching. They discussed confronting Augustine in the storeroom. He and the other three spherians were no doubt eating from the meager remaining supplies, gathering strength for the dig and their unthinkable barbecue. It seemed a better idea to lie in wait in the desert at dusk, in the deep shadows behind the rock formation. Lem would catch them in the act of exhumation and insist that Augustine and his comrades re-bury the coffin. Blair would capture it all on her phone for evidence in a trial on the outside, if it came to that. The footage would confirm Lem had violated Eden2's prohibition against weapons. But he'd argued for stricter law enforcement. After all, Mission Control stood firm behind a genuinely closed system, with no breaching whatsoever, for the full two-year term of the experiment and their contracts. Thus, neither sanity nor peace was guaranteed. He and Blair could only hope that thwarting the inconceivable would weigh in their favor.

Besides, though she didn't directly witness it, Blair was sure that Augustine had killed Kane.

"You don't know," Lem asserted two days earlier, after Blair found Kane, the aquatic manager, face down in the surf, head directed at the beach and feet pointed toward the water as if he'd washed ashore.

"I saw a bruise on his throat. It was *not* a heart attack. Kane was only thirty-six years old. He didn't drown either. He was an Olympic-caliber swimmer!"

Collectively, the spherians had envied Kane, who could pretend to be lost in paradise, surrounded by coral reef imported from Mexico. With real waves lapping at him, the walls of Eden2 disappeared and he experienced the best part of the terrarium. The rest of the group could only look on as they struggled to feed themselves from dwindling rations. It wasn't that Kane had it easy; he worked his ass off, rotating coral with the seasons, keeping them sunny in the winter, shady in the summer. He routinely scrubbed algae from the windows so visitors could see the ocean floor. He was a team player, except when it came to hunting galagos, tiny African primates with big eyes and bat-like ears.

Galagos resembled Pikachu—chubby yellow-furred rodents from the Pokémon cartoon—and they ran roughshod in the rainforest, chewing wires in Eden2's machinery and eating all the hummingbirds. Weeks earlier when Augustine announced he was going to capture the little bastards in bird snares and broil them, Kane took it upon himself to smash all the traps. Eventually, a fistfight erupted between the aquaticist and the rainforester. Kane's wife, Monika, ended it by giving

Augustine a nasty cut on his arm with a pair of garden shears.

"Bitch!" Augustine snarled at her.

"Don't eat the animals," she said to him.

He ate them anyway, ripping honeycombs from bee boxes and slaughtering the egg-laying hens. Augustine was now ignoring Eden2's original mission of scientific discovery—how to create and manage a closed-system biosphere—in favor of life's own objective, survival at any cost. In six months, Eden2 would be unsealed, the spherians released. Until then, Augustine and the others planned on consuming the ecosystem. Lem and Blair knew he was capable of anything. But did he straight-up murder a fellow spherian over an argument concerning monkeys?

"Six months," said Lem, back in their kitchen, gasping from the trip back from the library, before sitting down to eat his mush. "If we hold it together and keep our datasets intact, we'll have so much to report on, everything from soil samples and air and water measurements to entomology, eco-biopsychology—"

"He doesn't care," interrupted Blair, "about any of it. All he heard Mission Control say was: *No breaching.* Augustine has reduced this to a game."

"Well, game *over.*"

"What if he doesn't listen? What if you have to shoot him, Lem?"

He considered this.

"What I mean is," she continued, "let's agree that Augustine killed Kane. Then you're forced to kill Augustine. Killing a murderer to prevent cannibalism doesn't—"

"I'm not going to kill him. Just shoot his nuts off."

She smirked at his bravado, but only for a moment. "I can't blame him for eating the damn lobsters in Kane's reef. But I'll hate him forever for strangling our friend, because I *know* he did."

Lem shrugged. "Maybe not. Kane developed a condition when his weight dropped. Besides, Lopez is a physician. He did a postmortem and—"

"Lopez," she scoffed. "He might be crazier than Augustine, throwing scalpels at palm trees. Then again, you're the one who smuggled a gun into a biosphere."

Lem seemed to punctuate her statement with a stomp of his work boot. Cockroaches had infested the kitchen and with the chickens gone, no predators were left to eat them, except Lem. He often cooked them in a pan of olive oil.

They said nothing for a while.

"What about Monika?" he asked. She'd been grieving in her room since the funeral, getting high off an old PVC glue can and a plastic bag.

"You mean should we bring her tonight? I don't think so."

"She has to come. Otherwise, it's four of them against two of us."

"She can't fight."

"She scratched Augustine well enough. Tell *him* she doesn't have claws."

———

THE THREE OF them crawled out of a concrete-walled basement filled with broken grain threshers and algae scrubbers and into a night-laden wilderness. They waded through Kane's damp rainforest and followed the snaking stream. Along the way, Monika—stoned or out of habit—stuck her fingers in the soil, checking for moisture, and groomed the plants, removing wilted-brown leaves. Lem and Blair said nothing and kept navigating the savanna grasses, then climbed the cliff hanging majestically above the ocean Kane had designed and maintained. They paused to catch their breath, listening to the waves in the darkness, then pushed on.

Monika switched on the solar lantern as they made their way down a staircase threading between boulders and beyond the desert pyramid at Eden2's farthest end. They walked through thorned scrub until they reached Kane's gravesite and, behind it, the rock formation where Lem and the two women planned to wait for Augustine. Despite his marine science degree, Kane had been a fan of movie westerns like *Rio Bravo* and instructed his wife, if he happened to die in Eden2, to bury him in the desert.

"If there were a breeze in this place, it would make me feel human again," Monika said out of nowhere, standing over her husband's fresh grave. It was true, Lem knew. The total lack of wind deepened their banishment.

He motioned to them to follow. Together, they concealed themselves within the gloomy stone monolith, waiting for the would-be cannibals. Lem spotted a prickly-pear cactus pad on the ground, peeled it, and ate it raw. But it was so dry, it made him gag. When he offered a piece to Blair and Monika, they laughed, though without mirth. Lem recalled the javelinas that had been Noah's arked into the dome. They were curious creatures, always investigating and getting into trouble. Which is how they died, drowning in a pit of loose dirt where a malfunctioning sprinkler created quicksand. If he'd known how hungry he'd get, he wouldn't have buried those pigs. He would've salted them and made bacon jerky.

Footsteps now. Ahead they saw a flashlight beam scanning the desert floor. Lem heard Augustine's low voice talking to another spherian, probably Lopez. The two were always chatting about medical minutiae involving war or extreme sports.

Lem and the women waited. The digging proceeded steadily, and he wanted the evidence to be clear. Now and again, he glanced at Monika. She furiously rubbed her forehead, incensed at the men as much for tampering with her husband's coffin as she was at their intention to cook and eat the corpse.

He took a raspy breath and twitched his trigger finger a time or two. Lem hadn't fired his 9mm for years and that had been at a range, shooting under complete control at a stationary target. If he had to fire the gun now, he'd better hit his mark. The biosphere was hardly bulletproof and a breach would end the experiment, voiding their contracts and forfeiting their salaries.

He waited a moment, then tapped Monika on the shoulder, indicating it was time. He nodded at Blair.

As the three of them stepped out from behind the rocks, Monika lit up the diggers with the lantern. Augustine and Lopez dropped their shovels and shielded their eyes, the still-sealed coffin halfway out of the plot in front of them. Blair began recording. Lem spoke decidedly, decisively.

"Damn you, Augustine." He raised the gun. "This is disgusting and I won't have it. Pick up your shovels and put Kane back in the ground. You've violated the project's integrity and turned it into...into a...a *freakshow!*"

They bent forward to retrieve the shovels, but Lem saw Lopez reach for something in his boot. The doctor suddenly sprang up and threw whatever it was at Monika.

Scalpel.

Lem heard Monika gurgling as she dropped the lantern. Everything went dark.

"Asshole!" he screamed, aiming for where he expected Lopez to be. He pulled the trigger, once. The muzzle spit fire with a roar and in the glow of Augustine's flashlight, he saw Lopez collapse and spasm a few times before lying still.

Augustine was rushing Blair with the shovel, but she was ready. She swung a bicycle chain, glinting in the dim moonlight, and it whipped him between the eyes. He shrieked, dropped the shovel again, and fell to his knees, blood gushing from his lacerated nose and seeping into the cracked desert floor.

Lem walked up behind Augustine and pushed the barrel into the back of his skull.

"Kill me!" Augustine cried out for annihilation and Lem felt a surge of pity.

"Lem!" Blair yelled, her bony arms reaching out at him as if to magically push the gun from his hand. "Don't do it!"

On the ground, Monika death-rattled.

He closed his eyes...and squeezed.

YEARS LATER, at a docuseries panel at the Television Critics Association press tour in the Beverly Hilton, a young woman journalist asked Blair a question she'd dreaded. "How did you end up marrying the man you believe killed your friend?"

She took a long time before she spoke. She knew Augustine was watching, still under house arrest, and she wanted to reassure the man whose nose was still disfigured from the chain whipping she'd given him. The moderator was leaning into the microphone to move things along when she finally said, "I'll answer."

Staring into the distance, she said, "When Lem shattered the seal with a bullet, the nightmare was over. We reverted back to who we were before..." She caught herself before saying, "the fall." Instead, she said, "... before we launched our incredible mission. We discovered that we used to be kind. And after Lem died of skin cancer, the only person who understood me was..."

Just then, her eyes focused on the lavish trays of food available for brunch in the back of the luxury ballroom.

She blinked rapidly.

Someone asked the director a question about the ethics of documentary recreations.

THE FLYWEIGHT

When Lieutenant Dobbins discovered I could draw, he transferred me to Knuckle Company, and that's how I wound up with a bunch of Texans. A self-professed "funnies junkie," Dobbins assigned me to draw a strip, which I hastily pencil-and-inked by flashlight whenever I had a spare moment. Published in the weekly *Infantry Gazette*, the strip was called "Knuckle Company" and was loosely based on our missions in France. With the exception of Dobbins and myself, I caricaturized Knuckle Company by stressing their distinctive "cowboy" features: gap teeth, bowlegs, chew-drool. It never bothered them, though. Is there something inherently warm and fuzzy about cartooning? More likely, Texans are the stupidest people on this planet.

One of these Texans had an inferiority complex. He was only five-foot-three. Even today, I believe, you're not considered a Texan unless you're at least six-one. His real name was Bill, but Knuckle Company called him "Pecos." Every one of us despised him. He was not only the most mentally unbalanced of our group, but a loudmouth to boot. He was always showing off the toughness of his belly. "C'mon, punch me right here," he exhorted some newcomer to the company, pulling up his shirt to reveal a pale, undersized stomach. Inevitably, some greenhorn answered the challenge with a hard right, then Pecos—without recoiling— triumphantly wailed, "Steel-plated!"

He constantly bragged about the greatness of Texas, describing the varied topography: the piney woods and rich black soil of East Texas; the picturesque bayou-dotted flatlands; the subtropical fauna and fruit blossoms of the Rio Grande; and in the Big Bend, the haunting desert landscape. He went on and on about this kind of stuff and drove us all fucking crazy.

Strange as it may sound, though, he heard no argument from me. I conceded that Texas was underrated. And I told him it's still a fine location for getting a job, marrying a good girl, raising a family, driving a Cadillac, fearing God, et cetera. My main beef was that Texans thought they were superior even when national concerns demanded otherwise. During the War, gasoline rationing was the rule, but since Texans had plenty of gas in their own backyard, they felt they should be excused.

"Those are my people," said Pecos. "They don't let anybody push 'em around."

Each week, Pecos received an immaculately scripted letter from his younger sister Ginger, an aspiring model living in Dallas. Sometimes she included beauty shots of herself to let her brother know she was working. And let me just say that she was a very sexy blonde, tall and well proportioned, the antithesis of her malformed sibling. My heart tightened each time I looked at her. When he was in an upbeat mood, Pecos let me borrow the photos. I burned Ginger's face into my memory, drawing and redrawing her lovely mouth until I'd filled an entire sketchbook. I worshipped her, a Texas beauty queen, in spite of her brother, who committed errors so spectacularly dumb, they bordered on the psychopathic. And in France, that was deadly.

Once, after some brief small-arms exchanges, we regrouped under the tattered tarp of a demolished café to prepare ourselves for an advance of SS troops. What arrived instead was this guy riding a bright yellow bicycle. He wore a German uniform jacket, but with shorts, his bare legs working like a high-strung grasshopper's. A brown satchel hung across his thin frame. Obviously, he was a courier.

Obvious to everyone but Pecos.

He shot the guy off his bike. The courier received a gaping sucking chest wound. He flopped around for a few seconds, let out a horrid gasp, then fell still.

Dobbins turned to the murderous Texan and roared, "What the hell did you do that for!"

Pecos looked completely befuddled, as if a phantom had possessed him momentarily and pulled the trigger. Knuckle Company stared at him without sympathy.

Our position had been compromised.

The Germans opened up on us with a machine gun. Seconds later, things were downright scary: ten heavy-duty fifty-calibers in action, plus two of our rifle platoons burning magazine after magazine. I mean, we tore that place apart from both directions. Blasted shop windows. A cathedral's fractured dome, caved in by a mortar. A Nazi bullet must have struck one of our phosphorous shells, because the street blossomed with white sheets of fog. The air began to choke me with the vile taste of masonry dust. I hugged the ground behind a concrete park bench, trying to understand how all this came to pass. The Texan had shot a bicyclist and now the world was ending.

Things turned even more ominous when Sgt. Holt, wearing a black gas mask, crawled over and yelled into my ear, "Our radio officer is stranded at the church! Bring him back here!"

"Yes sir!"

"And take that son-of-a-bitch Pecos with you!"

I squirmed my way to a sandbagged ambulance, where I found Pecos cowering, and told him we'd been ordered to rescue the radio officer.

He rose clumsily and followed me along the tree-lined square, clutching his M-1. Whenever I glanced back at him, a wave of anger surged through me.

At the edge of the plaza, crouched behind a Red Cross stall, Pecos and I waited for a jeep to pick us up. By then, the Germans had switched to howitzers, pulverizing entire buildings. I'd never seen Knuckle Company in such a bestial state, their faces twisted in anger, transformed into fiends. So incensed was Spider that he'd overturned one of our 20mm anti-aircraft guns and was using it as a ground weapon to splinter a wooden cart that may or may not have been shielding enemy soldiers.

"Look what you started!" I shouted at Pecos over the din of death.

"He was a dirty Kraut!"

Shoulders drooping, the Texan leaned over to spit a glob of tobacco juice. It was evident in the weakness of his expression that he knew he was wrong. With the exception of women or children, couriers were about the most defenseless things you could shoot. I mean, he'd not only embroiled us in this hellacious firefight, he'd knocked us off of our moral high ground.

Anyway, as soon as the jeep screeched to a halt, sniper fire hailed down, shattering the windshield, bursting the tires. The driver took one in the neck and slumped against the wheel, gurgling. The Red Cross stall was now a target. The Texan and I ran for our lives. I spotted the concrete bench and slid for cover.

Machine-gun fire rocked the bench. The concussive noise rattled my skull and numbed my limbs. Dirt flew into my mouth, gagging me. I was either on the verge of euphoria or losing consciousness. The Texan held me like a child frantic for its mother, his fingers digging into my flesh. All I could do was return the embrace.

"Jesus Christ," he whimpered, his hot tears against my neck. "Don't let me die!"

It was an experience, that war.

WHEN THE ARMY cut me loose, I couldn't find work. With a return to peacetime, comic book sales had plummeted, forcing publishers out of business no matter what kind of comics they churned out—superheroes, science fiction, true crime. Only Westerns and romance sold. I couldn't draw horses too well and the world of *Young Love* was lost to me after what I'd seen in France. My cartooning career was over before it began. I was twenty years old.

So I started fooling around with the drums. I set them up in the storeroom of my uncle's restaurant in New York, where I occasionally worked as a busboy. Most nights after closing time, I went in there and played until dawn. It wasn't long before I figured out the Count Basie band style, the two hand-and-foot "sock" method with the high-hat cymbal positioned right next to the snare. Bit by bit, I made a little name for myself, filling in for house bands at places like the Deuce and the Spotlite. The money was decent, but I was restless, waiting for something to happen.

I'd just wrapped up a gig at the Deuce one night when Pecos came out of nowhere. I never thought I'd see him again, much less in a jazz club in New York. He looked fairly sophisticated in his dark blue cashmere jacket and gray pants, dressed to impress at five-foot-three. He bought drinks and introduced me to his friend, Dolly.

"Dolly," I said, reaching to kiss her velvet-gloved hand. "You're too much."

"Thanks, baby," she said. She was—as usual— thickly made up with rouge and mascara. Pecos asked us, "Do you know each other?"

"A hangout like this," she said, indicating the club, "makes for a small world."

I didn't have the nerve to tell Pecos that Dolly packed a bit more than other girls, so I asked about his postwar life. He'd dabbled in citrus down near the Rio Grande, but as a small investor, he couldn't ride out a year of low prices. He was a boxer now, a flyweight, still in training on his own; he'd yet to have an actual fight. He had a manager, though, a guy named Peppy Marino, a good-looking, well-dressed gangster-type, whose brother was a Mafia hitman. As it happened, I knew Peppy through my uncle from before the war. Back then, Peppy had owned a restaurant that featured a number of B-girls. Anytime you wanted to get laid, you went to Peppy's place where these brickhouse women sidled up next to you, drank with you for a while, and for a couple of bucks, one of them gave you a blow job. Peppy the pimp. Anyway, what the Texan needed now was a trainer.

"No one wants to bother with flyweights," he said. He sipped his drink. "What about you?"

Apparently, he'd seen me scuffle with a few pinheads in basic and saw I knew something about boxing. I brought up percentages and he offered me thirty. His first semi-professional fight was in six weeks and the purse was two grand, a lot of money in those days. I performed the mental arithmetic.

"To America," I said, raising my glass. "Land of opportunity."

"And to you, child," said Dolly, clinking a toast.

"And to Texas," added Pecos.

"Speaking of, how's your sister, by the way?"

We downed our drinks and ignoring the question, Pecos wanted to know, "So, do I have a trainer?"

"No problem," I said. "I'll get you into fighting condition."

And I did. I ran that little Texan all over the city. I

made him skip rope, lift weights, and quit smoking, drinking and transvestites. I fed him rare steak. He had to be in shape to use the things I taught him, stuff I learned from my old man: how to cover up and make a fist; when to step forward and unleash a three-punch combination; where to snap a punch or uppercut an opponent depending on whether he's against the ropes, off-balance, or out in the open. I trained Pecos to fight like a heavyweight, even though he weighed 112 pounds. Because they don't punch hard enough, flyweights always go the distance; they never get knocked down. They just jab each other to death. I didn't have the patience to watch an entire flyweight bout, so I encouraged the Texan to fight like hell for the first three rounds. If he didn't KO his opponent by then, I figured he'd be in shape and maybe win a decision. Besides, I was sure I'd lose interest and be useless to him by the fourth round.

I taught Pecos the dirty trick of leaving his belly exposed and feigning excruciating pain whenever his opponent landed a blow to the ribs. When the enemy became overconfident and cocky, thinking he could wither the Texan with a flurry of body shots, I instructed Pecos to blast away at the guy's face. The opponent was suddenly startled to find his ears ringing, his vision blurred, his nose broken and bleeding. True, it was amateurish; any experienced slugger with more than a brain cell would've ignored this dramatic jive. But it was still effective against the majority of imbeciles who participated in the sport of boxing.

Pecos learned fast enough and never questioned my advice or judgment. He obeyed me like I was Joe Louis. I amazed myself, given what little I had to work with. I mean, until I showed up, the guy hadn't the slightest clue about fist-fighting. In Texas, they must've taught him how to shoot off his mouth and his gun and nothing else.

Each day we went to work at a makeshift gym—an abandoned warehouse, really—on Eighth Avenue near 42nd Street. Pecos's manager had furnished a Prohibition-era canvas ring that squeaked whenever you moved around in it. The ropes were faded and frayed and sagged like wet noodles. In the afternoons, green-skinned junkies milled around outside, pacing the sidewalk, waiting interminably for their futile connections. Sometimes I lured one of these sad sacks inside for Pecos to pound. I tore a fiver down the middle, gave half to a small and particularly desperate-looking hophead, and say, "After two rounds, you get the other." Next, I handed the poor bastard a pair of decrepit gloves and helped him lace up—exacting, because an addict's hands tremble. Then I shoved him into the ring.

It doesn't matter how crazed a junkie is; a junkie is not a fighter. So Pecos went at it like a deranged automaton, clobbering every opponent into a state of near-unconsciousness. In terms of training for a fight, the benefit of knocking out drug addicts was dubious. However, I felt it strengthened the Texan's confidence in his ability to inflict bodily harm. Besides, Pecos seemed to enjoy the sparring sessions. I soon had to put a stop to it all, when junkies began lining up outside day and night, craving an opportunity to earn quick bucks. For a while, our gym was more popular than the blood banks.

We'd been training for three weeks when Peppy dropped the bomb. He showed up at the gym one day, wearing a ridiculous pink prewar zoot suit, a big cigar in his teeth, and said, "The venue has changed. I've arranged for a plane to Dallas. From there we'll drive to El Paso."

"Excuse me?" I said.

"You heard me," he replied in his tough-gangster voice.

"El Paso is practically in Mexico."

"If it's okay with Pecos, why should you have a problem?"

I glared at the Texan, who was pretending to tape his hands over by the speed bag. He blushed with shame.

"There's plenty of action right here," I said to Peppy. "How are we gonna make two thousand dollars in a faraway shithole?"

"El Paso is just another place," he said, like I was his boneheaded son. "In every country are people who have money and people who don't. The match will be attended by people with money."

I wanted to dismember him, but kept quiet.

Finally, Peppy added, "Get this man ready to kill your opponent," and without another word, he left.

I cussed out the Texan, calling him every name in the book. Then I went on to insult his mother.

"Does it matter where we go?" he said. "A fight's a fight."

Livid, I got him to don gloves and spar with me in the ring. I beat him badly. As he was lying flat on the canvas, I hissed in his ear, "Mexicans despise Texans."

Days later, Ginger drove up to New York from Dallas to help out her brother. During these last few weeks before the fight, her job was to cook and clean and generally tend to his apartment while we worked at the gym. The twenty-two-year-old bombshell arrived at our crummy little gym looking good enough to devour. Her blouse and skirt showcased her heavenly breasts, perfect legs, and an ass to die for. Her hair was a sun-enriched shade of blonde. She was better in the flesh than in the photos. I began to experience the ache and twinge of a profound lust. When she spotted us, she rushed to hug her freakish brother. Pecos stood on his toes to reach Ginger, who was nearly a foot taller. The difference—not just in height but in overall appearance —was astonishing. How could the two be at all related, let alone siblings?

After the introduction, Ginger said, "I've heard so much about you. Still drawing cartoons?"

"No," I said. "I'm a jazz drummer now."

She winked at me. I could tell she was a wild one.

"If you like music," I continued, "I know a great place."

"Hey, wait," Pecos said to me. "Don't take her to the Zodiac—"

"I'd love to go," interrupted Ginger.

So we went to the Zodiac and I showed her a good time. In those days, taking a freshly washed, dolled-up, White woman to a juke joint was analogous to waving prime rib in front of famished wolves. It could be done without hazard, but it was imperative to make the wolves understand that there was simply no way in hell they were getting any. The minute we walked into the Zodiac, I sent hard-bitten don't-fuck-with-me-and-my-girl vibes to everyone that gave us the once-over. For backup, a switchblade resting snugly in my coat pocket.

A band with drums and horns sound-checked, then rocketed into a set of boogie-woogie. Ginger grabbed my arm and practically dragged me onto the dance floor. I was good, but she was peerless. Winded after only a few numbers, I went back to the table to drink and watched her bump-and-grind with a few other guys. I seared holes into her partners with an evil stare, making it clear that if they stepped out of line, there would be serious consequences. The place began to reach maximum capacity. The music heated up. I could feel my shirt dampening.

Ginger returned, perspiring. She looked exquisite.

I introduced her to the couple from Detroit now sitting at our table. When I'd seen that they weren't dance enthusiasts, I invited them over. As soon as Ginger sat down, the man fired up what turned out to be award-winning reefer. To my continuing surprise, Ginger sucked in a huge hit and held it like a veteran dope smoker. I got a decent buzz going, so I whipped out my Bic and sketched the band's guitarist on a napkin. "I'm a cartoonist," I said.

"Yes, you are," said the man appreciatively.

In front of everyone, Ginger gave my arm a playful push. "You lied. You said you were a drummer."

"Jack of all trades," said the man's wife.

The couple was in town for the weekend, visiting family. The man said they had to wake up early the next morning and start the drive back home, where he made six dollars an hour in an auto factory, and she taught at a colored school.

"Together, that's great money," I said, and when

they laughed, I laughed too, though I wasn't joking. The wife offered to sell me a morphine syrette, and I politely declined. I was feeling sexy and didn't want anything to curb my enthusiasm. Ginger and I danced some more, then got ready to leave. We thanked the couple for their hospitality. I swapped addresses with the husband, Earl. "If you're ever in Detroit, look us up," he said.

Feeling giddy and invincible, Ginger and I hailed a taxi by pretending to drunkenly waltz into its path.

In the back seat, Ginger hiked her skirt to remove her black cotton panties and tossed them at me.

"Well?" She giggled. "What now?"

I knew right then I was in for a ride.

I stuffed the panties in my coat pocket. To reciprocate the immoral gesture, I handed her my switchblade. She flicked it open and began carving a star into the cab's leather interior.

"I didn't know you were Jewish," I said.

She replied contemptuously, "I'm from the Lone Star State."

"What's with the knife?" said the driver, having glanced at the rearview.

I rapped the courtesy glass. "Mind your business."

"I don't like weapons," he answered.

"The Ardennes would've been a bad place for you. Shut up and drive."

To this, the driver said nothing but gradually accelerated.

"You'd make a great oil man," said Ginger, "because you're crazy." She returned my knife and rested her head on my shoulder, purring, it seemed, like a sleepy tigress.

As soon as Ginger closed the door, she leaped into action, knocking me down and splitting my lip. I unzipped her dress. Even though I thought I knew every inch of her from filling sketchbooks with her images, I had to suppress a gasp when I gazed upon her in full uncovered glory.

Then she grabbed my tie and lightly garroted me.

"What?" I asked, a little puzzled.

Suddenly I caught on that she was roping me like a rodeo steer, bringing my face between her legs. She gasped and moaned and then, still employing the leash, guided me inside her. And so we had furious sex on the floor of a hotel room in Hell's Kitchen.

Afterward, sweaty and exhausted, we moved to the bed and smoked. The streets outside bristled with cars and the mirth of late-night partygoers. The moon hovered forlornly at the window. Somewhere, Charlie Parker fluttered on a cheap phonograph.

"I killed my husband," she said out of the blue. "Shot him dead." She glanced at me, gauging my reaction.

"Wow," I said.

"He was deeply troubled. He physically abused me. I got tired of it." She pronounced "tired" *tarred*. "One day I just snapped." She bit her lip. "I didn't want it to happen that way."

"In *what* way, then?"

"Well, I don't know." She sighed with the effort of confession. "Anyway, my brother was gallant. He hired the best lawyers. Three-year suspended sentence, but it was successfully appealed."

"Texans have no use for wife-beaters," I noted.

"The legal fees bankrupted Bill. He had to sell his citrus groves." At this point, a tear slid down her cheek and she rubbed at her eyes. "Never been a more devoted brother."

"I can see that."

"He worships you, you know," she said, rolling toward me. "He told me you saved his life in France. Shielded his body with your own."

"Not exactly. I fainted and fell on top of him."

"You're his savior," she insisted.

I stroked her narrow hips.

THE NEXT MORNING, Ginger and I toured the city, riding the subway and the crosstown bus. First, I treated her to butter-drenched eggs and English muffins at Reinzi's. Throughout breakfast, she seemed distant, distracted. It didn't take a genius to sense that I, or we, had crossed some sort of line and the thought that I'd never get that far again was so dismal that it caused me to suffer a moment of vertigo. Was Ginger ashamed to disclose to her brother that she'd been intimate with me? After a pot of coffee, I was determined to make things exciting again and quickly formulated a plan: I'd show her the wondrous and diverse beauty of the Big Apple. She'd be dazzled; the sights would convince her that Dallas no longer had anything to offer. After all, we were in New York, modeling capital of the world. So I took Ginger to see the transvestites parading on Broadway, the lesbian hustlers cruising Times Square, and the sulky beatniks in the cafés around Columbia

University, traipsing through Harlem, of course, to get there. We wandered through the Village and listened to the somber folkies strum their protests. In Washington Square, we watched a derelict skillfully roll an entire cigarette from discarded butts. All this and still her face remained impassive, cold. Nothing impressed her. For lunch, we ate Romanian—potato pancakes, stuffed cabbage, fried chicken livers, frothy steins of dark bitter beer. I talked too much and felt foolish—almost adolescent—in her presence. My efforts seemed useless; she'd already reached a decision about us.

Finally, she sighed. "We got too high last night. And went too far."

I said nothing.

"Last night was fun, but it can't happen again. Let's cool things down until the fight's over and done."

"That's three weeks away," I blurted.

"Well, anticipation is a good thing, right?"

That gave me enough hope to regain my balance, but I wasn't about to let on how smitten I was, and had always been, with her. "If it's okay with Ginger, then why should I have a problem?"

She gave me a puzzled smile, then brushed my face with her hand. "You're a good person," she said.

That afternoon I was left with her brother and a horde of rats, all of us sweating inside the world's nastiest gym. I was determined to transform Pecos into a homicidal maniac. When she saw what an amazing trainer I was, she would be mine. Each hour that passed without having contact with her fueled my efforts. Many times I wanted to phone her, but I checked myself. I wasn't going to be the one to break down.

But my phone never rang.

From time to time, she brought lunch to the gym, and as Pecos wolfed down a grilled steak sandwich ringside, I sat with her in the bleachers, made small talk, and listened to her describe her modeling try-outs. She seemed excited and hopeful about her career and this saddened me. I wanted her to be enthusiastic about us, not the catwalk. However, in retrospect, even if we'd carried on a relationship, I doubt it would have lasted, because during the final days of training, I was beat. The strain was almost too much.

In the mornings, I whipped Pecos through a series of drills, maybe a sparring session or two. Following lunch and a short afternoon nap, we went back to the gym to lift weights, spar, and pound the bags. At night, I hopped the subway to play the drums at various clubs, sometimes three or four per night, until sunrise. My hands were tender and blistered to the point that it hurt to merely grasp a cup of coffee, let alone drumsticks. To further complicate things, I'd finally scraped together enough cash to move out of Spanish Harlem and secure a slightly better apartment on the Lower East Side— better insofar as the new place had running water. Pecos helped me move in. Afterward, I noticed that he was looking around for an empty coffee can. To put him at ease, I threw him a metal pail and fetched some beers.

"Nice place," he remarked, wiping his lips with his hand. He sat down on a box.

"Plumbing works, anyway. How's Ginger?"

"She's good. She's been making the rounds, you know. Modeling agencies."

"Right."

"I'm surprised you two didn't hit it off better."

"Well, we're both very busy these days."

"Yeah. Think I got what it takes?"

Though I grasped the question, I said, "For what?"

"To be a boxer. A good one."

"Sure. Why not?"

"I worry sometimes."

I waited for him to go on.

"Know why I decided to fight?" he said finally. "Your comic strip. One you used to draw during the war? I still read them. Collected them all, every issue of the *Gazette*."

"Wow," I said. "I'm flattered."

"Know what I like about those old comics? The way you drew me, the way you drew *all* of us. Like we were champs, you know. John Wayne types. And it was authentic. Reading those comics is like watching newsreels. Or a documentary on the lives of real soldiers. And we were the soldiers."

"Huh," I said.

"When my citrus business failed, partner, I was down. I mean, *down*. In the dumps. And I had to take a long hard look in the mirror. It was sad, because I couldn't find a story that made any sense. For the life of me, I could not remember how things went. I knew there were moments of glory, in the war and everything. But I had trouble seeing a *pattern*. 'Knuckle Company' showed me a pattern. Your cartoons—the ones where I'm there getting punched in the gut and nothing happens and I'm standing there like a rock, the stone of Gibraltar? Those drawings held the answer. I gotta fight and be a fighter. I gotta *take* it as well as dish it out. *You*, partner—*you* showed me that. Just gotta be strong and believe in myself."

I answered, "See? That's exactly what I was trying to communicate."

WE FLEW TO DALLAS-FT. Worth with the idea that Ginger would drive us to El Paso in a rental car. I knew it was a dumb thing to do—invite a nice girl from Texas to a seedy boxing match. But she was anxious to see her brother in action, to witness the results of all those long hard days of training. At the airport, she looked lovelier than ever and gave each of us a hug.

"Easy, baby," said Peppy, subtly cringing. "This suit is pricey."

I asked her, "How are things?"

She answered, "Fine."

The drive to El Paso was a blur of barren ground, scattered towns and cities, silos and cultivated fields, horses, pigs, cows. Ginger sang along with the radio, completely ignoring me, and her husky, sensual voice heightened my melancholy. Peppy chewed a cigar and, strangely enough, filed his nails. I mostly sipped tepid soda and pretended to read comic books, the whole time trying to figure out where I stood with Ginger. And always coming to the same conclusion. Nowhere.

We crossed into a disreputable section of El Paso, the poverty intensifying with each passing block. Streets ceased to be paved, and sidewalks vanished. The color green became scarce. The neighborhood was worse than I'd expected. Naked children threw rocks at stray dogs. The smell of sewage hung in the air. The battered light poles—few that they were—leaned at extreme angles, like they'd all been smashed by out-of-control cars. Speeding cab drivers made intersections risky and chaotic. Fortunately, Ginger seemed to magically predict their moves and deliver us safely into town. She also spoke Spanish, so Peppy had her pull up to the courthouse and ask for directions.

"*Allí*," said a boy, nodding in the direction of ramshackle dwellings.

We pulled up in front of the largest of these hovels and got out. I nudged Pecos in the shoulder. He woke up with a jolt.

"You've got an hour to get ready."

Ginger stretched her long limbs. In her Henley and cropped pants, she looked like Katherine Hepburn. She sidled up to me and said, "I don't feel safe here," almost in a whisper. She glanced around as if the price of a stretch in this town was a savage beating.

"We might as well be in Mexico," I said.

"Don't worry," said Peppy, digging in his double-breasted jacket for a light. "I know everyone here."

I wanted to ask how, but didn't.

The fight took place in some kind of shack adjoining a tent that put on revivals. Inside, the hot polluted air was frightening. There were no seats or bleachers, just a dry dirt floor littered with cigarette butts. Scattered around were planks, barrels, an old washbasin. Above, three bare electric bulbs provided grotesque illumination. The bar was hardly larger than an ironing board. The ring consisted of water-damaged plywood and what looked like a decaying mattress. It was screened off with chicken wire to protect the boxers, but the mesh was flimsy. A paunchy man named Leon came forward wearing a dusty camel's hair overcoat and orange boots. He was the promoter—noisy, obnoxious, English-speaking. He and Peppy were obviously acquainted and got along magnificently, buying each other drinks, talking loudly about nothing, while the three of us stood around.

"Can your little dog fight?" teased Leon at one point.

Before the Texan could take offense, Peppy said, "Like a pitbull." Then Pecos made a guttural canine noise, which Leon thought immensely entertaining.

Back outside, we met the opponent, who was our age, maybe younger, calling himself La Máquina, "The Machine." He shook everybody's hand. Good-looking kid, jet-black hair, Indian features, wearing sequined shorts. He smiled slyly at Ginger, so I instantly despised him.

There was no weigh-in. There was no dressing room for us, so we took refuge in the shade of a rusted bus. The Machine shadowboxed with his people by the outhouse. I warmed up the Texan, getting him to throw punches with three-pound weights. We were next to a narrow two-lane road and as the cars shot past, we had to squint to keep out the dust. Then storm clouds suddenly rolled in and the sky opened up. The shower seemed to amuse the Machine, who tilted his head, opening his mouth to catch raindrops.

"Stick with me," I told Ginger and we re-entered the shack.

"Where's Peppy?" I asked Leon, who was getting plastered with a few Mexicans.

He shrugged. "He's around."

Ginger pulled me aside. "Hey," she said. "What's the situation here?" Her expression was one of fierce concern.

"Soon, Pecos will pulverize another fighter."

She shook her head. "None of this seems right. This place—"

"It's boxing. It's not exactly a refined sport—"

"My brother's a little slow," she cut me off fiercely. "Peppy's a dick, not to be trusted. But *you*!" I thought she was going to cry. Her lips trembled; her eyes grew moist. "What's *your* excuse? Why are you doing this to my brother?" She seemed startled by her own outburst.

"Look," I said. "I'm here to help." I pulled her close, until our faces were inches apart, but she refused to return my gaze. When I kissed her forehead, a little of the anxiety seemed to drain away, so I escorted her back outside.

We went in and I was immediately alarmed by the crowd. The place was packed with agitated spectators. The dim wavering lights infused the atmosphere with dread. It was obvious that this fight was a pretense for some kind of symbolic payback, for what I didn't know, unless it went all the way back to some imaginary act of revenge against the violent whites who stole Texas. Naturally, there was no trace of Peppy. Betrayed, I thought bitterly, with Ginger and me his unwitting patsies. But it was too late to turn tail.

Ginger, poor thing, gasped in horror.

I placed one arm around her waist, the other against the Texan's back, and together we advanced.

The Machine's people descended on the ring as Pecos stepped in. They screamed at the Texan, spitting, calling him "*gringo maricón*." The ref—a silent, no-nonsense type who acted like he would've rather been anywhere but in the midst of this—pushed the crowd back, allowing us to reach our corner.

My heart beating double time, I couldn't figure what was keeping the mob from wringing our necks even before the fight. Pecos looked a little queasy. He needed encouragement, so after the ref reviewed the rules and had them touch gloves, I yelled at him, "Now get out there and destroy this motherfucker!"

The bell rang; the fighters collided.

The Machine landed the first blow, a thumping left hook to the Texan's body. Pecos wasn't fazed, though, coming back with a left to the face and a stinging right to the body.

Ginger hopped in her heels ringside, a look of fear and relief on her gorgeous face as she watched her brother give as good as he got.

But then the Machine bullied him hard, driving him across the ring and against the ropes, causing him to clinch. The ref stepped in, and as they broke, the Machine shot a terrible right to the Texan's chin that made him go wobbly.

But only for a moment.

The Texan shoved the Machine into the center of the ring, then viciously double-jabbed the Mexican fighter. The crowd went insane, screaming at their hometown champion to knock out his opponent. And that's when my training and the Texan's stunning lack of self-preservation came together to generate an unforgettable moment in the annals of unsanctioned boxing.

Pecos refused to cover up, letting the Machine smash him several times on the forehead, inciting the onlookers to a feral intensity. To my shock, he wasn't cut; he didn't bleed. Instead, a supernatural energy seemed to charge him as he bewildered the Machine with a series of straight rights to the face.

Dazed by his opponent's sudden comeback, the Machine couldn't rally against the flurry of punches, the maelstrom of a Texas-style beatdown delivered by a pipsqueak avenger.

When the gong sounded, ending the round, everyone was stunned into silence.

"Oh my God, Bill!" screamed Ginger, clapping with joy.

Pecos walked toward me, standing in his corner, with his arms raised in victory, wearing a look of triumph, when a beer bottle came flying, cracking him on the back of his skull. He didn't crumple, though; instead, he scowled and scanned the audience, searching for the guilty party.

Then he was pelted with a blizzard of food.

Peppy showed up again at that moment, popping his .38 at the ceiling. Everybody scattered, running for their lives. Peppy pistol-whipped Leon three times, then searched the guy's pockets, pulling out a thick roll of green-as-the-hills American currency.

"Let's go," he said.

We hurried out of there and dumped water on Pecos.

Ginger brought the car around. "Bill," she leaned over to her brother's level. "Are you all right?"

He looked up at me with what I recognized as a pleading look on his face. "Did I do good?"

"Bill," I said, using his real name for the first time since I'd known him, "you did great."

"In more than one way, we won," said Peppy, re-holstering his gun.

Ginger, visibly shaken, drove us straight out of El Paso. Peppy suggested we stop in the next town to drink. On the way into a bar, Pecos staggered a little but regained his balance, approached the bartender, and ordered a beer. Her anger and fear having somewhat subsided, Ginger ordered a gin-and-tonic and sipped it through a straw, not looking at me. She placed her hand on her brother's shoulder, a comforting gesture. I asked for a bottle of cheap tequila and a pen. On a bar napkin, I drew a fanged gargoyle with tearing claws and dark wings. I felt tired and battered, like I'd been the one in the ring getting my face battered. The sharp taste of the lemon I sucked between slugs made me wince. I watched Ginger enter the ladies' room.

Peppy tugged at my sleeve. He led me over to a ratty-looking booth next to the kitchen. The smell of rancid fat was overwhelming.

"Tequila?" I offered.

"No thanks." He inclined his head, giving the bar a side glance. "I've got two thousand American dollars here."

"You mugged Leon," I said. "That was your whole point in this whole charade, wasn't it? To stick up some hood whose influence doesn't extend to New York."

He leaned forward. "Why don't we leave behind this dumb galoot and his sister? You've blown it with her anyway. Let's you and me split this straight down the middle, fifty-fifty, and go back to the city as friends."

I didn't care that I'd screwed it up by stupidly falling for this ruse. Right is right. I smashed the bottle across Peppy's face, knocking him out of the booth. As I was leaning over, taking his gun and the money, Ginger walked up to us, her eyes wide with surprise.

"Bill gets half," I said to Peppy. "You get ten percent."

With a pained expression, he tried to stand but fell back down. He dabbed his ear with a napkin. "What the—?" he spit. "What you do that for? The guy's an ignorant cowboy. An ass-for-brains Texan."

Only then did Ginger brighten. She came over and slid an arm around me, pressing close.

DREAM EVIL

Before his shift began that night, Kobran remembered something amusing. A minor starlet from the hit movie *High School Musical* had visited his AP English class earlier that semester to discuss the power of creativity. She asked the students to write down their dreams. Kobran jotted his list on a sheet of notebook paper using his missing father's Aspinal of London silver-sterling-and-leather pen.

Become an evil magician
Marry Beatrix
Give her babies

So the moment of reckoning had arrived for Kobran and he was rendered inert, thwarted by the dumbest of reasons. He couldn't find his hot bag for the extra-large three-top ordered for delivery by the most beautiful girl at his school. Beatrix loved vintage Norwegian black metal as much as he did, making her perfect. Hell, she *was* Norwegian, her surname Hertzenberg. She was also into Ouija boards and astral projection, which increased his certainty that they were soulmates. Her skin was deliciously translucent, her hair sunflower-yellow, her eyes crystal blue. He wanted to explore every part of her. He hoped that, after providing such a sweet deal (thanks to his employee discount) and driving far beyond Slices' delivery zone to bring Beatrix a pizza, she'd go with him to see Dimmu Borgir next weekend. Yet standing in the way of realizing his fantasy was a paltry, yet necessary, sack of black insu-lated polyester. In a frantic effort to find it, he knocked over the cardboard boxes, pre-folded and stacked in the stockroom.

"Hot bag!" he yelled in desperation. "Anyone?"

"Check your trunk," said his boss, Natalie, ladling tomato sauce onto a garlic-crust base.

Of course! He'd forgotten to bring it back into the store after his last delivery. He ran outside and, with the key, popped open the hold of his impossible-to-kill 1999 Toyota Camry. The trunk lamp had died long ago and the lights in the parking lot hadn't come on yet, so he used his phone light to examine the contents.

"Thank you, Satan," he said, locating the bag.

With a triumphant grin, he sprinted back into the store, causing the ribbon-strung brass bell that hung from the door handle to clang loudly against the glass. He slid and almost fell in a puddle of Fanta Orange a child had spilled near the entrance that Natalie had asked him to mop twenty minutes ago.

"Slow down," said his middle-aged boss, shoving another pizza into the conveyor oven. "You'll break your neck before you even get to kiss her."

He let up not an iota, throwing brown paper towels

on the spill, then grabbed the pie, which was steaming in its box, off the aluminum cool-down rack. He shoved it into the bag. "Can't give a hot girl a cold pizza."

"Fine, give her your icy corpse then."

Kobran mock-gasped. He opened the fridge to grab a liter of soda. "Too bad she's not into necro. Gosh, you really want me dead, Natalie?"

"On any other night," she said. "But it's Friday, so I'm giving you thirty minutes to impress that metal chick in the boonies. If you're not back, I'll send Lou out on deliveries and your last check will be waiting for you."

"Huh. That's an empty threat if I ever heard one. Lou doesn't even have a car," he said, hurrying past the register and into the lobby. He halted to check his reflection in the store window. He thought his long dark hair looked clean, yet very metal. He'd have to ditch his Slices polo, though, before handing Beatrix her pie.

"He can borrow mine," Natalie called after him.

Carrying the bag by its straps and with the soda pressed under his armpit, Kobran propped open the door for a gaggle of pot-scented college students. "You'd let Lou drive the Charger?"

"Just make it quick, Romeo!"

He laughed and scampered to his Camry. The driver's side door fell off its hinges, which ended up costing him a full minute as he struggled to set it right again before it closed properly.

———

He cranked his favorite disc, Emperor's *In the Nightside Eclipse*, and hollered along with the gnarly vocals that blazed atop a fury of serrated guitars, ghostly synths, and blast-beat drums comprising the song "Into the Infinity of Thoughts."

Then he noticed his fuel gauge needle sitting on the E. He cursed and pounded the steering wheel. Why hadn't he gassed up before his shift? A Shell was situated conveniently on his side of the highway up ahead, but he'd lose precious minutes. So he stomped the accelerator and got on the interstate. There had to be a gas station near Beatrix he could hit on the way back.

She lived on the edge of the valley, the northern limits of North Las Vegas. Her house was the only one whose construction was complete, nestled dead center within a labyrinth of unfinished, sprawling, cookie-cutter tracts called Playa Estates. He heard her father was a contractor who'd struggled to secure work in the aftermath of the recession. Now his business was thriving again, going gangbusters in Las Vegas, Phoenix, and St. George. But the recovery remained stalled in this part of the valley.

Kobran could see her enormous home glowing alone like an eerie beacon as he took the last exit and entered what felt like a lunar landscape patch-lit by dim, sporadic, solar-powered streetlamps. The sagebrush took on the appearance of spaceborne anemone, rustling strangely in the winds of a growing dust storm. He could make out something flickering in what looked like the backyard—probably a bonfire.

Suddenly, the shadowy form of a coyote, eyes burning like diamonds from the headlights, darted in front of his car and across the road. Kobran foot-tapped the brake out of instinct, then kept driving.

"Freakin' zoo out here."

He was running on fumes when he pulled into the cul-de-sac, cramped with at least six cars. She'd told him she was hosting a get-together, but he'd assumed it involved the few metal heads and punks she tended to hang out with during lunch and study hall. The number of cars made him anxious, concerned he hadn't brought sufficient food. Would she ask him to go back to Slices for more pizza? That would be a disaster. She had a loner streak, though, so maybe she planned to scarf the whole thing in her room with the door closed, while everyone else thrashed away on the Xbox.

He approached with the bagged pizza and soda, intending to ring the bell. Ascending the brick staircase, he looked up to see her waiting for him in the doorway. She was a vision, backlit by a radiant chandelier, wearing the shortest denim cutoffs and black Bathory half-shirt that exposed her flat tummy with pierced navel. He didn't normally care for bony girls, but the shape of her slender limbs revved his libido. She was barefoot, her painted toenails causing his throat to constrict.

"Nice uniform," she smirked, crossing her arms.

Crap, he forgot to change! He'd wanted to greet her in his Mayhem shirt. He had no choice but to follow his dear old dad's advice: Act like you couldn't care less if a woman admires you and she'll crave your company.

"Thanks," he said. "I can get you one if you'd like."

"I'll pass," she said. "But you can pass me the pizza."

Kobran shook his head. "I'm not a charity worker. Five bucks for an extra-large pepperoni, sausage, and mushroom. That's an eighty percent discount."

She haughtily cocked her hip and dug into her back pocket for the money.

He reached for it, looked at it, scowled, and still holding the bag, said, "Tip?"

She shrugged. "Out of cash."

"You can make up for that by coming with me to see Dimmu Borgir."

Her eyes went big. "You have tickets?"

"I'm pretty awesome." He unsheathed the pizza box and gave it to her, but she seemed disinterested in food. "Hey, don't drop that, Beatrix. It's the best in Las Vegas."

She balanced the edge of the box horizontally against her stomach with one arm, dangled the soda with the other, and looked at him. She was now, he could see, considering him in a new light, silently reappraising his value to her. He wanted to be judged favorably without letting on that he liked her. He noticed himself trembling, so he ran his fingers through his hair, feigned a yawn, surveyed the grounds, and sniffed the air.

"Your fire smells weird," he said. "Barbecue?"

She opened her mouth to say something, thought better of it, then took a step toward him. Her features went anime-soft as she said, "We're performing an evocation. You should join us. Actually, you *must*."

"Can't," he said, turning away, about to head back to his car. He hesitated, taking out his phone to glance at the time. He had exactly fourteen minutes to make it to Slices. "Working. Pick you up next Saturday, yeah?"

"Kobe," she pleaded, her hand grazing his wrist. Something about the vulnerability in her voice and the touch of her skin jolted him. "I need you to stay for a moment. The grimoire we're using...it's partly in Latin? You took Latin? You did that illusion for the talent show? And I know you know everything about the history of sorcery—"

"Not everything."

"Just give me, like, ten minutes. I need you to pronounce a few phrases."

"Why are you summoning?" he asked, unable to resist her lilting speech, her feminine presence. "Wait, *what* are you summoning?"

"We're calling forth a minor demon of success." She squatted to place the box on the ground so she could open the lid and remove a slice of pizza. Then she stood up to take a bite. "Mmm." She sensually put her gorgeous lips to the dough, catching the strings of melted cheese with her fingers, then licking them clean. It was erotic and absurd to watch a beautiful girl eating greasy food and moaning. He suspected he was being played, but his body responded and he lost the ability to speak.

After a beat, he said, "Ten minutes." He picked up his phone and quickly text-pleaded Natalie for more time. Then he said, "Where did you find a grimoire? If it's that goofy *Greater King of Solomon* book, you might as well—"

"No, no, this is *dual* translated into Arabic," she said. "It's an unholy text that Faridah—the girl with the pink hair from biology?—well, she found it in her dead grandmother's lockbox. She's in the backyard. Faridah, I mean."

"If the text is legible, I can pronounce it."

"Thanks," she said, stooping for another slice. "You're right, this pizza is fierce."

THEY WALKED into the house and Beatrix left the pizza box on the granite kitchen island. He brought along the soda in case they got thirsty and the bag so he wouldn't leave it behind. It was a normal Las Vegas luxury-suburban home with SKS appliances, and West Elm furniture, and a wall-sized Samsung screen in the living room. Completely unsurprising—save for the conjuring in the backyard.

"Parents gone?"

"They're in North Carolina for High Point," she said. High Point Market was an annual furnishings-industry trade show and Beatrix's parents were from that part of North Carolina, at least that's how Kobran understood it. "They're super-upset about my test scores, which aren't yet good enough for Duke, so I just need a boost."

"You need a demon for that? Just get a Ritalin script like everyone else." *Then study*, he didn't add.

"My brother had a terrible experience with that stuff. He ended up playing *Call of Duty* for five days straight and forgot to eat and sleep. He had a stroke and nearly died. He's twenty years old."

"Sure, I guess an evil spirit is safer." He imagined kissing lovely Beatrix and touching her pale breasts in one of her house's many bedrooms, but pushed aside the image. He wanted to impress her. He wanted to possess her. He'd been tasked with summoning a demon, though. Just another Friday night in Las Vegas.

They made their way through the back door and into the desert scape backyard. He put the bag and soda on a picnic table. The fire was raging and he could see pieces of furniture in the blaze. He was going to ask where the furniture came from, but decided to let it go. Some of his classmates gathered around in a half-perimeter, their backs to the house. When Kobran approached, there were no introductions. A few waved and said hey, but most simply nodded at him once, hypnotized by the dancing flames.

Wearing a Misfits skull shirt, skinny black jeans, and black Chuck Taylors, Faridah, the Moroccan-American punk chick, said hello. She held a book to her chest. "I know you," she said. "We were in bio together."

"Kobran Hammett," he said.

"Hammett, like the crime writer?"

He nodded.

"You know about old texts?"

"My dad's a rare-book collector."

"That must be cool."

"Haven't spoken to him in years," he said with a shrug. "What's that?"

Faridah handed him the grimoire. It looked bound in leather, but when he touched it, the book felt alien, repulsive.

"Interesting," he said. "Made from human skin?"

"We're not sure," said Faridah.

"Stop," said Beatrix, elbow nudging her. "Don't creep us out. Let's see if he manages the evocation. He doesn't have much time."

"I have to get back to work," he clarified, pointing at his shirt's Slices logo. His phone dinged and he looked to see that Natalie had texted him a poop emoji. Then a knife emoji.

Faridah nodded. With a finger, she indicated they

should move closer to the fire, so he and Beatrix followed her. He could feel the heat snarling at his face when he opened the book and, relying on firelight, found the page marked INVOCARE. The Latin was calligraphic with sinister flourishes. The script troubled him viscerally.

"Beatrix," he said, squinting. "More light."

She drew close to him and turned on her phone's flashlight, holding it over the pages. They coughed when the wind suddenly changed direction, engulfing them in a heavy cloud of firepit smoke. They fanned the air crazily, then took a few lateral steps, adjusting their positions so they could see and breathe again.

"I feel nauseated," he said, whether from the smoke or the book, he couldn't tell.

"Can you pronounce it or not, Harry Potter?" huffed Faridah. "I take the SAT on Monday."

He turned his head to clear his throat and spit. He didn't bother explaining that Latin pronunciation had changed over centuries and that since English took its alphabet from Latin, you spoke individual letters as you did in English. "I'm ready."

Beatrix again held the flashlight and he was about to begin when the crickets stopped chirping all at the same time and a giant blanket of silence seemed to descend on the abandoned suburban neighborhood. He hadn't noticed them until they went quiet.

Neither had Beatrix. "This book is legit!" she exclaimed.

"A coyote scared them is all," said the fat kid with the NIN shirt.

"Hush, Ryan," said Faridah. She rolled her wrist at Kobran, urging him to begin the evocation.

He licked his lips and began. "*Et veni, paulo diabolic*," he said. "*Fac mihi somnia vera facit*." He translated in his mind as he read aloud: *Come out, demon. Make my dreams come true.*

Nothing.

"Well, that totally sucked." Ryan chuckled.

SUCK.

The voice was horrible, dripping with hate. Kobran's spine went completely numb. The pages of the book he was holding came alive, fluttering like a captured pigeon. He fought the instinct to drop it. He suspected he would need it to contain whatever had arrived.

The demon slowly hobbled out of the fire on stumpy misshapen legs. Its body was a sewer lid-sized mass of oozing gray flesh, patches of flame burning on charcoal-like tumors strung across its sickening uneven shoulders and back. Its eyes were like pustulent vaginal slits, its mouth a clutch of broken yellowed teeth. The creature looked less like hellspawn, more like a damaged extraterrestrial that had crash-landed in the desert and learned to stoke fear with its disgusting voice. It smelled revolting, a portable toilet stuffed with rotting flesh and set on fire.

"Gross," said Faridah. She and the others began slowly, carefully, walking backward, away from whatever it was Kobran had summoned from an inter-dimensional hell.

The demon catapult-hopped directly in front of her, so fast it resembled a game glitch. She yelped, pinched her nose against the odor, and continued her gradual retreat.

DREAMS, the monster gargled, stumble-wobbling toward her. *TELL ME.*

Kobran found himself desperate to muzzle it. No one else could do it, so he started flipping through the book, whose pages had now settled, looking for a cage of confinement or a banishment spell. But all he could see was the Arabic translation and he knew nothing of that alphabet.

DREAMS!

"I...I want a perfect score," Faridah relented, whimpering. "On every exam I take. From now until I die."

FIRST BORN. I WILL HAVE IT.

"What?"

"No, Faridah!" Beatrix warned. "Don't agree to that. It wants your kid!"

"What kid? I'm not even—"

"It means any child you have in the future," explained Kobran, finger-tracing a sentence on the page —difficult, since Beatrix was no longer shining her light on the pages. He'd found the spell in Latin, though, and was cramming it into his brain so he could paralyze this talking dung heap.

Faridah stopped walking backward. She held her ground for a moment to say to the demon, "No deal!"

It growled with bestial dissatisfaction, then launched itself against her face, searing her skin with the ferocious heat of its grotesque flipper arms, toppling her into a sagebrush stalk. They thought they could hear the hissing of her flesh as it burned—or maybe it was just the demon's noise. But her scream was nightmarish.

Everyone except Kobran and Beatrix was racing to the house. It had to be now.

"*Adhuc manere, maccus,*" he intoned. "*Tu properas in quisquiliae inclusae sint.*"

The creature dropped from the girl's face and emitted a glass-shattering shriek.

"*Tace,*" Kobran added.

Like the crickets before it, the demon went mute. Its gash-like eyes were bulging as it strained against the containment spells, its body smoldering.

Beatrix tended to the wounded weeping Faridah as Kobran shut the book and rushed to the picnic table for the bag. He shook the soda violently, then opened it, angling the bottle so he was spraying the demon with carbonated liquid. The ploy seemed to work, cooling down the creature's temperature. Then Kobran used a nearby shovel to scoop-push the soaked gobbet of evil into the hot bag.

The demon barely fit and Kobran nearly singed his fingers sealing up the bag. He carried it gingerly, afraid of getting scorched, and walked over to where Faridah was lying on the ground. He kneeled to examine her. Her tear-soaked face was mildly scratched. The burns were mostly confined to her neck and looked first-degree, not serious enough for major scars or surgery.

"I don't think it's life-threatening," he said to Beatrix.

She nodded.

Ryan, the boy in the NIN shirt, brought over Ziplocs of ice to treat Faridah's blistering.

Beatrix and Kobran stood up, and she placed her hand on his chest.

"Thank you," she said with an expression of regret. "That was really dumb and I'm so glad you were here to help."

"You know," he said, "it was kind of fun. Until it went sideways." He went to kiss her.

She turned her blonde head and leaned back. "Um."

He looked at her sharply, as if to say, seriously? Not even a quick kiss? Then he did an abrupt about-face and started toward the house, intent on driving back to Slices to finish his shift with a new grimoire, a cooling minor demon in his pizza bag, and a tender heart broken by the ultimate rejection.

In the distance, a coyote was howling.

HE FOUND a gas station and kept his job. That night, he delivered ten more pizzas, each house well within Slice's area of service. He made a hundred bucks, but the cash felt like so many dead leaves in his wallet. There was no pleasure—without any hope of Beatrix in his future.

Shift over, he stepped into the walk-in freezer and shut the door behind him. He heard the sacked demon's teeth chattering like silverware during an earthquake.

Kobran opened the bag and said, "*Dico, qui stulti.*"

DREAMS. Its voice was a toxic secretion, but the teenage wizard wasn't about to let the monster move of its own accord.

"I want Beatrix," said Kobran. "Forever."

POSSESSION.

"And I want her to desire me. Forever."

SUBMISSION.

"One more thing: Five children."

IMPREGNATION.

Kobran arched an eyebrow. "And what do you require, little fellow?"

The demon didn't hesitate. *FIRST BORN. I WILL HAVE IT.*

He weighed it, but only for a moment.

"In that case, make it six children."

GLANDOMIRUM

L as Vegas that night sustained a deluge, the kind
of monsoon-season torrent that dumped two
inches in an hour, slicked the asphalt and neon
and disoriented weed-vaping rideshare drivers, snarling
Strip traffic and resulting in mournful horn honks and a
few scary moments when an impatient local—some
late-for-work employee speeding to a hotel-casino—
suddenly switched lanes, causing another vehicle to
hydroplane.

Airmid wasn't bothered by the gridlock, though.
She'd just finished her set at Cleopatra's Barge for a
rowdy group of tech conventioneers. They'd joined her
onstage for the rousing finale, a slightly alcoholic rendition of U2's "Desire." She hadn't needed to enchant
them. It was two weeks before Christmas and she was
in a magnanimous mood, eager to complete her latest
assignment, especially since it involved setting foot
inside the most god- and goddess-hospitable bar in the
southwestern United States.

The pub known as Glandomirum was superficially

Irish. It was located a mere tankard's throw from the Las Vegas Strip and Tropicana Avenue. At Glandomirum, the shabbier Celtic divinities hashed out their disagreements and blood-signed covenants. The bar served as neutral ground for a neutrality-challenged pantheon. But the bright charge of malted barley tended to heal all rifts—including the persistent wounds of rape and murder—and no one brewed tastier, more tranquilizing beer than Goibhniu. Maybe it was because he laced his product with hensbane. Maybe it was the heated metamorphic rocks—chipped from the Callanish stone circle in Scotland—that he plopped into a ditch of liquefied malt during the brewing process. Maybe it was nostalgia for the Iron Age.

Whatever the reason, Airmid swore that a goblet of Goibhniu-crafted ale could sweeten even the sour heart of the war god Neit. The only flaw she and everyone else noticed was that the beer reeked of a billy goat's nether regions. Still, they happily guzzled.

Goibhniu was wiping down the bar when Airmid sat down on a stool. He didn't need to look up to know there was an ancient deity in his establishment. The place was unusually slow because of the rain. A handful of college kids in UNLV sweatshirts playing pool and watching a basketball game on the TV screens was the only action.

She remained silent, patiently waiting for Goibhniu to finish. He never charged his fellow gods, but he didn't rush to serve non-payers either.

Finally, he poured two glasses of his signature malt from a stand-alone tap situated far away from the putrid commercial dregs he served to everyone else.

"Lovely Airmid," he said, placing a chalice in front of her. "It's been too long. How's business?"

"Thank you, kind sir. Business is slow when everyone behaves. I have less to do, but I can't resent a lasting peace."

"Well," he replied, "as my customers say this time of year: 'Peace on Earth.'" He toasted her.

They sipped, Airmid savoring the mugwort, carrot seeds, and nightshade. Together, they provided a dark smoky color and taste. "Your beer gets better over the centuries," she said.

He ignored her praise. "You imply everyone is behaving. Can't be true if you're here."

She licked foam from her lip. "I'm here because of Fintan."

Goibhniu stiffened his back and folded his arms. "He was here yesterday, of course. But I'm not hiding him."

"Never crossed my mind."

There was a lengthy silence. Airmid knew she wasn't at all intimidating. She had the soft feathery physique of a postwar North American torch singer. Which is why she sang five nights a week in Las Vegas. But her ability to heal the deepest wounds—even those induced by Balor's incinerating cranium rays—gave her status.

Eventually, Goibhniu leaned forward to take a swig and said, with empathy in his ragged blacksmith voice, "You know, maybe it wasn't a good idea, putting Fintan in a cave with fifty women. It made him feel a little... how can I put this?"

"Henpecked?" she said.

Goibhniu nodded.

Airmid shrugged. "Old news. Besides, how else was Ireland supposed to repopulate after the flood?"

"Have *you* ever tried it? Impregnating an entire platoon of ovulating banshees?"

She sighed, the beer so delicious it kept her from rolling her eyes. "*That* I have not. So where is he, then?"

"Says he's staying at the Golden Nugget. He thinks he's a salmon again."

"I went there before my gig. He checked out last night."

"He likes the pool. It has a giant shark aquarium in the middle of it. It's really the best place for swimming in this town. We have an aquarium over there, but it's freshwater. But maybe it's enough for Fintan." Goibhniu indicated a hefty thirty-gallon tank near the cigarette machine that contained a few blue-backed silver bass—a sport fish found in estuarine backwaters from Galway to Dublin. They looked bored.

"Swimming?" she repeated. "Salmon?"

"Yes. He came in here with that expression on his face he had back when—well, back when the Jewish God turned on the faucet and forgot to shut it off."

"In the desert?"

"What?"

"Salmon in the desert?"

"Airmid, your tolerance is shot. You should drink here more often, not just—"

She snapped her fingers suddenly, which caused Goibhniu to turn around and head back to his special beer tap.

"No!" she insisted. "Hoover Dam."

"We don't carry that."

She waved away his confusion. "The dam is where he's going, if he's not there already."

Goibhniu rubbed his long gray-streaked beard. "Hunh. That's good. I see now why they pay you for this." He meant the informal association of the Celtic immortals, who routinely hired Airmid as a fixer to remedy their day-to-day—or century-to-century—woes. She was a slender enchantress, an unassuming medic, and when things got hairy, a cunning resurrector of the dead.

But not of her deceased sibling Miach.

"I don't get paid," she corrected. "They let me sit at the grave of my brother and we get to talk for a few days before he turns to rot again."

Another prolonged silence ended only after the billiard balls cracked and there was unrelated laughter, a joke shared among university chums. Goibhniu chose that moment to clear his throat and asked Airmid to please join him in toasting the memory of Miach, her brother, slain by their hideous and evil father.

She drained her glass. Teary, she thanked Goibhniu and left Glandomirum to hop into her Nissan Altima and sleep before driving to the waters behind Hoover Dam.

Before that, though, she needed to stop at PetSmart to pick up a glass fishbowl.

THE RAIN WAS COMING down in sheets and the traffic was terrifying. It had been a few years since Airmid had visited the dam. But once she pulled in to the visitor's center from the Nevada side, she recalled her delight in the spectacle of the penstock towers, the sprawling spillway entrance, and the Mike O'Callaghan-Pat Tillman Memorial Bridge. She always enjoyed pagan displays of masculine strength and self-sacrifice and this was among the best that mortals had ever constructed. She especially relished the fact that more than 100 of them had given their lives to complete this monolithic nature-reversing monstrosity nearly a century ago.

"Such dedication," she murmured aloud, parking the car and digging in her back seat for a Harrah's umbrella.

Airmid walked through the exhibit's gallery of Depression-era murals and maps and into the darkened auditorium. A documentary devoted to the Bureau of Reclamation and its taming of the rivers was playing to a small number of spectators, one of them Fintan. She sat quietly a few seats away from the delinquent, shape-shifting, Gaelic god, listening to the authoritative man's voice drone on about how the federal government contributed to help settle the west and grow the food that fed a nation.

Movie over, the lights came up and the sparse audience exited. Airmid and Fintan sat alone in the theater, not sharing words. She noted how much he resembled Mr. Clean, the mascot for a chemical company. She had used the stuff recently to mop the dog hair and spaghetti sauce from her condo floor.

Finally, Fintan said, "When the waters rushed over the land and the mortals all drowned, I would've done anything to make it stop. I would've given my life."

"It wasn't up to you," said Airmid. "You never had a choice."

"I could've used a dam like this one. To redirect the water."

"Redirect it where?"

"Down the throat of that obnoxious fisherman from Galilee. The fisher of men whose big unhappy Daddy flooded the world."

"You're misremembering. Dude hadn't been born at that point. He didn't appear until after you changed from a hawk into a man and fought at Magh Tuireadh."

Fintan leaned forward, elbows on his thighs, to rub his furrowed brow. "I was covered in blood the entire time. I didn't hear of Jesus until Pelayo stopped the Moors at Covadonga."

Airmid snickered. "I always liked those Visigoths. They were fussy as hell—until you really needed them. And then they'd kill everyone to help a friend."

"Speaking of friends," said Fintan. "They sent the only woman I can stomach at this point to bring me back. But I'm still not going."

"You *have* to. You can't be a salmon. Such a waste to end up as bear food!"

"I'm not food," he said, and his form began to expand, hair sprouting from his bald head and fangs appearing in his mouth. "I *am* the bear."

Airmid stumbled out of her seat and struggled to get clear of his massive claw, which came swinging at her like a battle-ax. He'd nearly lopped her face clean off.

Seven feet in height now, his bulk expanded so quickly that the plastic seats around him splinter-cracked into flying pieces. He roared deafeningly, close enough that his gross grizzly spittle splattered her jeans.

She popped open her umbrella. "*Gaoithe*," she said.

Nylon canopy inverted, the metal ribs began spinning rapidly, causing a wind-tunnel effect that caught Fintan off guard, the skin of his snout distorted by the force of compressed air.

He uttered a bear-like grunt of surprise, took a step backward, and fell over a piece of broken furniture with a bone-crunching thud that made Airmid wince.

Because she wasn't sure of the extent of his anger, she quickly closed the distance between them and ripped the fabric from the umbrella so she could wield the sharpened ferrule like a dagger and bring him to heel with a few non-fatal stabs. But he had already reverted to humanoid form, curled in the fetal position, clothes shredded and mostly useless from his sudden transformation. He wept.

"Fintan," she said. "Stop crying."

The auditorium was empty save the two of them and the lights dimmed. The docu-film began playing again, opening with black-and-white newsreel footage of the series of dynamite explosions that eventually pushed the Colorado River's flow around the dam construction site and through the walls of Black Canyon. The theater's sound system was top-notch, the enhanced detonations rattling Airmid's teeth in her skull.

"I don't want to go back," blubbered Fintan, after the detonation sequence subsided. "I can't do this again."

"You're not going far. And it won't be long."

"The water. There's just too much water."

"*Ah-bur areesh aye.*"

"So—so why do we have to drown?"

"The world is parched, dry as a shite in the desert.

Every now and again, you have to add dilutables or else it all gets stuck, see?"

"No, I *don't* see. Help me, Airmid. Please don't let them—"

Suddenly Fintan was spotlit; he cringed like a vampire in the sun.

"What the hell happened in here?" A private security guard hired by the dam had lit them up with his flashlight. "Did you cause this damage, ma'am?"

"*Aisling*," she said, and the guard stood stock still and silent. His beam remained frozen on her, so she raised her arm to shield herself from the glare.

She turned to command Fintan to follow her outside, but he was gone.

She ran furiously, catching sight of him in the parking lot. He was sprinting for his car and *damn* he was fast, faster than a *mac tíre* dancing across greased coals.

"*Cuir ar foluain*," she said and her mutilated umbrella sprung to life, helicopter-launching her above the rows of vehicles like some improper Mary Poppins.

She landed a few yards in front of him and he skidded, planting his feet to switch direction. But she guessed his move and roundhouse-kicked him, the heel of her purple-glittered APL TechLoom Pro Sneakers crushing his jaw.

Flat on his back on the asphalt, he groan-gasped in pain. "Where'd you learn how to kick like that, Airmid?"

"Las Vegas," she said, a little out of breath, "is a big MMA town."

When Airmid walked into Glandomirum for the second time in twenty-four hours, she carried a fishbowl holding a single fish. Goibhniu was soaking the bar gun in a pitcher of club soda while biting into a corned beef sandwich, pieces of shredded cabbage falling off. The Proclaimers' "500 Miles" was pumping through the speakers, a song that normally filled her with dread, but it sounded great at the moment, having secured her quarry. Soon—probably tomorrow—she'd be chatting with her dead brother.

"That Fintan?" said Goibhniu through a mouthful of meat and bread.

"In the scaly flesh," said Airmid, plopping the bowl on the mahogany bar top.

"Was he agitated?"

"A little. He turned into a bear and nearly decapitated me."

Goibhniu guffawed. "He's all bark. A little dog can startle a hare, but it takes a big one to catch it."

"Wait," said Airmid. "Are you calling me a dog or a bunny?"

He laughed again. Then he thought about it a moment, and shrugged. "What's your next step?"

"We'll keep him in your aquarium, I think. Until we can be sure this isn't a broken agreement." She indicated the growing storm outside. The traffic lights were all blinking red from Boulder City to Las Vegas and the Strip was down to one lane from the flooding. The casino signage lost its glow in the inclement gloom.

Goibhniu squinted, trying to make out the chaos through the windows of his bar. "Think it's the big one?"

Airmid shrugged. "Not sure. I mean, there's global

warming, melting icebergs, and such. But maybe it's just plain ol' Old Testament rain."

He gestured toward the fish in the bowl. "Hope he's up for it."

"Ha! He did a fine job last time," she said. "The Irish and Scots are great fighters."

"Great artists, too," Goibhniu added, raising an eyebrow.

"Lovers."

"And legendary drinkers!"

"I'll drink to *that*," said Airmid.

Goibhniu went to the tap and poured them each a glass of ancient Gaelic ale.

They sat across the bar from each other and pitied the poor soon-to-spawn fish and listened to rain blanketing the concrete-stricken desertscape. He dreamed of her pale creamy thighs; she dreamed of her brother's cherry lips.

It came down for a very long time.

SWANSON

The headhunters lured all six of us away from our non-union casino jobs at the quiet end of the Strip. We were picked because we were young and looked good in clean white shirts. We accepted because a good paycheck was something we'd never known.

The first rule of our new business, we were told, was never to mention the Old Man's name or point him out while we were working. In the beginning, that was a bit difficult and awkward; from the moment we started training, we felt his approach, his unusual presence and strong personality. We chalked up his eccentricities as byproducts of moneymaking genius. But more than that, we believed that good times were here and our work troubles were now in the past.

The Old Man had wanted the best view of the Strip: the penthouse floor of the Dunes. However, when he learned that directly over that penthouse a dance club blasted loud rock 'n' roll every night until dawn, he instead set up shop on the top two floors of the

Desert Inn. All summer we slowly broke in to the strange new routine. We learned what he liked and what he didn't.

The Old Man loathed rock music; he thought the Beatles sounded like dumb teenagers. He preferred the schmaltz of Hollywood composers like Victor Young, a Chicago boy the Old Man had hired to score his own movie, *The Conqueror*, about Genghis Khan. It had starred John Wayne. The movie stunk up every screen it appeared on. Nearly everyone involved, including the Duke, died of cancer. The set, deep in a canyon of southern Utah, had been irradiated from the above-ground nuclear bombs going off at the neighboring Nevada Test Site.

Radiation is the reason the Old Man created the Caretaker 3000. For a while, the US military had been in the market for a combat mechanism that could continue to operate in the aftermath of an atomic war. They turned to the Old Man, a billionaire businessman, movie producer, and inventor, the last of which made him the Pentagon's de facto R&D guy. He manufactured a prototype, a titanium humanoid on treads instead of legs. For three, maybe four, years in the late '50s, the robot's funding was limitless. But once Khrushchev amassed an apocalyptic arsenal, there was no longer any point. No one would survive a super-power nuclear war. Soon the 3000's primary duty consisted of fetching the Old Man his nightly meal: a Swanson TV turkey dinner (white meat only) with apple cobbler. Which is why we rechristened the Care-taker 3000 "Swanson." Sadly, or so we initially thought, the Old Man considered the robot to be just another appliance.

WHEN HE WASN'T PASSED out on a concoction of
Valium and codeine, the Old Man sat completely naked
in a lounge chair, sifting through stacks of newspapers
and magazines piled around him. He read by lamplight,
towels, sheets, and aluminum foil obscuring the
windows. He summoned us by flicking a brown paper
bag with his fingers. He grew an unruly white beard
and his skin began to yellow. His vocabulary mostly
consisted of grunts and the occasional one-word
command. He collected his urine in Mason jars, looking
for signs of poisoning and organ failure. We dismissed
him as crazy and kept cashing our fat paychecks.
Because we did the Old Man's dirty work, we nick-
named ourselves the Dirty Half-Dozen.

Although he loved taking the military's money for
continued research, the Old Man wanted more than
anything to stop the atomic tests in the nearby desert—
tests that he felt were slowly killing him. Only the *Las
Vegas Herald*, a local newspaper, bucked his obsession,
consistently running editorials in favor of increased testing, citing the Cold War with the Soviets. The year was
1966, the aftertaste of the Cuban Missile Crisis still on
our collective breath. After a few weeks of absorbing
this pro-nuke propaganda, the Old Man did what he
liked to do when faced with a problem. He purchased
the *Herald's* parent company and soon the editorials
did an about-face, arguing for a worldwide testing ban.
The first anti-nuke article appeared on a Wednesday. It
was one of the first times we saw him smile, his yellow
teeth worked up into a grin, when the paper, sheathed
in a sterilized plastic bag, was delivered to his room.

I⊤ WAS DALE, a slot machine tech who'd seen a lot of
sci-fi movies, who'd reprogrammed Swanson from a
military prototype into a TV-dinner automaton. Dale
was the only one of the Dirty Half-Dozen with an engi-
neering background and he seemed to know what he
was talking about. Back in the late '50s, when it was
called the Caretaker, Swanson's mission was, in the case
of atomic conflict with the Soviets, to defend whatever
Americans were still alive after a nuclear attack by
eradicating any and all invading armies. Dale erased
Swanson's aggressive responses and substituted care
and concern, making the robot an invaluable part of our
team.

Whenever the Old Man got a wild hair up his ass,
one of us, usually Guido, grabbed the telephone and,
for example, called the Baskin-Robbins ice cream
company and got them to take a special order for the
Old Man's favorite flavor, banana nut. Or someone else,
usually Seth, the limo driver, jumped in the car to pick
up an Arby's roast beef sandwich after the Old Man
saw a commercial on TV. Or the smartest guy on duty
dusted off the typewriter and postmarked a letter to the
governor of Nevada, demanding he halt a test blast due
to the wind.

But gradually, we dumped every one of our respon-
sibilities on Swanson. Dale outfitted him with a crude
but effective voice box for phone conversations and
installed some new circuits that enabled him to type.
Driving was actually possible, too, since the Desert Inn
was centrally located on the Strip, with plenty of conve-
nient fast-food joints nearby. A trench coat and hat

were usually enough to get him through a late-night drive-thru without being spotted for what he was. Behind the wheel, the five-foot-tall, goggle-eyed Swanson resembled a little old lady wearing thick spectacles who could barely see over the steering wheel. Toward the end, Swanson did everything but earn a fat paycheck every two weeks and become modestly wealthy. We handled that much.

Through the windows, we watched the sun rusting down into the hills. Some nights we doped up the Old Man with drugs, ate the ice cream Swanson brought us, and fell asleep, dreaming of what our lives might have been like if we hadn't signed on for this improbable escapade.

Eventually, the Old Man settled into a pattern of watching Westerns on TV. That made our jobs even easier. But he had moments when anger sparked up within him for seemingly no reason. He threw a cup of coffee against the wall when he deemed it too cold. He demanded we all write letters to the governor when a little ghost town on the edge of the Nevada Test Site called Lockhart defied his wishes. Apparently, the residents sold their uranium mine to a rival company from California for a great deal of money. The Old Man had wanted the mine for years and he'd come close to acquiring it, only to lose it at the last minute when his dummy corporation, which had made the initial offer, was accidentally unmasked by a goofy *Herald* reporter researching a totally unrelated story.

"Should've carpet-bombed those Lockhart cocksuckers with my F-22!" the Old Man yelled. Apparently, he'd personally flight-tested aircraft at Lockhart's nearby lakebed years before. At least one of the planes had crashed, though the Old Man had walked away without a scratch. "It's not too late. It shall be done!"

We yawned, exhausted from listening to a maniac, and shot him full of heroin.

———

He raved like this for weeks. And then Swanson arrived one afternoon with a human hand severed just below the wrist—prominent silver skull ring on the middle digit, calloused, dirt under the fingernails. The robot placed it in the Desert Inn's walk-in freezer with the 350 gallons of Baskin-Robbins banana nut ice cream.

Visibly distraught, the Desert Inn executive chef came up to the penthouse to alert us. None of us had law enforcement contacts and there was no way to determine who'd been mutilated or if Swanson was, in fact, the perpetrator. Certainly, the robot had the strength necessary to rip a guy's hand clean from his body, but Dale assured us this was highly unlikely. We looked at Swanson's own four-fingered (with opposable thumb) metallic mitts, their pincer-like appearance, and we could sense a shiver run down the spine of Kimball the Mormon. When Kimball questioned the effectiveness of Swanson's reprogramming, Dale reminded us that the Old Man's military subsidiary, American Tool Company, had never inputted any arm-ripping directive into Swanson's circuit mind. According to Dale, The Caretaker 3000 was equipped with primitive armor and weapons and was really nothing more than a glorified blast door with arms, legs, a head full of sensors, and twin 50-caliber machine guns mounted on its shoulders. Oh, and a nuclear warhead that would self-destruct when necessary. But that had been neutralized.

So what in the hell did Swanson need with a severed human hand? Where did he get or find it? And where was the handless victim?

IT WAS AGREED that Dale was the best person to interrogate Swanson. He did so for hours in one of the empty rooms on the eighth floor that we rented as a noise buffer. He came out looking tired, despite having drained several pots of coffee. Swanson had revealed nothing, Dale told us. The robot acted as if the incident had never happened, that he hadn't brought a severed hand into the hotel. Swanson didn't have a face capable of humanesque expression, so all we had to work with was his eerie synthetic voice. Emotionless. Yet, as Dale told us in no uncertain terms, it was *wrong* somehow. It all seemed charged with something nefarious.

Ignoring Dale's advice to let it go, the rest of us presented the mystery mitt—packed in ice inside an Igloo cooler—to our contacts in what was then considered the Mob at an Italian joint on Sahara and Valley View. We asked if anyone in their crew was missing something important and, oh by the way, did they recognize this ring? Something about the whole thing must have irritated Esposito, one of the New York Mob's top "advance men" and a bona fide gangster, because he started yelling, going off about how if any of his people were missing five fingers, *he'd* be coming to *us* for answers and not the other way around. Then he threatened to detach our cocks and shove them up our mothers' asses. So we thought: Now might be a good time to exit.

We didn't pause to collect the hand, later figuring that Esposito might put it to good use.

WE TOOK the issue back to Dale, who suggested that Swanson had merely found the hand lying in the desert somewhere and brought it back to the Desert Inn to ensure that none of us was injured. That caused a collective shrug. Or maybe Swanson brought the hand to the Old Man the way a dog fetches the morning paper. We weren't about to ask him about it.

When we did ask Dale what Swanson was doing roving the desert all by himself, he revealed for the first time that our errand boy had taken to conducting early-morning strolls through Red Rock Canyon on the very western edge of the valley, where the fiery rock formations could take your breath away. Swanson let the cool night air saturate his overheated circuitry in preparation for another day of laboring for us in the Old Man's inner circle.

Dale said Swanson revealed this during another more recent interrogation. We would've probed the robot ourselves, but a big part of us wanted to let Dale deal with this aspect. We couldn't determine if Swanson was lying. We didn't know how to approach a conniving military prototype. Dale alone did.

We believed and trusted Dale absolutely. He had a degree from MIT. The only time we looked at him askance was when he complained of headaches, which got so bad, he sometimes described them as feeling like an alien presence in his mind. We urged him to stop working so hard, take some time off. But we knew he wouldn't, couldn't. He was the sole conduit between us and the ongoing mystery of Swanson.

We had figured Swanson parked himself in the empty eighth floor every evening, plugged himself into the wall socket for a good night's charge, and counted electric sheep. Instead, he was out wandering the desert, feeling crushed under an existential weight that robots must feel. Bravo for him, we thought. Even robots need to carve out a little personal time.

That was what we told ourselves—until the evening Swanson showed up with a sackful of Arby's roast beef sandwiches and off-the-chart Geiger-counter static, clicking so rapid that it blurred into white noise and woke the Old Man from his slumber, nearly causing him to hyperventilate, his emaciated body twitching like a lunatic undergoing a heavy shock treatment.

"Get that thing out of here!" he rasped through a thick haze of prescription narcotics.

———————

AMONG HIS MAGAZINES and urine containers, the Old Man had had us install Geiger counters in all the rooms, the kind found at the Nevada Test Site, in the event strong winds should blow radioactive dust into Las Vegas. They'd never gone off before, but something really hot had affixed itself to the shell of our iron companion. The clacking of the machines was enough to make us believe the apocalypse was finally here.

The idea that Swanson had been out humping

atomic bombs actually crossed our minds. Did he realize he was contaminated? Where did he go to get so severely irradiated? He looked at us innocently, the blank stare of a lifeless mechanical doll, albeit steel-reinforced and tank-treaded.

"The Test Site," said Dale. He had a faraway look in his eyes, Swanson's betrayal at once definite, yet beyond his understanding. The Old Man had saved the robot from the scrap pile and this is how Swanson repaid him? By trying to poison a man who feared radiation more than anything?

The possibility chilled our blood as we, wearing protective suits the Old Man had provided each of us on our first day at work, took turns scrubbing down Swanson inside a "survival-center" warehouse on Industrial Parkway. We left him there for several nights, trying to figure out what the hell had happened to him.

EVEN CLEANED UP, Swanson continued to register low-level radiation. Dale wasn't sure why. He figured it had something to do with the new counter's sensitivity. It was an expensive and highly sophisticated instrument, perhaps *too* efficient.

We started observing Swanson twenty-four hours a day. One of us tailed him wherever he went. He was no longer allowed to serve, or even see, the Old Man and his home base was now the warehouse, so we watched to see what he did with all his newfound free time. If we had to pee, we used our walkie-talkies to have someone cover for us. If we noticed erratic behavior, we called Dale right away to have him approach Swanson and determine what, if anything, was wrong. Dale knew how to talk robot-ese, we joked.

One night, a few of us monitored Swanson as he rested his gears and servos in the darkened warehouse. But those of us stationed outside must have fallen asleep for a significant length of time—a lapse that would cost us dearly.

No one heard it when his directional lights suddenly came on, his motor whizzing in preparation for movement. Apparently, he snuck out of Industrial Parkway and toward the rows of apartment complexes of what was then known as Naked City, a nod to the many showgirls who sunbathed topless poolside and partied late at night on the roofs of the more fashionable and luxurious buildings.

Swanson of course, ignored the festivities. Instead, we later learned, he broke into and hotwired a Cadillac parked on Florida Street and, tires screeching, got on the I-15. But then he went the speed limit, careful not to draw attention.

By then, we'd realized he was gone. Thanks to the radiation connection, we managed to pick up his trail and the six of us, the complete Dirty Half-Dozen, tailed him for what seemed like forever.

———————

WHEN WE PULLED up to a town in the middle of nowhere, we scratched our heads. Why would Swanson come here? Before we could even ponder an answer, he emerged from his Cadillac and, clumsy from the dust, churned his way down the road's cracked pavement and onto the dead main street. The sun came up behind us.

There, in the center of town, was the blackened burned-out shell of one of the Old Man's F-22 fighter jets. Could it be the prototype version—the plane the Old Man had crash-landed into a desert lakebed decades ago?

Dale sat in the back seat of our car, fidgeting. We sensed him rifling through the possible reasons for all this. He took a deep breath and wiped the sweat from his brow with a handkerchief.

For at least a minute nothing happened. Finally, we got out and walked, our dress-shoe heels crushing the desert sand.

"Catch the name of this place?" said Dale.

We shook our heads.

"Lockhart," he said.

This was the ghost town the Old Man had shouted about obliterating.

———

WE STOPPED in our tracks when we saw them.

A dozen misshapen figures dressed in dirty rags. Vaguely human. Sporting massive basketball-sized goiters and growths on their heads, necks, and shoulders, tumors that no doubt challenged their balance. Limbs either swollen or attenuated. Patches of hair sprouted from sunburned flaking scalps. They resembled monstrously rendered characters from the pages of an EC horror comic book, a juvenile-delinquent's gruesome hallucination. They stumbled out of the shadows, but with eerie confidence, calmly, as if they'd waited years for us to arrive, for this terrible moment when they'd finally confront us.

One particularly ugly creature with no legs used his arms to ambulate. He wasn't any shorter because his arms were extended and bent, a fleshy upright variation on a grasshopper's femur and tibia. He progressed faster than the others and rushed out to greet us. Or maybe butcher us. We couldn't be sure. The creature's distorted face was twisted, grooved, pockmarked, a grotesque mound with moist glistening raisins for eyes. No eyebrows or lashes, so he didn't blink at all. Those eyes simply glared at us, emanating evil and promising focused insanity and rage.

Dale inexpertly pulled a .38 from his lab coat, an act that failed to instill us with any confidence. We stared across from one another, the Old Man's flunkies squaring off against a gang of ghost-town troglodytes, a mere football's throw apart. Swanson stood with them, albeit quietly, motionless. There were six of us, all men, but being outnumbered lacerated our guts.

The worst part, though, was when the creature spoke. He turned our hearts to ice, mainly because he didn't rely on his vocal cords. He instead used his terrifying mind.

"Oh god," Barron whimpered aloud.

"Did...did whatever *that* is just say something?" Luis stuttered in disbelief. "Inside *your* brains, too, I mean?"

"Telepathy," Dale suggested.

Magic, the creature corrected. *The Bombs give us magic and our powers grow stronger. We want the Bombs to come back. We will make them return with the Old Man's death.*

"The Old Man is going to die?" Dale said aloud.

"Of course. The radiation weakens him. We finish him off by driving him out of his mind."

We didn't know how to respond to this, so the creature continued. "You haven't noticed?" He cackled like a demented crow. "My name is Alter, by the way. *And these are the people of the town of Lockhart. We—*

"You're downwinders," Dale interrupted. "Aren't you?"

Of course. Alter scuttled closer, waddling like a mutilated crustacean. *We were caught in the black ash of the tests. But we do not begrudge the government like other towns. The US military and its scientists have blessed us. We are happy! Happy for the gift of magic.*

"Not magic, I'm afraid," Dale countered. "It has to be a rare genetic alteration, an unusual malformation somewhere in your frontal lobe that's allowing for...for thought-transference."

The thing called Alter found this deeply amusing. His laughter boomed and reverberated inside our skulls. Confused, we covered our ears with our hands, which only increased the volume.

The gun suddenly yanked itself free from Dale's grip and hovered in the air like a hummingbird, barrel swiveling until it pointed directly at Seth—and discharged.

Seth instantly clutched his chest with both hands. Glasses sliding off, he collapsed to the ground, blood leaking in the dust. We looked at him, stunned and horrified—but then the revolver went flying, a rocket shooting across the desert. A puff of sand hundreds of yards away confirmed it: No matter how far we might run from Alter, he could eliminate us.

"Psychokinesis," Dale mumbled, barely audible.

Alter's shabby apostles gathered before the remaining five of us. They were groaning perversely, as if achieving a simultaneous and shared orgasm. The sound filled us with loathing, nausea.

See? said Alter, slathering our minds with the ripe sensation of senseless murder. *Magic. Now get back into your car and go home, if you want to survive. The Old Man's end is near.*

"How do you mean?" Dale replied. The color had drained from his face, but what he said next belied his obvious fear. "You bunch of freaks will never make it to Las Vegas!"

Laughter like stabbing icicles again. Alter raised an insectoid arm, gesturing behind us. We fought the urge to flee, shit our pants, curl up and die right then and there. Instead, we turned around to watch the lid of our car trunk pop open with a sickening click. Alter was bending our reality to his every nightmarish whim.

———————

SWANSON CAME ALIVE AT ONCE, tearing off toward the vehicle. Rotors whirring, he leaned into the trunk and carefully, almost gingerly, lifted out

Last chance, warned Alter. *Go.*

We went. Just as we reached the vehicle, while we were catching our breath, Dale said something jaw-dropping. "I know why Swanson is registering low-level radiation."

Swanson was primed, explained Dale. The robot, which to our ire had never demonstrated a capacity for collaboration before, had worked with Alter to figure out how to reactivate its internal warhead. He'd gone from meals on wheels to silver-plated doom.

Guido, puke clinging to his chin and collar, found the testicles to wonder, "Wait. You never removed the warhead?"

"It's called pit-stuffing," sighed Dale. "You basically cram the tritium tube, which is inside the plutonium hollow, with a whole bunch of wires. The only way to get the weapon to work again is to dismantle it, remove the pit, cut it open, remove the wire, remanufacture the pit, and reassemble the weapon. It's a very long and very costly and somewhat dangerous process."

Barron offered the obvious. "These weirdos seem to have plenty of time on their hands and a tidy profit from selling their uranium mine."

Dale opened his mouth as if he might say something, closed it. Then he said, "You'd need the right tools. And I'm afraid—"

That you provided those tools yourself? Alter said, piercing our minds again. *In your workshop, perhaps? Why, yes. Yes, you did. You made it so easy for us. And sifting through your unlocked head for the activation process was a cakewalk.*

Dale's headaches. The presence he'd described as alien. Goddamn it.

Standing by the car, we were much farther away from the mutant horde at this point, maybe fifty yards. But we could still make out what happened next. To our amazement, one of the mutants raised his arm, which was clearly missing a hand. But then the creature grinned with his razored rictus, an anglerfish haunting a dried-up ocean floor. We looked on as a disembodied hand with a distinctive silver skull ring on the middle finger crawled up from the dust, onto his leg, and along his radiation-ravaged frame until settling and fitting perfectly at the end of what had been, just moments earlier, a mitt-less stump. We imagined one of Esposito's street soldiers trying to explain to the boss that the hand simply got up under its own power, opened the door to the restaurant, and headed up Sahara Avenue.

Christ, we'd been played for fools by the mutant-gimp inhabitants of a Nevada ghost town.

You helped us. We're grateful. The town folk of Lockhart thank you. Now leave and let the good citizens of Las Vegas know that the Children of the Bomb are coming. That soon we shall inherit the earth and humanity shall return to dust.

We all stood stock still, blank-eyed, in utter silence, waiting for someone to open a door on the vehicle so we could all pile in, peel off, and get as far away from this nuclear freak show as possible. Of course, Las Vegas would be incinerated by an atomic bomb Dale had failed to defuse inside a robot that was supposed to protect human life, not snuff it out like a cheap party candle.

Our thoughts raced. No more bountiful checks for doing little to no work. No more of the good life in Sin City. No more blow jobs from beautiful call girls, mountains of shrimp and lobster, golf with the buddies, betting on the Packers, all-night blackjack games, treating our families to everything they wanted. Hell, no more families.

No more anything, period.

Those fucking bastards had ruined us.

Finally, Dale shrugged. "Maybe the Old Man has a safe word that shuts down Swanson."

Wishful thinking. We all knew that any such shut-off was lost in the Old Man's shattered mind, sealed off in his traumatized body, locked in his oozing heart.

Lockhart.

Dale coughed into his fist, lab coat flapping like a flag of surrender. He looked exhausted, ill. For some reason, he reached in through the car's open window and turned the ignition key. We were paralyzed. Or we were trying to think up a plan of action. Or a course of action had already been decided for us.

"A Hard Day's Night" came on the radio. Someone cranked the volume knob, and we sang along, in unison, with the bittersweet chorus.

Magic.

———

AFTER THAT, no one said anything—not a fucking word. Past caring about our puny selves, we had a plan to fight back one last time. We lifted every nearby rock and stone we could find, tossing them into the trunk. Rather absurdly, Luis threw in a Gila monster that had been hiding in a hole, grabbing it by the tail. Then we all jumped into the car, hoping that our combined weight would be enough to thwart Alter's psychokinetic powers. We wanted to drench the fender in his blood, the blood of all the bad citizens of Lockhart, Nevada, where testing had unleashed pure evil. Where testing had unearthed unlikely preposterous heroes.

Dale stomped the gas pedal, hurtling us toward the mass of mutant gimps with minds like razors and hands that could be severed and reattached at will. Alter's psychic screams all but decapitated everyone in the car.

First, Guido's skull caved in, a rotten pumpkin yielding to an invisible sledgehammer's wallop. Barron's head imploded seconds later.

Windshield fractured, dashboard and back seat wet with gore and bone fragments, the vehicle rushed on. Tires hissed. Radiator crumpled, releasing steam as it impacted the first few bodies.

The final image we took to our graves? Swanson on fire, heading right at us.

And as we knew would happen: White light swallowed everything.

SON OF MOGAR

P erched high above Hollywood Boulevard, my house borrows much of its dark atmosphere from the wreckage below.

Where I live, I've simulated a world from another era. There are clues: framed lithographs of gorillas; a portrait of a giant robot, a woman trapped in its pincers; a small ivory dragon, fanged and hideous. This place is a shrine, really, a testament to my early years in the profession and to a friend who remains a profound influence on my life.

Growing up in Hollywood, I met a lot of intriguing people, but none compares to Hirose, who moved here from Japan to work as a suit actor. Dead ten years now, he is an obscure champion. Today, one might accidentally discover his films on an online horror fanzine. Sometimes a brief segment of his work pops up in a prime-time sitcom, where it is disrespected, ridiculed. The fading of Hirose's star is hard for me to accept, because the man looms so large in my memory. I write this in remembrance of the father I almost had.

Hirose trained to be a bomber pilot when he was sixteen. In the battle of Midway, his plane was hit by a gunner from a Grumman F6F Hellcat. The bullet made a tiny entrance, but the exit, Hirose saw, was larger than a softball. Wind violently rushed into the cockpit through that hole, rattling the cabin and scattering his flight documents. He gripped the controls and turned the plane around. After executing a perfect landing with a damaged engine, he went immediately to a noodle house near the base, where he drank wine and paid for a tattoo of a woman fornicating with an octopus.

When the war was over, Hirose secured a job as a driver in the motor pool of the Occupation Forces. He was amazed by the Americans and their emphasis on specialization. In Japan, versatility was considered indispensable. He was scolded for changing a tire. "For tire problems, there are tire men," the officer said. "Stick to the steering wheel." A few years later, Hirose was arrested by the American military police for speeding, thrown in jail, and fired.

He bummed around on his savings until he saw an ad for a one-year training school for actors and when the year was over, he eventually found work with Imamura Pictures. Soon he landed small parts in various samurai flicks and later in big-budget war epics. Highly regarded by important directors, he was frequently cast, appropriately enough, as a bomber pilot.

One day Imamura's casting director, Endo, invited Hirose to a private screening of a print of the 1933 *King Kong*. Having seen few if any American productions,

Hirose was dazzled by the eerie power of model animation. The giant ape seemed truly alive!

Yet even as a young man in his mid-twenties, he
recognized the cost and time that such effects
demanded. He was sure that he could do a better job on
the screen than a flexible toy and a stop-motion camera.
Indeed, the movie kindled something pure and atavistic
inside him. He was stricken with the urge to climb
skyscrapers, swat at fighter planes, clutch women like
Fay Wray. But he needed a mask, a costume. The idea
took shape in his mind just as the projector cast out its
last fragments of light. Hirose convinced his friend
Endo to approve the research and development of a suit
for a picture titled *Mogar, the Monster-God!*

First came the sketches. Working with artists in the
costume department, Hirose made the creature's face
tight, compact, brutal. During the construction phase,
he asked for a wire-controlled tail and a low center of
gravity. Despite the latter, the original design was still
too top heavy and the test for walking in the suit ended
ignobly, with Hirose falling and breaking the proto-
Mogar's jaw. The second design lacked a sufficient
number of breathing holes and was difficult to remove.
Finally, the suit was ready, according to Hirose's now-
exacting specifications. Mogar resembled a bipedal dog
with reptilian features, or rather a gigantic mutant
terrier with scales.

Hirose approached his role with enthusiasm and dili-
gence. Frequently, he visited the zoo to study the movements of animals, theorizing how best to portray a
radioactive creature from a mysterious uncharted island.
Inside the suit, it was very dark, lonely, isolated, and obvi-

ously more cramped than the bomber cabin he had been confined to during the war. Each morning before heading to the studio, Hirose meditated for a full hour. He choreographed all the monster battles well in advance, advising the set builders where to place the miniatures. He was even involved in the script and came up with the twist of having the scientist's daughter steal the oxygen destroyer.

When it came time to shoot, the production tested his physical limits. In the samurai pictures, he'd worked summer days in full armor; the suit itself presented little problem and dehydration was never a concern. But now the studio lighting caused him to swoon. The sensitivity of film was terribly slow at that time and shooting a movie required severe brightness. The director used ten-kilowatt lights and the surface of the latex suit softened to the point of melting. Hirose's sweat evaporated; salt leaked from his pores. He had to move rapidly so that in the editing, the speed could be slowed down, creating the effect of an immense and naturally plodding Mogar. Fortunately, principal photography was completed in less than three months. Imamura Pictures initiated a marketing and distribution campaign. Meanwhile, they had the negative stored in a warehouse.

But the warehouse burned down.

Soon after, a competing film company began production on its own giant-monster flick.

Employing a similar rubber suit instead of model animation, this new movie caused a sensation at home and overseas. Hirose was devastated. He quit Imamura and worked sporadically in a bowling alley. He drank heavily. He paid for another tattoo. At the age of twenty-six, he felt washed up. It was agonizing to have been beaten to the punch, robbed of his personal vision. He'd nearly suffocated, shriveled into a human prune, and came close to being hospitalized. For what?

Meanwhile, Hirose's friend Endo gave up his job as casting director, married an American correspondent, and moved here to California. He found a job as a stagehand for a small production company. Four years later, he'd ascended to the position of special effects director, working on genre cheapies like *Zombie Ranch* and *Bride of Robot Spider*. At some point, he came across a script for a killer gorilla movie, which called for a suit actor. He thought of his friend Hirose and wondered what had happened to the talented young man. In a fit of nostalgic curiosity, he wrote a letter to the heads of Imamura. The reply saddened him. The actor had hit the skids. He lived in a seedy district and worked sporadically, if at all. Tattoos now covered his body. For all this, Endo felt somehow responsible. Perhaps he could have pushed harder for a release date on *Mogar*, in time to have made his young friend a star. Endo bought Hirose a one-way third-class ticket to the States. The year was 1957.

I was ten years old and a Hollywood orphan. My father, who is best remembered for his role as the comical cross-dressing pirate in *Black Mast*, had died in an alcohol-related car wreck when I was a baby. My mother, successful in her own right, was an amphetamine addict and eventually went psychotic, garroting her hairstylist with a belt and running over a producer with her silver Corvair. A well-intentioned and elderly vocal coach named Polly Steckler adopted me shortly after my mother entered the asylum.

Polly was gray-haired, round, a cat-lover. We lived

in a cottage tucked away in the back of the lot where she gave lessons. I can remember her sitting opposite B-movie starlets, her chest rising up and down, trying to get her pupils to speak from their diaphragms. She possessed a beautiful voice herself and the actresses, before leaving, always kissed her on the cheek. As devoted to me as any mother could have been, she packed my lunches for school and inquired about my homework.

Polly taught into the evening, so I got to wander the studio lot. I loved the sound stages, those great caverns of darkness as big as aircraft hangars. In the hours before dinner while the actors were on set, I messed around in the makeup department, applying pancake powder, mascara, false eyelashes, and lipstick and studying my face in the bulb-lined mirrors. Then I went to the set and pestered the prop man, Dexter. He had everything that might be needed in a scene. Phones, lamps, cut flowers—everything you could imagine. Drinks, too: coffee, tea, soda, even booze. Yet he never let me so much as taste the liquor. Looking back on it, I can see that everyone at the studio was very protective of me. I'd been adopted not only by Polly, but by the stagehands, directors, assistants, other actors, the entire studio. That year, I became especially close to Hirose, though I saw him as peculiar and possibly dangerous. Gradually, he grew into a sort of father.

I first met him on the set of *Drums for the Death-Ape*, a box-office turkey, but now something of a cult classic, mostly due to the prolonged and titillating scene in which the murderous gorilla strips actress Lora Romero down to her undergarments and ties her to a sacrificial altar. His gorilla suit was sophisticated for its time. It sported chest bladders and leather skin and was covered in genuine animal hair. Hirose was in the suit, mask, and everything, preparing for the director's next move, when he must have seen me reach for one of Dexter's props, a whiskey flask.

"Do not drink that," he said, his voice muffled, his furry hand taking the flask. "It will turn you mindless."

I mumbled, "Yes, uh, sir," then walked over to the standby painter's gear and pretended to rummage. Wiping off my makeup, I felt sick with embarrassment and fear.

Hirose had scared me; it was unnerving to be repri-manded by a gorilla. He must have felt bad, too, because minutes later he asked me—this time without the mask—to help mend his suit, which he'd torn in a poorly choreographed fight with a knife-wielding voodoo priestess. I saw then that he was Japanese and asked if he knew any kamikazes. He said yes; many of his childhood friends had been trained as Zero pilots and had given their lives to the war effort. Taro, for instance, died in a futile attempt to crash his plane into the U.S.S *Archerfish*, hitting only water. He told me that when he was a driver for the Allies right after the war, he struggled to learn English; even then, his fluency was still imperfect, but he was always under-standable and entertaining. For the rest of the day, as the electricians wasted time arguing over whether to use an existing power source or an independent genera-tor, I helped my new Japanese friend stitch his suit.

He told war story after war story. Then, when he related Mogar's awful fate, I recall that I had to thread the needle, because his hands shook slightly.

"What's it like?" I asked. "To act like a gorilla."

"It is a freedom," he said. "I do what I want and no troubles for me."

Hirose was a perfectionist and when he failed to meet his own impossible standards, he drank, although never in my, or anyone else's, presence. He drank by himself; after all, he was a foreigner and Japanese at that. He lived alone in a trailer on the studio lot, out near the animal-training grounds. As it turns out, I was his first real American friend.

To keep in shape, he regularly played handball with some of the lanky black carpenters in the late afternoon and on the weekends, he lifted dumbbells. He woke me at sunrise to time him on his early-morning runs around the studio's parking lot. Tapping on my window, he called, "Get up, get up! Let us run!" I rubbed sleep from my eyes, ran a comb through my hair, changed, and tied on some tennis shoes.

To simulate the conditions of a monster suit, he wore three T-shirts, a sweatshirt, a heavy coat, and pull-on sweatpants over a pair of jeans. I yelled, "*Go!*" hit the stopwatch, and he practically sprinted the entire distance. In retrospect, I'm surprised he didn't give himself a heart attack. We had the parking lot measured and he could run five-minute miles one after the other, like a machine. Afterward, I helped him remove all those layers, so he could shower, then we headed to the studio's cramped cafeteria for breakfast.

"Heart and lungs must be strong," he said, sipping his hot tea. "Else the monster is sickly."

After a tiny bowl of oatmeal and some fruit, we walked to the gym for a quick series of pull-ups, push-ups, and sit-ups. He ripped right through them. If I succeeded in doing some, he bought me an ice cream and comic book at the studio's soda fountain after school let out.

One day he picked me up in his Cadillac and disclosed some spectacular news. The studio had cast him to star in an upcoming giant-monster movie. A larger production like this meant more screen-time and more money. In addition, the slightly higher cost of such a project might, one hoped, might translate into a better film.

Happy and garrulous, he puffed dramatically on a cigar. "I owe you everything," he said. "You have helped me with English, with my physical fitness. You are my best friend. Here is a token." He handed me a small statue, an ivory dragon, and cranked up the radio.

"Thank you!" I yelled over the blare. "And congratulations!"

Unimpressed, Polly sat in her chair, patching a pair of my jeans, glasses angled against her nose. "I suppose it's an enjoyable way to make a living," she remarked when I told her the news. "In the absence of creative talent, one can always release the destructive tendencies." She didn't look up, but persisted in working her needle.

I can't really blame Polly. Like most people, she perceived no decorum or technique in Hirose's performances. As a vocal instructor and former concert singer, she believed very much that these qualities had to be self-evident for one to call oneself any kind of artist or craftsman.

I paused, puzzled by her sardonic note. Ice cream melted down my hand. "You don't think Hirose is creative?"

"It seems nasty to break things."

"Nasty?"

"Cruel. Savage. Inhuman."

"Yes," I said. "That's what I like about Hirose. He's inhuman."

Being a top-notch suit actor was not easy. Even if you were in peak condition, strong enough to maneuver effectively in the suit, you still had to perform stunts as well. In *Vaporize All Dinosaurs!* Hirose executed a dangerous underwater scene, using scuba equipment inside the costume. A cart was placed on rails on the bottom of a pool and towed by a rope tied to a truck. Hirose rode on the cart, his head below the surface. But the truck had accelerated too quickly. He gradually rose out of the water, which rushed fiercely against his face. By some miracle, he managed to retain his scuba mouthpiece. Had it been knocked away in the torrent, he surely would have drowned. Again as a dinosaur, in *Planet of the Burrowing Lizards*, he was buried alive under a mountain of dirt and had to emerge on cue to combat a gargantuan moth. As a gravity-defying alien in *Martian Conquest*, he was hooked with wires, attached to a crane, and swung about wildly until he banged against a boom microphone and smashed the catering table.

His suits had to be patched regularly. He owned three: gorilla, dinosaur (T-Rex), and metallic alien, this last doubling as robot duds. For repairs, Hirose used anything and everything, from resin, fiberglass, and gelatin to urethane, tar, and chewing gum. If a suit became too worn and he had money saved, he replaced it, buying a new custom-made one from a designer in Oregon. Occasionally, the studio loaned out Hirose to star in another company's A-picture, in which case the other company's special effects or costume department provided a lavish outfit for him to work in. Such a deal was rare, however. Although they paid him a pretty good salary, Hirose was contracted to a small production company that specialized B-grade films and the terms of the agreement dictated that he supply his own equipment. He didn't mind; he cherished his suits and preferred working in them. They gave him a feeling of independence, insofar as he didn't have to rely on anyone, any studio, to transform into a credible monster. He especially prized his gorilla suit. Once, I crept into his trailer and caught him talking to it, as if the hairy lifeless thing in his arms were a woman. He brushed it carefully, lovingly, with his fingertips. "Darling," he whispered to it. No doubt he'd been drinking.

It was after an all-you-can-eat dinner buffet in Hollywood that he drove out to the beach, where he liked to practice some slow, deliberate, rudimentary judo he'd picked up in the Japanese Imperial Navy. He stood in the soft sand, poised, right leg drawn, as if to execute a kick. He performed peculiar motions with his arms. The sun allowed itself to melt into the Pacific. Sea gulls called, swooping down across the surf. I collected shells and poked a dead crab with a stick, flipping it over to reveal its underside. After a while, the sky grew dark and Hirose turned on the car's headlights. We sat on the hood, listening to the waves, waiting for the stars to emerge. That night, Hirose told me about the flight deck of the carrier *Shinano*. It was covered with a mixture of concrete and sawdust, to provide traction for aircraft landing gears. More important, the Japanese Navy had installed twelve arresting cables that went up and down by compressed air and were supposed to snag planes and keep them from rolling off the deck. Also, there were huge barrier nets in case aircraft missed the cables. "The metal nets stopped you," he said. "But they crushed your wings. Bent propellers like noodles.

"Let me say that I knew young man assigned to *Shinano*. He found below deck a jade propeller. The young man attached the propeller to his fighter plane and never lost in combat. He was forever victorious. He exploded many enemies. Nothing could touch him, not even machine guns. Also, the propeller allowed him to speak with the ghosts of dead enemy pilots and they forgave him for everything. But the young pilot had a jealous friend, who wanted the propeller for himself. One night, this friend secretly switched propellers. The next morning the young man took off, crashed immediately, and died.

"The jealous friend flew through the air like an invincible bird. He avoided sneak attacks and his bullets struck every target. He defeated all his enemies and returned to the *Shinano* to land his plane. But he descended so quickly that the arresting cables missed the plane. The nets were ready to stop him, but the jade propeller cut right through the metal, like it was tissue, and the jealous friend rolled his plane off the deck and into the water and he drowned. Today, the skeletons of the young man and his jealous friend lie at the bottom of the ocean next to a propeller that glows green."

Hirose was silent then. So was I. The stars began to appear. He asked if I wanted to drive back to the studio and I said yes. Hirose sat in the passenger seat, scanning the radio dial. He located Bo Diddley's "I'm a Man" and gave it a little volume. He tapped the dashboard all the way home. I drove with the utmost care, to show that I was mature enough for the task. I remember thinking that I'd heard one of his greatest war stories, even if I didn't quite grasp its meaning. I looked up to Hirose as a man, because he was one, just as Bo Diddley insisted—physical but contemplative, tough but romantic, brave yet vulnerable. Of course, up to this point, I had every reason to admire Hirose. He was at the top of his game.

"Can anything hurt you?" I suddenly asked, making the turn up the freeway entrance ramp.

He said, "Only myself."

Diddley's song stuttered to a halt, then a spot came on, a plug for what was arguably Hirose's finest, most impressive accomplishment, *The Day the Earth Ruptured!* in which a giant iguana obliterates all the major cities of the world.

For a short while, Hirose dated a bony beehive-haired stenographer named Joyce. He'd met her in the downtown courthouse, where he planned to protest a speeding ticket, and, I imagine, he was captivated by her sunny aura of healthy all-Americanness, her pageant beauty, her thick makeup and conical breasts.

He said to me, "I have met an angel."

"Does she know you're a giant monster?" I asked.

He winked. "Not something you tell pretty girl right away."

They went out on a few dinner dates, and I remember thinking they looked good together. I had apprehensions, of course. For one thing, I surmised that she was a vapid gold digger with an unnatural affinity for Cadillacs and she did, in fact, utter remarks that suggested she didn't have much going on upstairs, but I didn't dare discourage my friend. Even a child, such as I was then, could recognize that people need other people to lessen the perpetual ache of loneliness. With Joyce beside him, Hirose acted like the world was boundless and bubbling with possibilities. Their relationship seemed to be progressing just fine, but then Hirose took Joyce to see *The Day the Earth Ruptured!* in hopes of impressing her. The movie was sneaked at the Cornell Theatre in Burbank and after the show, they had coffee at the Smoke House. Much to Hirose's dismay, Joyce said she didn't want to see him anymore. "If that's the kind of picture you make, I don't think this relationship is going to work out." She wanted him to star in movies like *Show Boat*. Hirose tried to explain the unfeasibility of producing that kind of movie in five days for under $50,000, but she'd made up her very limited mind. He never saw his angel again.

In the days that followed, Hirose feigned ambivalence, joking that at least he'd gleaned something from being dumped: to abstain from women whose hairstyles produced more sheer terror than his suits. But I could sense that he'd been wounded. One evening after a grueling non-union shoot—in which the 142-pound Hirose had nearly given himself a hernia carrying the 100-pound actress Lori Paget across a gopher-hole-ridden field out near the Santa Anita Racetrack—we returned to his trailer to relax with steaming cups of green tea and a few slow-paced games of checkers. With the windows open, it was yet another warm spring evening on the periphery of Hollywood. We listened to the radio turned low, hoping to catch a decent R&B number or at least radio spot for one of Hirose movies. Moths battered themselves against the screens and in between moves, Hirose blew cigarette smoke on them.

Point blank, I asked, "Did Joyce break your heart?"

He shrugged. "I can no longer be injured," he said. "My heart died many years ago." He looked visibly irritated as he exhaled another cloud into the frenzy of moths. The subject was dropped and never broached again.

The relationship between Hirose and Endo was a mysterious and complex one. As soon as he'd found Hirose employment with the studio, Endo had jumped ship and signed on with the studio's lesser competitor, the Santa Monica-based National Releasing Company, which specialized in buying the rights to Italian sword-and-sandal flicks, producing stories around the special effects sequences, and selling the results as double features to drive-ins from Little Rock to Pittsburgh. Endo's job involved fashioning new films out of the Italian footage. From what I gathered, he was highly critical of Hirose's profession and whenever the two came together, Endo urged his younger countryman to give up suit-acting and move into production work.

One afternoon on the set of another automaton-gone-amok movie, I spotted Endo, talking with Polly near the sound equipment. I approached Hirose to tell him what I thought was good news—someone was here to visit him!

But Hirose remained cool, his voice betraying displeasure. "Endo despise what I do, this direction. He hate everything about me."

Bewildered, I said nothing.

Back in Hirose's trailer, as I toweled the sweat of his performance from his neck and back, the door opened and in walked Endo, smiling. He was in good shape, tanned, dressed in an electric-blue jacket and a black turtleneck. "Hello there, Hirose," he said. "I really like new movie. Suit looks great."

Hirose, dryly, replied, "Thanks. I'm so glad you *like*."

"No, really," Endo said, unruffled. "You have great effects team here. Much energy and intelligence." He gestured in my direction, indicating that I was a crucial cog in the larger mechanism that was Hirose's greatness.

Feeling awkward in my silence, I blurted out, "Yeah. Lots of energy."

Abandoning his successful persona, Endo tried his best to be just another effects-member-in-the-trenches, but Hirose showed only disdain. I was stunned; I'd expected open displays of affection or at least the mutual warmth of longtime friendship. Had they fallen out recently? Had Endo disparaged Hirose's latest performance? The tension was unbearable, so I left to join the crew outside for snacks and soft drinks.

Half an hour later, I re-entered the trailer and everything had changed. Hirose was smoking and smil-ing, totally absorbed in Endo's plan to repackage a Spanish gangster movie. It was mind-boggling: detach-ment and disregard one minute, enthusiasm about forthcoming projects the next. What did these two Japanese friends really think about each other?

One day not long after this, I found myself in line for groceries, standing next to Endo. I asked him what Hirose had meant when he said his heart had died. Endo nodded grimly. He invited me to dinner at his ritzy house in the Topanga Canyon, where he described

Hirose's wartime ordeal in hideously altered Techni-
color, sparing no awful detail, until I could imagine,
projected on the screen in my mind, the wasteland that
was once a place utterly enveloped in a spectral cloak of
radiation. Hirose's family was among the casualties at
Hiroshima. This came as a shock to me. I'd understood,
of course, that Hirose had no family in the States, but
he'd never mentioned anything about the bomb.
Suddenly, Hirose's life story expanded to cinematic
proportions. Doomsday pictures coruscated through my
mind, like those prompted by the psychotic ravings in a
radio spot or a promo trailer for one of Hirose's movies.

"Hirose showed up soon enough to suffer what no
man should suffer," Endo said.

Scouring the makeshift hospitals pitched along the
waterways, Hirose had hoped to chance upon a
surviving member of his family. He gained entry into
the camp closest to the bombsite, where his younger
sister was sleeping in a cot. Her face was bandaged and
her fingernails had turned black. Hirose sat by her
bedside until she lost consciousness the next morning
and her heart stopped. He later learned that the rest of
his family had died in the blast, their bodies crushed
beneath the rubble of their homes.

"Hirose is a man full of pain," Endo told me. "He
goes crazy from time to time. He drinks too much, and
he hurts others."

"He's never hurt me."

Endo nodded. "I believe you. But I've had to deal
with his wretchedness for too long and I see him differently. He is under death spell. Because he has known
death, he thinks he must suffer life of grief. He is
masochist. He gets pleasure from reliving event over

and over again. I say to him, 'Hirose, leave the past and look to the future.' But he doesn't listen. He no embrace the present. He choose instead the nightmare of history."

I'd been abandoned, too, but my abandonment was brought on, for the most part, by my parents' poor, or rather all-too-human, choices and not as a consequence of any cosmic irrationality like war or, especially, a nuclear holocaust. I hadn't been forced to look on helplessly as some real-life fission-powered nightmare suddenly killed everyone close to me. I'd always figured that, since we were both lacking an immediate family, Hirose and I shared a similar alienation and grief. But now I was aware of the chasm of difference between our circumstances; they were radically unalike and mutually exclusive. I had an entire community of showbiz professionals to support me, like Polly and Dexter. Hirose had no one, except for me, a little kid. It's not that I compared our respective traumas and determined that mine was altogether insignificant. More simply, I now perceived his sadness as being too much for one man alone to carry around. At only twelve years of age, I could sense that Hirose's sorrow isolated him and threatened to destroy him.

I never told anyone this, but sometimes Hirose visited Endo in Santa Monica and while he was away, I snuck into his studio trailer. Under the mattress, he hid Betty Page bondage mags, which I often swiped and swapped with the cameramen for comic books. Beneath the sink next to the cleansers, he stored his liquor, mainly vodka. He stashed cigarettes in the medicine cabinet. I went through his closet and pulled out the suitcase that contained all his Japanese-inscribed medals. In a shoebox, he kept a messy pile of photos taken during the war. Pictures of him, smiling, in uniform, walking the streets of Tokyo, or on the deck of the *Shinano*, looking out on the water. A wide-angle shot of him in flight gear, helmeted, standing with his teenaged crew, all of them smoking cigarettes and wearing the same serious—or was it frightened?— expression, the bomber squatting ominously in the background. His suits hung in the kitchen walk-in, the driest and coolest part of the trailer.

I stripped down to my underwear, stepped into one of the suits, and pulled the top up and over my head. Through the eye slits, I saw myself in the full-length mirror. In the thing, I felt invulnerable, blameless. As if I could lay waste to anything and not be held accountable. I stood outside of convention, beyond good and evil. I pretended that Hirose's trailer was a metropolis and that I was Mogar. Sofa pillows were tanks; I threw them around. I scaled the La-Z-Boy as if it were a skyscraper, then emitted banshee screams and thumped my chest before falling to my doom. For hours, I imagined these and other scenes, until I worked up a sweat and became exhausted. I was always careful to place the suits back on their hangers. Polly figured something was going on when I got busted at school for smoking.

"Where did you get the cigarettes?" she asked.

"I stole them from Hirose."

She gave me a serious look. "No more. Don't take things from that poor man."

"Why is he 'poor'?"

She sighed. "He always has to play a monster."

THE STUDIO PERSONNEL may have looked down on Hirose's profession, but they admired his work ethic. In spite of his Japaneseness, which they didn't know what to do with, his stoicism made them feel petty, his commitment made them feel weak. He never complained, always showed up early and left late. He was quiet, polite, approachable, intelligent, forbearing. As a consequence, people were mesmerized by the ease with which he seemed to go from mild to wild. I loved to watch him on the sets, the way he disappeared into roles. Like Orson Welles in *Citizen Kane*, he could explode without warning and be on the rampage at a moment's notice. He became a savage whirlwind, snapping power lines, careening through a gauntlet of mixed artillery, mowing down chemical refineries, pile driving lobster-clawed behemoths. Nothing stood in his path. His demolitions were exhaustive and oddly therapeutic, not just for himself, but for the audience as well. An instinctual actor, he nonetheless had a definite, if somewhat limited, intellectual understanding of what he was doing.

Hirose got me interested in special effects, at first by encouraging me to observe his repair work. Eventually, I started fixing his suits and when I wasn't in school, I was his personal assistant on the set. After I turned eighteen, the studio hired me. I mostly worked on miniatures, scaled-down recreations of cities. Hirose believe that well-constructed and well-placed miniatures were essential to an effective giant-monster performance. He worked closely with set builders and directors to ensure sufficient room for the choreographed tussles with no screw-ups. Still, things went wrong. Now and again, the staff pulled the rope too soon, collapsing the building before Hirose made his approach and pelting him with debris. Or the pyrotechnics were too fierce and his suit caught fire. Sometimes model tanks and airplanes assaulted him after the scene had already been shot, as he was taking off his costume. Or the other suit actor drop-kicked him at the wrong moment. In spite of all of this, Hirose was both patient and forgiving, a far cry from what his screen presence might lead you to expect.

Yet wearing the suit, day after day, movie after movie, eventually took its toll. During the shooting of *The Plastic Eaters*, Curtis Bennington, the director, pressured him to dance a jig after thrashing the Atomic Avenger. Bennington was an anemic, effete, pipe-smoking Hollywood has-been, a real hack who dressed like a beatnik from one of those campy teen exploitation flicks, complete with shades and beret. Hirose adamantly refused to dance. Usually, the two got along. But now Hirose maintained that he was an actor, not a ballerina.

"Our hands are tied," said Bennington, shrugging his shoulders, signaling the best boy to fetch him another brandy. "The studio wants to market *The Plastic Eaters* as a children's movie. This thing has got to be lighter in tone. It's too disturbing—there's a lot of nuclear paranoia going on here, man."

Hirose, dinosaur-garbed, grabbed the bullhorn, stepped in front of the hapless director, and inches from the man's face shrieked, "Paranoia? Say to two hundred thousand incinerated Japanese! And if you do, tell them hello for me!"

As Bennington fell backward, Hirose flung the bullhorn aside and stormed off to his trailer. The crew looked at one another in confusion. Someone, perhaps the camera operator, muttered, "Prima donna." I suggested that we break for lunch. We all looked at Bennington, who got up, adjusted his sunglasses, cleared his throat, and nodded his approval. The best boy appeared with the brandy and Bennington finished it off before the kid had a chance to ask what happened.

It wasn't long before the scandal made its way around the studio until it reached the company's secretary and main gossip, Susan Lychack, an excellent cook who always prepared a terrific spread of corned beef and Jewish dishes for the wrap parties. Susan passed on the story to the company's accountant, who shuddered at the notion of spending another thousand dollars on an added day of principal photography.

The producers summoned me to their office and implored me to talk some sense into Hirose, so that evening I knocked on his door. Standing outside, I heard the clink of bottles and the recorded twang of Chuck Berry's guitar. "Come in," he said.

Dressed in jeans and a plaid shirt, Hirose presented a bright smile. Tattoos slithered out from under his sleeves. He mock-punched my arm and gestured toward the sofa. "Sit, sit," he said. "Shall we dance to Chuck Berry?" He did a brief sing-along with "Too Much Monkey Business," after which he gave a sudden sharp "Hah!"

I sat down and he brought me an iced tea. He lit a cigarette at the table. We looked at each other uncomfortably for a minute. Then he gazed at the empty TV screen, nervously flicking non-existent ashes. I chewed ice. Chuck Berry played on for the souls of the burger-munching teens. The trailer's spare furnishings gave the moment the air of a legal proceeding. I tried to present the situation in a positive light.

"Big nasty creatures are no longer the rage," I insisted. "These days, nothing is oversized. Everything is small and shows up in swarms: insects, spiders, killer bees. Look at Hitchcock and his pigeons. Or else you've got natural disasters—typhoons, tidal waves, earthquakes. There will always be a need for suit actors, but not in the same capacity. Look, little kids never tire of giant monsters. So maybe children's entertainment offers another avenue for today's suit actor, you know? More employment opportunities? Kids can't watch *The Plastic Eaters* if it's all about Armageddon—"

"Hold a minute," he interrupted, exhaling smoke. "I do not agree. I cannot base life's work on fads and whims of babies. I am suit actor because I have no choice and so I must act with dignity. Not with dollar signs blocking my vision. No, no, I refuse to dance for money." He stood up to extinguish his cigarette. "I will pump gas instead."

"Fine," I said. I leaned forward to grab his arm. "Don't dance. But your principles won't make any difference. Bennington will simply get Pepe to put on the suit. Bennington will film him doing the Monster Mash and the scene will appear next month in drive-ins across the country. Your performance is already compromised."

He yanked his arm away. His face turned an angry red. "Not with my suit, they won't!"

"Listen to yourself. The designer in Oregon manufactures the suit and sells it to other studios, other actors. It's not *yours*."

He picked up a chair and smashed it against the wall. The whole trailer shook. The needle skipped right across the record. A picture frame fell, crashing to the floor.

Just as suddenly, Hirose was restrained again. "Am sorry," he said, brushing his hair back into place. "But I will not dance for children find me amusing. Let us go to eat." He threw me the keys to his Cadillac.

———————

BENNINGTON HIRED someone to put on another Space Reptile costume, shot the dance scene, and included it in the final edit. When Hirose found out, he was livid. Emboldened by too much liquor, he broke into Bennington's home one night and threatened the director with a tire iron in front of his wife and children. Luckily, the studio heads arranged things so that no charges were filed. I promised everyone that I'd monitor the actor's behavior and intervene the next time I saw his fuse getting short. The damage had been done, however; from then on, the company labeled Hirose as a potential liability. They also saw me as a babysitter, a kid who had to shoulder the responsibility of caring for an unstable veteran actor.

The Plastic Eaters scored a hit with the kids, spawning two sequels and a TV spin off. Up to this point, giant monsters had been suffering at the box office; the genre seemed to be running out of steam. Because of the overplayed nuclear war concerns present in many of these movies, the plots for the most part were dull and formulaic. To limit production costs, the studio insisted that we use stock footage of Space

Reptile and the Atomic Avenger leveling San Francisco and other cities. Even Bennington, unimaginative and corner-cutting director that he was, expressed his displeasure. Thus, the productions ended up being little more than mish-mashes of clips from already-screened movies. Even so, the studio kept churning out these special effects-deficient, ineptly scripted clunkers and the tykes ate them up. I spent more time in the editing room than on the sound stage. It wasn't long before I longed to return to miniatures. I had an over-whelming desire to construct a small metropolis, no matter how rickety or short-lived, no matter how cheap the materials. But my aspirations were never fulfilled and my miniature-building skills languished.

I Iirose, on the other hand, had entered a new phase of his career. Bit by bit, the hard facts penetrated his brain. Children's bad taste in cinema made it possible for him to draw a weekly salary. So he began to warm to the idea of dancing. He put his pride on the shelf. Pushing fifty, he experienced the indignation of actu-ally juggling fake boulders in his ape suit—in front of the TV camera, no less! Mercifully, the series was canceled after two seasons. Hirose continued to find work, albeit the kind that only the most hard-core sci-fi and horror fans could stomach. I'm talking grade-Z. Worse, he picked up some more dreadful television gigs. As I grew older, I could see that despite remaining in some demand, Hirose's glory days in Hollywood were on the wane.

Now in my late teens, I started hanging out with the makeup department in between shoots and mastered tons of tricks: bald caps, hairwork, injury simulation, aging facials, prosthetics. I even learned about kabuki, which impressed Hirose a great deal. By the mid-sixties, people in the industry were beginning to take notice. Rival studios offered me lucrative salaries, signing bonuses, box-office percentages. They couldn't tempt me, because I felt guilty about Hirose; I wanted to help improve his movies and make him look scary again. Usually, he was pleased with my work. However, one time I offered to add blood-tubing effects to his gorilla mask for the final showdown in the 1967 *Ape vs. Android*. And he took offense. He accused me of endeavoring to corrupt his aesthetic and philosophical beliefs and claimed I was striving for offensive and immature goals. "Blood and guts will distort film's message. It will contaminate performance."

"I want to bring a sense of realism to your work."

"There is nothing real about ape-socking robot," he insisted.

I saved the effects for what today would be considered an R-rated movie called *Gore-rilla*, which starred a Filipino suit actor, a newcomer named Cruz. Hirose had been offered the role, but after reading the script, he passed on it; in his words, it was "intended for shitheads." So the studio brought in Cruz for less than half of what they would've paid Hirose. From then on, he lost more and more work to actors like Cruz, willing to work for scraps. Also, the industry that Hirose had cut his teeth on here in the US no longer played by the same rules, what with the sixties coming to a close, the dismantling of the factory system, the weakening of the Production Code. My friend found it almost impossibly difficult to adapt.

"Who is Cruz person?" he once asked after reading in the trades about a new movie, *Tentacles!* slated for production. Hirose hadn't been offered the role. We were in the cafeteria, finishing breakfast. "He gets all the jobs but has no talent. Casting directors smoke grass! To play octopus, need to be ambidextrous. Cruz has bad left arm."

"The tentacles are wire-controlled," I said, but then the expression on his face made it clear I'd given something away.

He narrowed his eyes. An uneasy period of silence. Then: "Why you not tell me?"

"Tell you what?"

"That you were hired on this movie. That you now Cruz's best buddy."

I fiddled helplessly with the silverware. "I'm not his buddy."

He shook his head. "Will octopus require your makeup skills?"

"No," I said. "I've been promoted to special effects director."

"Oh, even more *new* developments. Tell me, after you signed, did you ask director to consider *me* for part?"

"Yes."

"And what did he say?"

I looked down at the floor. "He said he wanted someone younger."

Hirose made no reply, but sat motionless, the paper splayed in his hands. He gently folded it, took a sip of tea, and left.

For weeks afterward, he resolutely avoided me.

I felt terrible. But the truth was, Hirose was too old for his line of work. His choreography had become stale, his movements less convincing. He couldn't disas-

semble the Hoover Dam with the same mechanical effi-
ciency, snatch a body with the same alien dexterity,
savage a White woman with the same ape-like convic-
tion. No longer the consummate suit actor of yesterday,
he refused to come to terms with the irrefutable fact of
his advancing age. Why was he hanging on? After all,
he had money saved. He could afford to retire, take up
gardening, travel, find a woman, relax. He depended on
the ritual of performing in a suit, but people like Cruz
threatened to render him and his performances obsolete. Twenty years Hirose's junior, Cruz had speed,
superior strength, better mobility, increased stamina—
all the necessary traits one must possess in order to wear
a cumbersome octopus outfit. With all my heart, I had
wished, hoped, and prayed for Hirose to cinch that role,
but the producers and casting agents were calling the
shots. I had a say only in matters pertaining to special
effects.

Eventually, the studio's financial backers heard
grumblings that Hirose was having trouble working in
the suits. He fainted a few times during a crucial week
of shooting, delaying the schedule and costing
producers money. They called us in to talk and as soon
as we showed up at the office and sat down at the
conference table across from these blank-faced executives with their garish ties, we both knew the news was
bad, if not dire.

Hirose stood up and said, "I'm not going to retire."

In his fierce determination, he spilled his Styrofoam
cup of coffee, causing hot black liquid to shoot toward
the laps of the panicky executives. One of them had the
presence of mind to grab the napkins out of a box of
doughnuts sitting at the end of the table and block the

oncoming stream. When the president of the company, Jim Osterberg, realized that the immediate threat had been averted, he replied, "We don't want you to leave. However, we feel it's time to renegotiate. Everyone in this business knows your talent is incomparable. You have reached a level of experience that most of us can only dream of attaining. But twelve movies per year is too much strain for a man of your age, in spite of all that you bring to the sets. Maybe now is when you start thinking about the future. We want to give you a chance to ponder life outside the world of rubber suits and the spotlight. Now, if we were to trim down your workload to, say, six movies—"

"No," Hirose said, shaking his head, arms crossed unyieldingly. "I am perfect health. The problem is suits need better ventilation." He looked directly at them, but not with defiance. Instead, his face took on the aspect of that of a petulant child and for a moment, I thought I might burst into tears.

Osterberg sighed. "I was afraid you might take it badly. Your health isn't the issue, Mr. Kumata. Monster movies are bombing at the box office these days. It's all been done: giant lizards, giant apes, giant crabs, giant amoebas, giant chickens. Unless someone comes up with an original concept, we simply can't risk investing in sci-fi horror, while blaxploitation and martial-art flicks continue to make the money. And since you're neither black nor a black belt, this means we really can't use you that much anymore, because the fact is we just don't need to rely on suit actors the way we used to. We hate to force phased retirement on you, but our hands are tied. The giant monster has fallen on dark days."

Following this, I tried to console Hirose by treating

him to a seafood platter at Lindsey's. He picked spirit-lessly at his fried clams and made perfunctory attempts at conversation. I did my best to steer our talk away from moviemaking, but I inadvertently blundered into describing a new experimental recipe for realistic-looking internal fluids and organic structures.

Having heard enough of my prattle, he put down his fork. "What will I do now?" he said miserably.

I told him I didn't know.

For the remainder of the sixties, Hirose picked up extra work, mostly no-budget features that paid him very little. Of course, money wasn't a concern for Hirose; he'd saved a good deal of his earnings. It was the work that mattered, that gave his life purpose. From time to time, I stopped by his trailer with a gift of vodka, for which he sheepishly thanked me, and we discussed the latest developments regarding the industry and the fading genre of giant monsters. He was always happy to see me. In time, however, my visits became less frequent; after all, I had my own career to tend to. I was twenty years old now.

During the seventies, things got worse for Hirose. The blockbuster was back and the B-movie industry took a nosedive; it was quickly displaced by high-concept high-priced extravaganzas. This was part of a trend, like disco music and bell bottoms. Every two-bit producer in Tinseltown wanted a *Star Wars* or his very own *The Godfather*. Nobody wanted another *The Plastic Eaters*. Drive-ins, those teenage passion pits, were closing all over the country, the looming screens torn down to make room for shopping malls. As a result, company policy suddenly changed and the studio retained the production crew but laid off the actors, all thirty of them, Hirose included. They gave him a gold watch. At age fifty, he found himself without not only a job, but also a place to live.

"This is my saddest day," he said, stuffing his suitcase with aloha shirts and khaki pants.

"Hardly," I said. "Just wait. You're going to enjoy retirement."

With little fanfare, he packed up the rest of his few belongings and took up residence in Endo's garage. Because her pupils also were let go, Polly, too, was unemployed. She moved to Florida to spend her remaining days shuffleboarding, ingesting various medications, clipping coupons. I called her every Sunday until her death a few years ago.

As for myself, now that my two reasons for loyalty to the studio had been dumped, I quit, began freelancing for the majors, and quickly established a reputation. Soon afterward, I married a stuntwoman, Dolores, and during our few years together, we lived in a pricey house in Beverly Hills. About what became of Bennington, Osterberg, and the others, I have no idea, nor do I care.

After being canned, Hirose auditioned for roles, but nothing ever came of his efforts. It didn't help matters that the encroaching presence of digital technology soon put everyone out of work, and not just suit actors, but also go-motion experts, animatronic specialists, puppeteers. But it wasn't only directors and talent agents that Hirose failed to impress; he also failed to impress himself. Consequently, he hit the bottle more and more. Hanging out in creepy grossout bars on Sunset, he started getting into fights. He was arrested twice for drunk and disorderly behavior.

Tired of posting bail, Endo eventually kicked him out.

Hirose was rotting away in a filthy prostitute-harboring motel when I landed him a menial gig with one of my effects teams. It was humiliating work, I see that now. I had him making bug guts, which meant that I was paying him to take part in something that at one time, he'd been entirely opposed to. It wasn't long before he started showing up for work completely intoxicated, unable to perform the simplest tasks. He left, and I never heard from him again. Still, I kept in touch with Endo, who every few months invited me to lunch and brought me up to date on Hirose. Although plagued by deteriorating health, he'd managed to find satisfactory housing in downtown San Francisco. I had always intended to pay him a visit, but my busy career made it hard for me to plan a trip outside LA. I heard he'd found a woman who understood his weird energy and not only didn't mind, but actually liked, the shrine. Together they had a couple of kids.

Ten years ago, Endo called to say Hirose had died of cancer. I came up with the money to pay for the funeral, which was very small, and the meager headstone that marks his grave. Besides Endo and myself, Dexter and Cruz showed up and appeared earnestly doleful. The priest muttered some suitably religious words and tossed dirt on Hirose's casket. Afterward, we all went out for drinks and I struggled to recall what made our Japanese friend seem, on the one hand, so touchingly sensible and on the other, so hopelessly lost. I mumbled something of the sort to Endo and he responded, "Hiroshima."

I suppose I see something of my own fate in

Hirose's story; inevitably, a computer programmer—
some whiz-kid with a college degree and a filmic
memory that goes back only as far as Steven Spielberg
and George Lucas—will render me obsolete and
useless, too. Late at night, safe in the present, comfortable in my spacious home looking down on a dark and
disordered prospect, I drink a little Chianti and imagine
this young geek, motivated by vague loyalty and subtle
remorse, building a modest shrine to me and my anti-
quated ways, a shrine that resembles to some degree the
one I've built here. If I close my eyes, I can see the
programmer now, asleep in his luxury house,
surrounded by the relics and replicas of a world he
helped devise and then destroy. He is dreaming fitfully,
I feel sure, of an enormous creature that, upon being
startled awake by a murmur of unhappy voices, is
forced to confront a shrunken metropolis, a city
marvelous in its intricacies, yet obscene in the sheer
magnitude of its folly.

A LOOK AT: GUNPOWDER MOUNTAIN: A WESTERN NOVEL
(KID CRIMSON BOOK 1)

Step into the 1860's Wild West with Gunpowder Mountain, the thrilling first installment of the new Kid Crimson western series.

Join Kid Crimson as he flees his abusive past, navigating the treacherous landscapes of the Confederate South to find refuge in the bustling boomtown of Virginia City, Nevada.

As the youngest and most ruthless hired gun in town, Kid faces off against brutal gangs, all while capturing the attention of the town's loveliest saloon girls. But Kid's life takes a dangerous turn when he uncovers a Confederate plot to assassinate President Abraham Lincoln during his secret visit to Nevada—a conspiracy that involves a hydrogen machine, air balloons, a mountain of gunpowder, explosive-sniffing hogs, and even a poisoned stew.

Caught between two women vying for his affection and a looming miner's revolt, Kid Crimson must navigate a perilous path to keep Lincoln safe and secure his own future.

AVAILABLE NOW

ABOUT THE AUTHOR

Photo courtesy of Becca Schwartz/UNLV.

Jarret Keene is an assistant professor in the Department of English at UNLV, where he teaches American literature and the graphic novel. He is the series editor for Las Vegas Writes, published by Huntington Press, and is the author of *Hammer of the Dogs*, and the middle school grade books *Decide and Survive: The Attack on Pearl Harbor* and *Heroes of World War II: 25 True Stories of Unsung Heroes Who Fought for Freedom*. Keene has been interviewed by *Writer's Digest*, *Publisher's Weekly*, *EcoTheo Review*, *Library Thing*, *Black Fox Literary Magazine*, and Coast to Coast AM.

www.ingramcontent.com/pod-product-compliance
Lightning Source LLC
Chambersburg PA
CBHW012240260626
47157CB00025B/3294